A KILLER'S MARK

An Aidan O'Reilly Thriller

Angela Kay

First printing, June. 12, 2021

"Serial killers kill for the power and control they experience during the murders and for the added ego boost they get in the aftermath from community fears, media coverage, and the police investigations." —Pat Brown

"Evil hiding among us is an ancient theme." —John Carpenter

To my grandfather, Roy Scarborough, Jr.

1

LIEUTENANT JIM DELONG STEPPED over the dew-laden grass, his boots leaving a trail of disturbed droplets in his wake. As he approached, the stillness of the scene before him seemed almost surreal—a stark contrast to the chaos of the arriving police and forensic teams.

His eyes were immediately drawn to the solitary figure lying by the water's edge. A woman, her body positioned with an eerie serenity, lay as if gazing up at the breaking dawn. Her arms were folded across a black dress that seemed to absorb the morning light, and in her hands, a bouquet of white carnations stark against the dark fabric. But the peacefulness was a lie. As DeLong drew closer, the grim details became apparent—the unnatural angle of her neck, the two puncture wounds marring her skin, and the dried blood tracing a path from a deep cut.

The world seemed to hush around him as he kneeled by her side, the reality of her final moments written in the bruises and desperate scratches on her arms and the blood beneath her broken fingernails. It wasn't just the brutality of her death that unsettled him; it was the calculated placement of an envelope, a silent sentinel against the white of the carnations, bearing a name that would draw him deeper into the mystery: *FBI Special Agent Aidan O'Reilly.*

As the lieutenant contemplated the scene, the first rays of sunlight broke through the trees, casting a mournful glow over the woman's final resting place. DeLong felt a familiar tug at the edge of his consciousness—a mixture of resolve and dread. Another life taken, another story ended too soon, and another puzzle to piece together in the hope of finding justice in a seemingly unjust world.

With his gloved hand, he took the envelope, staring at the letters on the front. But he didn't open it. Instead, he passed it over to a nearby officer with instructions to contact the FBI Resident Agency. Although he wasn't familiar with anyone in the bureau, he trusted they would locate the named agent.

As DeLong wondered if this woman meant anything to the FBI agent, he took notice of one of his men interviewing the teen-aged couple who'd reported the crime. Scattered in the distance of the waters, divers searched beneath Clarks Hill Lake, and the rest of the team scoured the surrounding area for evidence. So far, they had found none.

DeLong's frown deepened as the medical examiner rose, having completed her initial examination of the deceased.

"From what I can tell, and based on the body temp," she said, removing her latex gloves, "she's been dead for about six or seven hours. I'll have a better idea once I do a proper autopsy. I'd have to say the cause of death was strangulation by a thin wire of some sort."

As she spoke, the officer who had contacted the FBI stepped next to him. His face was stoic and professional, betraying no sign that the brutal crime scene affected him. Without uttering a 'thank you,' he ended the call, clipping the cell phone on his belt.

"Sir, I spoke to Assistant Special Agent-In-Charge Tara Monroe myself." He glanced at his notepad as he recited the name. "She's dispensing agents to the site. We're not to move the body until they've arrived."

The lieutenant's interest in the investigation continued to peak. He arched a brow. "Did she give you details we may need to be aware of?"

"No, sir."

DeLong smiled to himself. Of course not. The FBI had their own way of doing things.

The lieutenant switched his attention to the medical examiner with a single nod. "You heard the man. But once she's released to you, she's your priority."

"Understood."

He stepped over to where the teen-aged couple stood. As he neared, he noted the young man saying, "Can't believe I actually found a dead body."

"I don't think I'll be able to sleep tonight," the girl said, a shiver in her words. The light wind bristled through her brown hair, sweeping a strand in her eyes. With a frown, she brushed it aside and hugged herself. "It's so awful."

"This is just like watching a TV show, isn't it?" The boy scoffed, his gaze lingering on the body.

"This isn't a joke," DeLong said. "A young woman's dead."

The boy swallowed hard, his gaze settling uneasily on the lieutenant. "I didn't mean—I was just saying—"

DeLong ignored him with a wave of his hand and looked at the officer. "What did you get?"

"Wrong place, wrong time," the officer said. "They planned on spending the day here, but found her instead."

"Are you going to arrest us?" the boy asked.

"No," DeLong said. "Thank you for calling it in. You're free to go home, but the feds may need to speak with you later."

"Let's get out of here." The girl, tugging at her boyfriend's hand, led him away from the scene." He followed with reluctance, his eyes glued to the body by the water.

DeLong said, "All right, men." His officers looked his way, giving him their full attention. "When the FBI arrives, I want us to be as cooperative as possible. Understood?"

His men muttered their agreement.

DeLong returned to where the body rested. She had no ID on her, nothing to give him a clue of where she belonged. What was her name? Who were her family? Noticing the wedding band on her finger, he wondered if she and her husband had children.

"It's tragic," one of his sergeants said, standing next to him.

DeLong didn't respond. He didn't need to. During the years he'd spent as a police officer, he'd seen unimaginable things.

And he knew it wouldn't be his last.

2

THE PERSISTENT BUZZ OF the cell phone shattered the stillness of the early morning, its vibrations echoing against the wooden bedside table. In the dimly lit room, Special Agent Aidan O'Reilly stirred, a groan escaping his lips as the remnants of a rare, peaceful sleep clung to him. Reluctantly, he fumbled in the darkness, his hands searching for the intrusive device. As he squinted at the caller ID, the burden of his responsibilities pulled him back from the fleeting respite of dreamland into the all-too-familiar world of unforeseen crises.

"Honey," Cheyenne mumbled next to him. "Are you going to get that?"

Rather than answering, he groaned, searching through the darkness for the phone, and glanced at the caller ID. Aidan blinked to let his eyes adjust enough to read the blurry words. *SAC Hansford*. He frowned as he touched the screen to answer the call. The special agent-in-charge of his field office in Atlanta wouldn't be calling unless it was an emergency, knowing he wasn't due to report in until Monday. As it was, Aidan and Cheyenne had come home from Boston three days earlier than they intended. When they discussed their plans last night, Aidan had voiced his thoughts that he didn't want to spend a hectic week helping his younger sister in her wedding bliss, then spend hours driving home for work soon after. He wanted to relax for a few days, considering he'd been working a full caseload.

"O'Reilly." He sat up and rested against the headboard of the bed. After a few more blinks, he became lucid enough to focus on his boss's voice.

"I'm sorry to call you on your vacation, but are you back in town?"

Aidan hesitated before telling his boss that he was.

"Good. I need you to report to me ASAP."

Aidan glanced at the red numbers on the bedside table and saw it was seven forty-three in the morning. He frowned again, realizing they'd only returned to their apartment an hour ago, and he had slept a little over thirty minutes. But he didn't tell that to Hansford. Something serious was brewing. If it wasn't the edgy sound of Hansford's voice, then it was a feeling rising to his throat.

Aidan cleared his throat. "What's going on, sir?"

"We've been notified of a homicide in Augusta."

Hansford hesitated, and the feeling in Aidan's nerves went into overload. He was almost afraid of what his boss would tell him. He searched his mind for the date.

June the twelfth.

The date alone was enough to tell him everything. How could he not have realized it?

"What is it?" He closed his eyes, praying it wouldn't be true. "You wouldn't be calling me in for just a murder. What's going on?"

"The local authorities advised me they found an envelope addressed to you attached to the body."

Aidan's heart seemed to freeze in his chest.

No.

It couldn't be.

Part of him knew it was. But another part hoped the anniversary would be overlooked.

"They also informed me this body had..." Hansford paused again, "... been tased."

Aidan's heart leaped to his throat, and he clambered out of bed to leave the room, so Cheyenne didn't wake up to overhear the conversation. His legs felt like jelly, and his throat was raw. He wanted to scream in anguish, but fought to keep himself composed. It'd been hard to manage, but he *had* to stay in the investigation.

"Tased?" he repeated, keeping his voice low.

Hansford's silence was all Aidan needed for confirmation.

He sat at the kitchen table in the darkness. Memories of the case as a rookie agent came flooding back.

He'd worked the investigation on and off throughout the years.

Most members of law enforcement had the one case they dreamed of every night.

The one case that just wouldn't let go.

The Carnations Killer was his first serial, and he'd been killing every year since he started. Unfortunately, he had outsmarted even the best of the best. And now, it was his tenth year anniversary.

"I need you to come in. I'll brief you on what Lieutenant DeLong of the Columbia County Sheriff's Office said. I also already forwarded his email to you."

Hansford's words faded as Aidan considered the information. His mind raced wildly in all directions. There were times when it seemed he was closing in on the killer, but no. Every time...*every single time*, the serial killer escaped unscathed while the bodies of his victims were scattered around. And every single time, Aidan renewed his vow to find the killer and bring him to justice once and for all.

And tonight was no difference.

Aidan clutched his cell tight in his hand, the device almost embedding itself against his palm.

"Agent O'Reilly?" Hansford said after a while of silence.

"I'm here," Aidan said. "I'm on my way in now."

After he ended the call with Hansford, he made a pot of coffee. He didn't want to take the time, but it only wasted a few minutes, and he needed the caffeine in order to get his thoughts in order. As the coffee brewed, he hurried through the hall to his room. He didn't bother with a shower, but splashed cold water on his face and ran three strokes of his comb through his hair.

Aidan pulled on a white dress shirt and a pair of black slacks, then shook Cheyenne's shoulder. Her snoring, the only thing about her that ever bothered him, ceased, and she moaned, her eyes fluttering open.

"Hey, sorry to wake you, love," he whispered. "But I've got to cut my vacation short."

"Why?" she said, half-asleep.

"I've been called in. I'll explain later." He kissed her cheek, telling her he loved her.

She mumbled a response and turned over.

As Aidan hastily prepared to leave, his mind involuntarily drifted to the past encounters with The Carnations Killer. Each unsolved case, each life taken, flickered in his memory like a haunting slideshow. He remembered the first time he'd come across this nemesis – the frustration, the sleepless nights. The killer had become his shadow, a ghost in his life, always there but just out of reach. Clutching the coffee thermos, a grim resolve settled in his heart. This time, he silently vowed, things would be different. He would not let the killer slip away again, not on this, their grim anniversary. With a final glance at the quiet apartment, he stepped out into the early morning, the determination to end this decade-long chase burning within him.

❖

ALTHOUGH THE ATLANTA TRAFFIC was spreading thick, it took him only twenty minutes to arrive at the massive building that housed the Federal Bureau of Investigation team.

Aidan now sat in Hansford's office looking over crime scene photos the lieutenant from Augusta had emailed.

Hansford spoke as Aidan studied the photos. They've recently learned the victim's name was Maya Gibson, age twenty-eight. She was married to Clark Gibson, an elementary school teacher. Like the other victims he had investigated in The Carnations Killer murders, she was blonde and in excellent shape. The killer posed her as if she were sleeping, holding a bouquet of white carnations against her chest.

Aidan's hands shook, and he tried to conceal it.

"Where's the scene?"

"Clarks Hill Lake in Augusta," Hansford answered, his throat scratchy from years of chain-smoking two packs a day. He scratched his curly gray hair. "I already have a helicopter ready for you. Lieutenant DeLong is sending a car to collect you and take you to the crime scene."

Aidan nodded. "Thank you, sir. Anything else?"

Hansford heaved a heavy sigh. "I'm sorry to ruin your vacation, O'Reilly."

He forced a weak smile. "Comes with the job, sir. Maybe after ten years, I'll get lucky."

"Let us hope."

They rose and shook hands.

"I'll see what I can do on my end to help catch this guy once and for all."

Aidan never told him—or anyone—how deeply the Carnations Killer affected him, and he never could. The Bureau would remove him from further investigations, and that was one thing Aidan refused to permit.

With the file containing the details about Maya Gibson clutched in his hand, Aidan left the office and made his way to the helipad.

3

AIDAN'S ARRIVAL AT CLARKS Hill Lake was met with the cold embrace of an early morning breeze, carrying with it the solemnity of the scene that unfolded before him. His trained eyes scanned the perimeter, absorbing every detail – the scattered investigators, the somber divers in the distance, the lifeless form that lay hauntingly still by the water's edge. Each element etched itself into his memory, a silent testament to the gravity of what lay ahead. As he stepped closer, the weight of the killer's return pressed heavily upon him, a familiar adversary emerging from the shadows of his past.

Aidan showed his credentials to the officer standing behind the crime scene tape. When she waved him through, Aidan continued to where a crowd of police investigators was still surveying the scene. A tall man wearing a ball cap and a top and blue jeans, stood next to an equally tall, dark-skinned man near the body. They spoke, faces in deep concentration as they considered the scene. Aidan assumed the one of the men was Lieutenant DeLong.

Once he introduced himself, Aidan found he was right, and the other man was Agent Shaun Henderson, the senior resident of the field office in downtown Augusta.

Aidan shook their hands—DeLong's shake was wilted, while Henderson almost crushed his fingers.

When Aidan politely referred to Henderson as "agent," he'd requested to be called by his first name, stating they were going to be working long days together trying to track the killer.

With an affirming nod, Aidan turned his attention to the body, kneeling for a closer look. He noted every bruise, the black dress, white carnations, the taser marks.

With a single look at the crime scene, it was obvious the killer he'd hunted for the past ten years had returned, and Augusta was his new hunting ground. The memories made Aidan's heart drum against his rib cage. He balled his fists in anger, then released them, hoping his new peers didn't take notice.

Aidan remembered the chilling call he'd received the night before the killer's last victim met her demise. It was a simple phrase meant to taunt them.

To taunt him.

And he remembered his bitter laughter.

I can kill, and you can't catch me.

Aidan wanted nothing more than to erase the voice from his memory, but it was something he thought about almost every day. He wondered if he would spend the rest of his life hearing that voice.

"Do we have the approximate time of death?" Aidan asked, trying to push his thoughts to the back of his head.

"M.E. believes it to be around seven hours from the time the body was found," DeLong said.

"Any personal belongings?"

"No. And my forensic team combed through every inch of this place. It's clean."

Aidan nodded. The killer planned the murders long before he ever approached his victims.

Aidan imagined the killer studied his victims' daily routines. He knew who they were with. He likely knew what grocery store they frequented and the day of the week they took out the trash.

He planned it to the tiniest detail.

But Aidan also knew after eluding capture for so long, most killers were bound to make a mistake. He hoped this would be the case with The Carnations Killer.

"The husband?" Aidan asked.

"I have men questioning him as we speak," Shaun said.

Aidan asked about the letter, the reason he was called.

DeLong passed it over.

They hadn't opened it but had slipped it into an evidence bag. Aidan pulled on a pair of latex gloves, dragged it out of the protective bag, and removed the letter from the envelope.

He glanced between DeLong and Shaun before reading the letter's contents to himself.

FBI Special Agent O'Reilly—
How good it is to see you again. I've really missed you. Have you missed me? Well, I left a present for you in hopes of making up for that. I do hope you enjoy her. You always seem to have to come to me, don't you? Well, I decided I'd do you a little favor and come to you for once. Ah, it's so good to be back in your acquaintance, isn't it? I'm looking forward to us continuing our little game.
Your friend,
The Carnations Killer

Every part of him wanted to rip the letter into pieces. Aidan noticed his hands shaking, so he replaced the letter in the bag to mask it. It had been hard enough returning to Boston for his sister's wedding. He hadn't been back since he first came across The Carnations Killer ten years ago. And now to come home to this?

"Why do you think he's singling you out, Agent O'Reilly?" DeLong burst into his thoughts, drawing him back to the real world.

Aidan hesitated as he looked at DeLong, then Shaun, and back again.

"He's killed fifty women," he said, clearing his throat. "That we know of. He likes to leave me notes. He's always seemed fascinated by me. I don't know why."

DeLong frowned. "Are you telling me we really have a serial killer in my city?"

Aidan nodded and continued glumly, still looking at the note the killer left for him.

"They are all blonde, in excellent shape. That's the only common link for our victims. As far as we can tell, none of the previous victims knew the other." Aidan kneeled next to the body, using his hand to show the two marks on her neck. "He first uses a taser to subdue them. Then he takes his victims elsewhere. I think he gets off on the abuse. He uses a rod or something of that nature to torture them. After holding the vics for about a week, he strangles them with a wire to finish them off, then dumps the bodies where he knows we will find them."

Standing directly behind him, he heard Shaun let out a soft curse. "I've heard talk about the killer in the past."

"The killer redresses his victims in a black dress, leaving off their undergarments," Aidan continued. "He usually poses them in this manner, except for the last victim. He seems to enjoy going out with a bang. Last year, he chained his victim to cement and dumped her in the middle of the Hudson River. He had anchored the boat, called to give us the tip, and when we came to it, a note told us to 'look down.'"

Aidan pushed to his feet, his eyes on the lifeless shell of the young woman.

"What's with the carnations?" DeLong asked.

Aidan hesitated before he spoke.

"Black dresses are usual funeral attire. It's his sendoff for the women. As for the white carnations, I believe it's a message for us."

"What's that?"

It was Shaun who answered. "It means 'good luck.'"

Aidan nodded his agreement.

DeLong released a loud sigh that came out as a whistle. "As soon as the medical examiner finishes the autopsy, I'll make sure you get a copy."

"I appreciate that." Aidan looked up at Shaun. "After I pull together some information, I'd like to have a debriefing. I think eleven will give me enough time."

"Of course," Shaun said with a single nod.

Aidan turned to DeLong. "You're more than welcome to join us. Actually, I highly recommend you do. We're going to need to work together on this. The killer's known to kill for a few months and disappear. We need to work quickly and the more people we have on our team, the better."

DeLong nodded. "I'll see you at eleven."

"If you're ready, Aidan, I can drive you to the office," Shaun said. "We'll get you settled with your own car shortly."

"That'd be great."

Aidan turned to where the media and other bystanders had gathered to watch the scene. The buzz of the audience grew as they neared, and the reporters were brash at trying to get their story.

He'd dealt with a lot of things that got under his skin throughout the ten years of being a federal agent, but there was nothing he despised more than the media.

They had to walk by them to get to Shaun's vehicle. As usual, the reporters bombarded them with questions the media knew they wouldn't—or couldn't—release right away.

"What's the victim's name?"

"Do you have any suspects?"

"How long has she been dead?"

"What interest does the FBI have in this murder? Do we need to worry about a serial killer?"

The reporter who spoke jammed his microphone under Aidan's nose.

"At this time, I'm not at liberty to say anything about the circumstances." Aidan pushed the microphone away from his face.

"You're not at liberty, or you don't know?" the reporter asked.

"We're still assessing the situation," Aidan said, trying to remain calm. "The FBI and the Columbia County Sheriff's Office will release a formal statement later this afternoon."

Before another inquisitive reporter had the chance to press for more information, Aidan and Shaun slipped underneath the tape and headed for the car.

"You heard it here first," the reporter said to the camera. "This is Jordan Blake reporting live at Clarks Hill Lake."

"I hate reporters," Aidan said as he opened the passenger's side of the car Shaun indicated was his.

Shaun chuckled. "They are a feisty bunch, aren't they?"

After they settled in the vehicle, Shaun buckled before turning his head to look at Aidan, raising a brow. "So, you've been investigating The Carnations Killer for ten years?"

Looking over at his new partner, Aidan said, "I was fresh out of the academy."

Shaun whistled, turning the ignition.

"And he always requests you?"

Aidan hesitated with a frown as faces from previous murders flashed in his mind. "Yeah. It's one of life's greatest mysteries of why."

4

"THIS IS MAYA GIBSON," Aidan said, using the clicker to change the slide to a photograph of their victim. He glanced at the large projected picture of the young woman, a broad smile plastered on her face. She wore her blonde hair in a ponytail. Her right ear had several earrings lining her lobe, while the left only had one.

Aidan cleared his throat before continuing, turning his attention to the assembled agents in the conference room.

"Her husband reported her missing last Tuesday night when she didn't come home from her yoga class."

Aidan hadn't had the chance to meet the handful of men and women who sat in their chairs, but they kept their concentration focused on him as he spoke. Lieutenant DeLong sat in the back corner of the room, his eyes glancing from one federal agent to another.

"Date of birth is May 5, 1988. She was attending graduate school at Augusta University." Aidan paused and looked back at the team. "She moved here with her husband and two children three years ago from Utah." Pushing the clicker button again, the slide changed to the crime scene photos. "Two teenagers found her at six-fifteen this morning at Clarks Hill Lake."

"While we don't yet have the autopsy reports, based on the previous murders we can assume that Maya hadn't been sexually assaulted. We'll keep you posted as information comes in."

Aidan pressed the button again on the clicker and fifty small images he'd compiled flashed on the screen.

He knew their stories by heart. They would be embedded in his mind every day and night.

With a hard swallow, Aidan told the agents what he could. "We believe the man responsible for the death of Maya Gibson is the same man responsible for the deaths of these women. The media refer to him as The Carnations Killer. You'll find the names of the victims in the database. They were all murdered in a ten-year span across the United States. He'd resurface every year on, or around June fifteenth. All of these women have been beaten, tased, posed. Their commonalities are that the women had good figures and blonde hair. He would contain them for about a week before dumping the bodies the night he murdered them. And always in a location where they would be found the following day. If the killer learned we hadn't yet discovered a body, he would call in an anonymous tip. We have yet to find evidence of the killer at the crime scenes. He left no DNA, no fibers, nothing."

"What do we know about the killer?"

He looked in the speaker's direction. It was Tara Monroe, the assistant special agent-in-charge. When Shaun and Aidan arrived at the downtown office, Shaun introduced them. She had graciously shaken Aidan's hand, thanking him for joining her team on short notice.

Tara was two inches shorter than Aidan's five foot seven, slightly on the round side, with thin legs. She wore red lipstick, just enough pink blush to give her cheeks a soft glow, and her black hair in a tight bun.

She hadn't been in the room when they began the briefing, so she had at some point crept into the meeting without Aidan realizing. She stood by the door, a large file resting in her arms.

"The only fact we have is that he's hedonistic," Aidan said. Before resting his eyes on Tara, he scanned the room. "He enjoys torturing these women, but doesn't kill for sex. The killer uses a taser, probably to subdue them at first. Then he kidnaps them. He plans the details before the actual abductions. I believe he takes the time to study their routines. He's careful. And he craves attention. He wants us to know we can't get him. So he leaves the white carnations trademark on the victims' bodies." Aidan swallowed. "And the notes to me."

"Could it be a copycat?" an agent in the middle of the room asked.

"Highly unlikely. He tased Maya, and we've kept that information confidential in the other killings, as well as the notes addressed to me."

Aidan set the projection remote on the table, grabbed his water bottle, and took another sip.

"The Carnations Killer murders three to seven women within six months before disappearing. It's vital we work together quickly and efficiently. I want each of you to look over the information on the intranet. This is our priority. We must stop him before he kills again."

"How do you propose we do that?" one of the female agents asked.

"To start, I want teams to go over the previous victims. Familiarize yourself with them. Find differences and similarities in the victims and the autopsy reports. I want you to re-question the previous victims' families if possible. We're going to treat this with a new set of eyes."

AFTER THE DEBRIEFING, AIDAN sat at the desk they chartered out to him, staring at the photos of Maya Gibson as though the answers he sought would reveal themselves. He scanned the notes from her crime scene versus the other victims'.

However, nothing new stood at attention, and after a while, his vision blurred.

Aidan stopped to rub his fingers against his eyelids, trying to erase the sleeplessness and apprehension.

Shaun was at his desk making phone calls, and Aidan wished he'd hurry. They'd planned on a quick lunch before making their way to Maya's yoga studio. Aidan wasn't hungry, but he hoped eating something would boost his metabolism. He left the apartment before grabbing breakfast, so he'd need to have a little food to fuel his stomach.

Aidan closed the file and snatched the landline from its holder. Punching her number on the keypad, he called Cheyenne.

Although it wasn't anything new, Aidan knew Cheyenne wouldn't be too appreciative that he'd abandoned her for work when he was supposed to be on vacation. They had hoped to spend a few days together, doing nothing but enjoying each other's company. It was a rare treat because, often, something would come up.

Case in point.

"Hey, honey," Cheyenne answered.

"Hey," Aidan said.

"You're not supposed to be back at work until next week." He could almost see her lips turning into a frown.

Aidan smiled. "It's better than hearing that raucous snoring you had going on."

"I don't snore," she said.

"I'm sorry, love," he said. "But they needed me."

"Will you be coming back this weekend?"

"I don't know," Aidan said after a brief pause. "I'll try. But..."

She cleared her throat, then added, "You know, my sister lives in Augusta. Maybe I'll call her and visit."

"I don't know about that," Aidan said. Although Cheyenne didn't fit the profile, the thought of her being in the same city as a serial killer didn't appeal to him.

"I've been wanting to see her anyway," Cheyenne said. She already seemed to have decided.

"Okay." Aidan sighed. When his wife made a decision, there was nothing he could do to make her change his mind. Besides, at least he'd be able to keep an eye on her. "I guess that'll be fine. Let me know when you get to her place, so I know you're safe."

"I will."

"Good. I'll find time to stop by later today, okay?" he said.

"You better," she said. A pause. "Be careful, Aidan."

"Always." Aidan spotted Shaun walking his way, so he told Cheyenne he loved her and ended the call.

"Wife?" Shaun asked him, a smirk playing on his lips.

"Yeah."

"Ah, I see. I'd like to learn more about her. Ready for lunch?"

Aidan grabbed several folders from the desk and rose. "Yeah. Let's go."

5

Downward Dog was a small yoga studio tucked in the corner of a strip mall. If it weren't for the large sign on the side of the road, Aidan would have overlooked it. The parking lot was full, so Shaun parked along the side near their destination, and they climbed out of the car.

Aidan had been staring at his notes for most of the trip, muttering to himself about the information in the federal database.

The killer's first known victim was a young woman named Sherry Finch. She was thirty-three, married to a law professor from Harvard University. One child. Sherry had long blonde hair that she always kept in a ponytail. She had a pretty face, wore no makeup except for a light-colored lipstick. She had a college degree in English, however, became a stay-at-home mom rather than pursue a career.

Originally, the prime suspect in Sherry's murder was a man by the name of Albert Cross. The police had arrested once him for peeping through her bedroom window and watching as she dressed. Other than that, his rap sheet was clean. Shortly after Albert Cross left jail, someone had kidnapped Sherry in the night, tortured, and strangled her to death by a thin wire. Her posed body was discovered a week later by an elderly man taking out his trash. The killer posed her, put her in a black dress without undergarments. He placed a white carnations bouquet in her hands. As with the victims following, she'd been tased.

A few weeks after Albert Cross' arrest for suspicions of her murder, they found a second victim on a folding chair at an apartment pool. He'd obviously had an alibi for the second victim, and the police soon discovered that Cross was in New York during the time of Sherry's murder. So they released him.

Over a few months, three more victims popped up with no leads on who may have killed them.

Aidan followed Shaun into the yoga studio, hoping they would catch a break. Maybe the killer had messed up and kidnapped her while someone watched.

Aidan doubted it, but it was always a possibility.

The studio was large on the inside, containing two rooms and a reception desk. People doing various yoga moves occupied both rooms.

The receptionist typed furiously at the computer, her eyes narrowed in deep concentration as Aidan and Shaun made their approach.

Aidan set his credentials on the countertop.

"Good afternoon, miss. I'm Agent Aidan O'Reilly, this is Agent Shaun Henderson."

"Hi, um, can I help you?" She blinked, taken aback by the interruption.

"I hope so." Aidan noted her name tag read *Brianna*. He handed her a photo of Maya Gibson. It was a recent picture her husband had given them earlier in the day. "Do you recognize this woman? She used to come here."

Brianna took a long look at the photo before she nodded. "Yes. She attends classes every Tuesday and Thursday night."

"Have you noticed whether she may have seemed bothered by anyone?" Shaun asked. "Maybe he was trying to pull advances, and she didn't like it?"

Brianna shook her head. "No. Not really." She narrowed her eyes. "Did something happen to her?"

It was Shaun who answered. "I'm sorry to inform you, but we found her body earlier this morning."

Brianna fell back against her seat, her eyes wide. "Oh, I'm so sorry. That poor woman. She's always been so nice."

"Anything you can think of would be a great help," Aidan said.

Brianna bit her lower lip as she thought. "I don't know. I mean, some of the guys would look at her. She was absolutely perfect. I'd kill to have that body, you know? I think they all knew she was happily married, so they didn't come on to her or anything. But I guess it's possible one of them may have. I've just never seen it."

"Did she ever go out with anybody from her classes?"

"Yeah. Every Tuesday night, they'd go for drinks. Mostly it was the women, but sometimes the men would join in. Mrs. Gibson was the type you can't help but love, you know?" She shook her head. "Mrs. Gibson made friends with everybody. She invited me a few times."

"Has anybody new begun coming to the studio? Particularly on the days she's usually in attendance?"

"We get a few new people just about every day. We do keep a list, but I'll need to check with my boss and make sure it's okay to give it to you. He's in the back."

"We'd appreciate it," Aidan said.

The receptionist said she'd be back, then walked past the two yoga classes and entered through a door on the opposite side of the building.

Aidan watched as the class nearest to them did a pose. Cheyenne enjoyed doing yoga from time to time, and she'd mentioned a few pose names, but Aidan couldn't remember what this one was called. They were in a squat position, arms wrapped around the back of their bodies, hands linked. Most of the group seemed to perform the pose exceedingly well, except for one or two. The yoga instructor weaved around the room, fixing bodies the way they needed to be.

"Pasasana," Shaun said from behind Aidan.

Aidan turned to see Shaun leaning against the reception desk, his dark arm blending with the black counter.

"What?"

He motioned toward the yoga room. "That pose. Called Pasasana. Or Noose Pose."

Aidan realized he must have been muttering to himself, as he'd done several times when in deep concentration trying to figure something out.

"Looks painful," Aidan said.

Shaun set the brochure he was skimming through on the counter and flashed Aidan a smile, his teeth white, almost reflecting off his skin. "Takes practice."

"You do yoga?"

"Shocked?"

"Actually, I am."

Shaun shrugged. "It's one way for me to release stress. But as you can see, I'm a big guy, so it's hard for me to do some of the poses. They are, as you said, painful." He grinned again.

"What's your other stress-reducer?" Aidan asked.

"Punching things," he said simply.

Before Aidan could ask him what things, he spotted the receptionist returning, a man trailing after her. He allowed the conversation to fall into silence.

"Agents," the man said, extending his hand. "I'm Craig Jones, the manager."

Shaun and Aidan accepted his hand.

"I understand you're looking into Maya Gibson's murder?"

"Yes sir," Aidan said. "We were hoping to get a list of your newest customers—dating back to the beginning of last month."

Jones nodded and looked over at his receptionist. "Give it to the agents." He looked back at them. "When I heard Maya was dead, I couldn't believe it. It's horrible what happened to her."

"How long have you known her?" Shaun asked.

"Two or three years," the manager said.

The printer whirred as it spit the documents onto the tray.

"Do you have any suspects yet?"

"We're prohibited from discussing the investigation," Aidan said. "As soon as we can, we'll release the information."

"I hope you catch this guy soon," Jones said.

"Did you see her leave with anyone last Tuesday night?"

Jones shook his head, exchanging glances with the receptionist, who stood by the printer. "Brianna and I were both closing up as usual. I think Maya was the last to leave, but I can't be sure. You never think about how unsafe the world is until it's too late."

"That's true," Shaun said.

Brianna finished printing the pages and passed the documents to Aidan. Jones told them Maya was well-liked. She was soft-spoken, didn't get into confrontations.

"Thank you both for your time," Aidan said. "If you remember anything else, call us or the sheriff's office." He left his card, and they turned to leave.

6

He watched as news reporter Jordan Blake recounted what the federal investigators had released so far. As usual, it was nothing. He'd always been much too careful to leave evidence that would lead to his capture. After all, he was a professional. They only knew what he wanted them to know. Once, he left a riddle for the local law enforcement, but they weren't smart enough to crack it. Or maybe he was smart enough to write a riddle stumping even the best of the best.

Either way, they never grasped it.

Well, not in time, anyway.

He had tried to give them just enough time to save one of his targets before her demise, but they were an hour too late.

It was a shame. But it still brought a smile to his face.

So far, the reporters didn't seem to realize the new girl—according to the reports, her name was Maya Gibson—was his newest woman.

He was sure the police knew about it. They had to know. Especially since Special Agent Aidan O'Reilly more than likely told them. Law enforcement had that irritating habit of hiding things from the public.

But he'd soon change that.

He wanted to be sure the world knew he'd returned.

He wanted the world to fear him.

They needed to know he could—and would—strike anyone. He'd make the women wish they were dead. Then he liked to watch as they squirmed on the floor, trying to escape.

It never worked out for them.

Still, they never seemed to learn.

They always—*always*—pleaded for him to let them go.

I won't tell anyone. I promise. Just please let me go home. I have a family. Please.

Waaaa.

It was funny how the tears of the women were like clockwork.

Why were they like that, anyway? Why did people cling to hope when they knew there was none? Why did people pray when they knew it wouldn't be answered?

He'd asked one of his targets a few years ago.

But all she did was whimper and try to crawl away.

He had struck her across the temple with the tire iron, then demanded an answer from her. She offered none.

It was irritating.

He was only naturally curious about why people hoped bad times would turn out good. What good was it when you knew, when you just *knew*, you'd die anyway?

Maybe there was a hidden answer to that riddle of life after all.

Maybe because they realized they were going to die anyway, the only thing left to do was hope.

A paradox.

It was a very curious concept.

Anyway.

Back to Jordan Blake.

He could tell the reporter was getting ready to sign off.

The reporter's birthday was in a few days, so he planned on leaving a card for him. He planned it so that shortly after receiving the card, Blake would get a text on his phone.

And all he would have to do is watch as Jordan Blake—a young man eager and desperate to make a name for himself—told the world The Carnations Killer had returned.

People like Jordan Blake were such easy targets.

They were also the most fun to use.

And easy to blame if ever it came to the time he needed a fall guy.

The key was to always plan the escape.

And he did so to the tiniest detail.

It was a game, really.

Much like playing chess.

You can't play a game without first understanding the rules. It was no fun otherwise. And to understand the rules and play the game well, you had to know the move you're going to make long before you made it.

Before he took—what was her name again? Ah, yes, Maya something. Before he chose her as a target, he had already started developing a plan for Agent O'Reilly. It was only polite, wasn't it? After all, they'd worked together for ten years. It was their anniversary. It was a milestone, so he needed to do something for the agent.

Something special.

It was going to be the going away gift.

He wasn't sure what he wanted to do yet, but he had a few ideas to sort through.

But first, things must fall in their natural order. That was part of the rules. Jumping the gun would only cause him to make a mistake, and Agent O'Reilly was smart. O'Reilly had done very well in his career, which made him both a threat and a thrill. He helped bring down not one, but two drug trafficking rings, and he'd arrested a serial arsonist who had killed four men and one woman, injuring many others. Those were only a few of O'Reilly's commendations.

It only made him more pleased to be in the forefront of O'Reilly's mind.

Yes, he enjoyed playing with O'Reilly.

Games were no fun unless you had a worthy opponent, and Agent O'Reilly was the perfect pawn.

The news report was now over, and while Jordan talked to various people, he gathered his things and headed for the reporter's office.

It was time.

7

Jordan Blake stepped into his office and found Kent, his cameraman, holding an envelope to the light, trying to get a read on its contents. The glare of his wire-rimmed glasses bounced off the white packet, making it a little more difficult for him to see what was inside.

He glanced over at Gary Short, one of the news station's field technicians, and rolled his eyes.

"What are you doing?" Jordan said.

Kent dropped what he was holding and spun on his toes, his hands clamped across his chest. His eyes seemed to bulge from his head. When Kent realized it was Jordan, he closed his eyes, letting out a breathy curse. "Man, Jordan. You scared the living daylights out of me."

Jordan arched his left eyebrow and crossed his arms. Next to him, Gary chuckled, resting his shoulder against the jamb of the doorway.

"Well, maybe if you weren't in my office trying to read my mail, I wouldn't have had the pleasure of scaring you so much."

"Sorry," Kent said. He scratched his auburn head of hair and leaned down to retrieve the envelope and passed it over. "I saw some guy slip this under your door. I was just curious. Usually, it's a hot chick that's fawning over you with those ridiculous love notes."

Gary watched the two banter. His voice filled with amusement when he spoke. "As much as I'd love to stick around and watch you beat each other up, I'm going to take off. Promised my girl I'd stop by the store for some bread and whatever else she needs."

He patted Jordan's shoulder and headed down the hall, leaving the news reporter glaring at his cameraman.

"Ever hear of 'curiosity killed the cat?'" Jordan snatched the object from Kent and made his way to the small desk.

"Good thing I'm not a cat, then," Kent said. He motioned to the mail. "What is it?"

With his letter opener, Jordan sliced through the top of the envelope and pulled out a card. It was a custom-made greeting card. The sender had taken the time to cut out block letters and glue them to the front.

"Hmm. It's an early birthday message," he said, grabbing a strawberry from his fruit basket a young fan sent him yesterday afternoon. "'Happy happy birthday to you. Here's to a great day. Have you heard of The Carnations Killer? Listen to what he has to say.'"

Again, Jordan's eyebrow rose, this time with curiosity. He grabbed another strawberry and opened the card to read the typed message.

"Dear Jordan," he said.

Kent moved to peer over Jordan's shoulder. He cleaned off his glasses with the tail of his shirt and slipped them on the bridge of his nose.

Jordan continued reading. "'I've watched you for a while and I decided I want you to be the first to know. In a few minutes, you will receive a text with the exciting news.'"

"Intriguing," Kent said. "Do you really think The Carnations Killer returned? Do you think he was the one who killed that girl at the lake?"

Jordan wasn't paying his cameraman any attention. He gnawed on a Granny Smith apple as he slipped deep into his thoughts, his mind reeling over why The Carnations Killer would want to send him a cryptic birthday card.

And why send a text? Why not just tell him in the card?

"Yo," Kent said, shaking Jordan's shoulder. "You've got a text."

Jordan snatched his phone from the table, his mind still thinking about the mysterious card. When he looked at the cell, he almost dropped it.

Do you want to make a name for yourself? Help me help you. Tell the world The Carnations Killer is back.

Jordan looked at Kent, whose eyes grew. It was obvious he had read the message as well.

"Man, that's ... scary," Kent said.

"Who did you say left this card?"

Kent shrugged. "Didn't see his face. Kind of tall, black hair, something like that. His back was to me."

Jordan rose so he could look into Kent's eyes. He was half an inch shorter than the cameraman. "Well, looks like he's giving us the big break we've been looking for."

"I don't know," Kent said with a frown. "Maybe you should go to the cops first. See what they want us to do."

Jordan shook his head with fervor. "Going to the cops could ruin our chance at a breaking story. He wants us to go on the air. And besides, doesn't the public have the right to know? You know how cops are. They wait until it's too late. That agent at the scene today told us 'no comment.' We know something now. Don't you think we owe it to the people to comment?"

Kent frowned, and Jordan knew he hit the spot with his cameraman.

"Fine," Kent said. "You're right. They should be aware."

"Well, then, let's get ready to go on the air."

AFTER JORDAN FINISHED WITH his makeup artist, he double-checked his reflection in the mirror to be sure he was camera ready. He ran his fingers through the thick mass of black moussed hair and checked his teeth to be sure nothing was in them.

Standing in front of the blue backdrop, he took in a deep breath and released it.

Kent stood behind his camera. "All right. Ready when you are."

Jordan pulled in one more deep breath and pushed it out. "Great. Let's do it."

After Kent counted down with his fingers and pointed at Jordan, he flashed his trademark smile for the camera.

"This is Jordan Blake, reporting live at WJFX News. A few moments ago, I received an interesting birthday card that someone slipped under my office door. And here's the kicker. It was sent to me by the infamous Carnations Killer himself. He wants us to know he's back."

Jordan told the camera and the people who watched his channel what had already been released to the public about The Carnations Killer. He informed they would release no other information at the moment, but to stay tuned.

He ended by saying, "Our recent victim—Maya Gibson—fit the profile for The Carnations Killer to a T. Could he really have returned? Or is it a copycat playing games? Do the police suspect The Carnations Killer? If so, why do you think they are reluctant to tell us? After all, the FBI stated earlier this morning, they would release a statement to the public this afternoon. When this afternoon, agents? It's almost two o'clock now, and the public is anxious to know whether or not their lives could be at stake. This is Jordan Blake, and you heard it here first."

After he signed off, Kent told him it was okay to break character.

"How was that?"

"Perfect," Kent said. "But you do realize nothing good will come of this? This guy's probably only seeking attention."

"In this world, my friend," Jordan said, "we're nothing unless we have attention. This guy's the most sought-after serial killer since the Green River Killer. And we've got the breaking news. How can we not run with it?"

As he spoke, Jordan saw his boss appear around the corner. By the look on his face and the stride of his gait, he didn't appear happy.

"What do you think you're doing?" His booming voice carried into the room.

"Making sure I have longer than fifteen minutes of fame," Jordan said with a shrug.

"Next time you want to run with a story, you come to me first. Thanks to you, I just got a call from the FBI."

"That was fast."

"And they aren't happy at all." His boss crossed his arms. His cheeks flushed red, as they always did when he was angry. "They're on the way. They want to know more about this card of yours. And for that matter, so do I."

"Sure," Jordan said matter-of-factly.

"I want no more surprises. I mean it."

"What are you going to do, Thomas? Fire me?" Jordan crossed his arms over his chest.

"That's exactly what I'll do. You think you're irreplaceable? Well, you're not." Thomas turned on his heels. "Be in the conference room in twenty minutes."

8

Cheyenne called to let Aidan know she'd arrived at her sister's. So, after he was situated with a bureau vehicle, he headed to Laura's house.

His eyes growing heavy with each tick of the clock, Aidan wished he had time for a catnap, but he knew it wouldn't be possible. There was too much to do. There were a lot of pros and cons that came with his job. Lack of sleep and few vacations were definitely a con.

He knocked on the door, and Cheyenne's younger sister, Laura, appeared in the frame. When she saw him, her grin stretched wide across her face.

"Well, if it isn't my favorite FBI agent."

"Laura," Aidan said, reaching out to wrap her in a tight hug. "It's been a while."

Though they only lived three hours from each other, with Laura's job as a traveling nurse, it wasn't often that they could see her. She'd always been one of Aidan's favorite people. And one of the wildest.

He pulled from the embrace. "Where's your other half?"

Laura tilted her head. "Out on the deck. We're having lemonade. Would you like some?"

"No, thank you," Aidan said. "I won't be able to stay long. I didn't get to talk to Cheyenne before I left this morning, so I was hoping to make it up to her."

"Yeah, she told me." Laura swatted his shoulder. "That wasn't very thoughtful of you, O'Reilly."

They made their way through the house to find Cheyenne. As they did, Laura told Aidan they would have the house to themselves because she was heading to Florida for a few months. Aidan asked when she was leaving, and she informed him early Monday morning.

When they stepped into the heat, Cheyenne regarded Aidan, smiled, and jumped from her chair. He pulled her into his arms for a kiss. She released a contented sigh as she wrapped her arms around his neck.

"I've been missing you today."

"Not nearly as much as I've missed you," Aidan said.

"Let's call it a draw," she purred against his lips.

"Get a room, guys," Laura said in mock disgust as she sat.

"Do you hear something?" Aidan asked Cheyenne.

"No, not really. I think it's just white noise." She kissed him again as his cell phone vibrated in its holder on his pants. "Is that you or your phone?"

"Aww geez," Laura said.

Aidan laughed as he reached for his cell to see who was calling.

It was Shaun.

"Sorry, love," he said. "I've gotta get this."

She frowned, but nodded In understanding. He answered the call as she turned to resume her conversation with her sister.

Aidan didn't pick up what Laura whispered, but Cheyenne laughed, and play punched her in the shoulder.

"Yeah, Shaun, what's up?"

"We've got a problem."

Aidan narrowed his eyes. "Another victim?"

"No." A sigh. "I think you better turn on the TV to WJFX."

Aidan hurried into the house, making his way to the living room. After grabbing the remote from the coffee table, he turned the television on to the channel. He watched as a reporter talked about The Carnations Killer's previous victims and suggested that Maya Gibson was his latest. He ended his report by accusing law enforcement of withholding information the public had the right to know.

Aidan's blood boiled.

He recognized the young reporter as the one at Maya's crime scene earlier. He was the one who jammed the microphone into his face and had asked whether or not a serial killer was on the loose.

"I didn't miss the press conference, did I?" Aidan asked, knowing it was not the case.

Cheyenne and Laura must have taken notice of his haste to come inside because they lingered in the doorway, watching, eyes wide.

"No," Shaun said. "Apparently, someone slipped a birthday card underneath the reporter's office door. And now he just told millions of people the card was from The Carnations Killer claiming he's back."

Aidan threw out a round of angry curses. Cheyenne glared at him through her square-rimmed glasses, her hands on her hips. But Aidan didn't care. There were reasons they kept certain information silent until they were ready to announce it to the public. Now, because of a certain reporter, the city would be in chaos, the FBI and local police were shamed, and they'd have to figure out how to do damage control.

If that were even possible.

Aidan cursed again, jamming his thumb on the power button of the remote and tossing it toward the couch. It missed the cushion by an inch and hit the wall with a loud crash.

"I'm on the way to the news station now," Shaun informed him.

"Yeah, yeah, I'm on the way."

Aidan ended the conversation and slipped his cell back into its holder.

"I've got to go," he told the girls.

"I really wish you would quit that," Cheyenne said, fitting her glasses more comfortably on the bridge of her nose.

"What?" Aidan asked as he made his way to the door.

"You know what—that profanity you do," she said. "It really bothers me. I tell you all the time."

"I know," Aidan said. "I'll work on it. But right now, I've got to get back to work."

He kissed her cheek, and she told him to be careful. Telling Cheyenne he loved her, Aidan said goodbye to Laura and hurried out the front door where the bureau car waited.

9

AIDAN PULLED INTO A parking space in front of the WJFX News building as Shaun climbed out of his car. He pushed his door closed and waited until Aidan parked and turned off the ignition, then met him at the driver's side. Shaun pulled open the door.

"This is a mess," Shaun said.

"You're not kidding," Aidan said, unbuckling. "We've hardly started the investigation. Now the state's going to be in panic mode. We're not sure yet if it *is* The Carnations Killer." He climbed out, slammed his door, straightened his dress shirt, and released a heavy sigh.

Another wave of sleepiness overtook him, and he attempted to mask it by shaking his head.

Shaun looked at him curiously. "Are you saying you don't think it's The Carnations Killer after all?"

Aidan frowned and crossed his arms. "I'm saying we know nothing yet. Until we do, there isn't a need to cause undue panic." He paused, then in a low voice said, "But I have no doubt in my mind The Carnations Killer murdered Maya Gibson. We have to proceed carefully. All he wants is attention. Fear. That's why he contacted this reporter in the first place. And because of Jordan Blake, that's exactly what he's about to get."

They began walking, and as they reached the door, Shaun grabbed the handle. Before he opened it, he regarded Aidan.

"Do me a favor and don't punch this guy."

Aidan eyed him, wondering how he could tell what he was thinking. They'd only met this morning, and he seemed to read his mind.

"Why not?" Aidan said. "He deserves it."

"Because if you were in his shoes, you would have done the same thing," Shaun said. "As would I."

Aidan rolled his eyes.

"Fine," he said after it was clear they wouldn't be proceeding without an agreement. "I won't punch him."

"Good," Shaun said with undeniable satisfaction, pulling the door open.

They walked into the building side-by-side, and a few minutes later found themselves in a conference room. Jordan Blake was already waiting, sitting comfortably in his chair, one leg over another. Next to him sat the cameraman who attended him at Clarks Hill Lake.

"Agents," Jordan said, a smug smile playing on his lips.

The sight of him made Aidan want to deck him.

Before he had the chance to respond, the door opened, and another man stepped through.

"Agents O'Reilly and Henderson?"

"Yes," Shaun said, extending his hand.

"Nice to meet you. I'm Thomas Blake."

After shaking his hand, Aidan looked from Jordan to Thomas.

"What I'm sure you're thinking is correct. We are related. The conceited young news reporter over there is my youngest nephew," Thomas explained. "He's full of himself but is a dang good reporter."

"I see," Aidan said. "But that doesn't give him the right to go on the air and—"

"So, the first amendment doesn't apply with reporting serial killers?" Jordan asked.

Aidan squared his jaw.

"The point Agent O'Reilly is trying to make, Mr. Blake," Shaun said, "is that informing the public there's a serial killer in the vicinity without prior authorization, does nothing but create havoc within the community."

"But don't they have a right to know?" Jordan asked.

"They do," Shaun said. "However, we need time to assess the situation."

He waved his hand and took a seat across from the reporter. Aidan followed suit, remaining quiet. He opted to let Shaun do the talking. Aidan decided his new comrade seemed like he'd handle it much better than Aidan ever could. Aidan worried he may make the situation worse if he spoke.

"But what's done is done." Shaun cleared his throat and folded his hands together. "Can we see the card?"

Aidan followed Jordan's gaze toward his uncle, who remained standing by the door. Thomas gave him a slight nod, resulting in a light sigh from the reporter. He leaned toward the floor and removed an envelope from his bag and set it on the table, pushing it across the table.

Shaun used a tissue to retrieve the envelope. He used another tissue to remove the card. They read the note.

"Did you see who left the card?"

"Kent was the one who saw the guy," Jordan said.

Aidan regarded Kent, who shook his head.

"I didn't get a good look at him. He was white, black hair. I saw him lean down and slide the card underneath the door. Then he walked away. At the time, I thought it was a fan. Jordan gets a lot of fan mail, and with his birthday coming, he gets plenty of cards and gifts."

"We're going to have to admit this as evidence," Shaun said.

"Think you'll be able to get fingerprints off it?" Jordan asked.

"Doubtful," Aidan said. "But we're going to try. It doesn't say anything about him returning. Where did you get that information? Or did you only speculate?"

"He received a text message shortly after reading the card." It was the cameraman who spoke.

Jordan fished for his phone and searched his messages.

"Wait a minute," he said after a few minutes of silence ticked by. His eyes grew. "It's gone."

"What's gone?" Shaun asked.

"The text. It was there. I promise. Kent saw it, right?"

"Yeah. I mean, it came shortly after he received the letter. It said to tell the world The Carnations Killer was back."

"What's your number?" Aidan grabbed a notepad and pen from his shirt pocket. He scribbled the number Jordan recited and packed his things. "We'll have our techs check to see if they can't find out who sent the message to your phone."

Aidan looked across the table at Jordan, who was tapping his phone's screen. He assumed the reporter was still trying to find where the text message may have gone.

"In the meantime, Mr. Blake," Aidan said. He waited until Jordan looked at him. "In the meantime, if this guy contacts you again, please don't go directly to the camera, okay?" He slid his business card across the table. "If he contacts you, I need you to call us. Day or night."

Jordan nodded slowly.

"I'm being serious," Aidan said. "If you do this a second time, I'll have you arrested for obstruction."

"I get it," Jordan said coolly.

"Perfect." Aidan pushed to his feet, Shaun following his lead. "Thank you for your time, gentlemen."

They made their way out of the conference room, Shaun studying the note as they walked.

"Curious stuff, isn't it? The Carnations Killer contacts Jordan Blake and tells him to report he's back. A text message disappearing from Blake's phone?"

"It's not unheard of that serial killers reach out to the media," Aidan said. "It's their way of crying for attention, while taunting us. And there are technologies that allow you to remotely delete a text message. I'll stake my career on it that the text message was sent from a burner phone, so we won't be able to trace the sender anyway. But we now learned something we didn't before."

Shaun considered it. "He's tech-savvy."

Halfway to the cars, Aidan unwittingly released a yawn.

Shaun glanced at him and it was obvious he noticed.

"This was supposed to be your last week of vacation," he said. "Why don't you let me write the assessment into the database? I'll finish the day and you go on home. Get some rest."

"I'll be fine," Aidan said.

They reached their cars.

"You left Boston around three yesterday, right? I think that was what you said earlier during lunch."

Aidan nodded, not liking where he was going.

"So, you said you drove non-stop to get home to Atlanta. It takes at least fifteen hours from Boston to there, so you probably got home around six thirtyish in the morning. And you arrived at the crime scene around eight-thirty. And now it's almost four." Shaun frowned. "Which means you've been up for twenty-four hours, give or take. You need sleep, Aidan. You've done enough for the day. Go home, finish your vacation. We'll regroup on Monday morning. The investigation isn't going anywhere, and you know as well as I do that you have to be alert to do the job well. I don't want to tell Tara that the agent Atlanta sent us is falling asleep on the job."

Aidan fought back another yawn, knowing Shaun was right.

"Okay," he said. "You win."

"Good. I'll let you know if something comes up. In the meantime, get some rest and I'll see you soon."

Aidan opened the car door, climbed in, and turned the key, listening to the engine rumble.

"Thanks, Shaun," he said.

"Anytime, buddy."

10

AIDAN PULLED IN FRONT of the open garage and climbed out of the car. He stepped across the stone walkway to the front door, and, using his key, opened it. When Aidan strode inside, the smell of spaghetti sauce greeted his nostrils. He found Cheyenne in the kitchen, leaning over a pot, stirring its contents.

"Hey, you," she said with a warm smile.

Aidan went over and wrapped his arms around her waist, kissing her neck. He muttered against her skin that the sauce smelled delicious.

"Thanks," she said with a light sigh. "It's a new recipe. Very spicy. I wanted to make Laura's favorite dish." She turned to face him. "What are you doing home? I thought you were going to work late."

"Shaun—he's my new partner—insisted," Aidan said. "Insisted I sleep off the drive from Boston."

"Good for Shaun," Cheyenne said with a small smile. "I like him already. I hate it when you chase bad guys in your sleep."

"That's all I ever do," he said with a scoff. Almost as soon as the words came out of his mouth, he realized his joke was a bad one. "It's just not always easy to leave work at work."

"I understand." She caressed his cheek. "I just worry it's going to get the better of you. Before I left, I picked up the mail. You got another letter from that guy at Quantico. They still want you to teach."

Aidan groaned and walked to the refrigerator to pull out a bottle of Michelob. "I told you I don't want to teach, Cheyenne. A field agent is all I've ever wanted to be. I can't imagine doing anything else."

"Can't you just think about it?" Cheyenne asked. "If we moved to Virginia, and you taught, I wouldn't have to spend my life wondering if today's the day I'll get the news you've been killed. You'll have a steady job and no more late-night calls. We could start a family."

"Cheyenne—"

She pressed her fingers against his lips. "Just consider it. That's all I want you to do. Please? Whatever decision you make, I'll support it. But think about it."

"Fine," he said. "I'll consider it."

She kissed the tip of his nose before turning to continue stirring the sauce.

"Where's my wild sister-in-law?"

Cheyenne pointed to the ceiling with her wooden spoon. "Changing the sheets in the master. We're going to sleep in there while she's away."

He watched her taste the sauce, savor it, and then dump a dash more of oregano.

"Tara is going to deliver the press release shortly," he said. "I'm going to go watch it."

"Okay."

Aidan kissed her cheek before walking to the living room. He switched the channel to WJFX, his new favorite station. From now on, he'd be watching it. He needed to keep his eye on Jordan Blake.

The current news anchors were discussing the weather—it was supposed to storm this weekend—and something about a man finding a baby on a park bench. He apparently took her to the hospital, and now the police were in search of the mother.

Thinking about the park baby made Aidan consider his relationship with Cheyenne. He had been with her since his move to Atlanta almost seven years ago. He had met Laura at the local grocery store and before he realized it, they'd made a date. Soon after, Aidan met Cheyenne and knew at that moment he wanted to spend his life with her. He'd asked her to move in with him a year after dating, but because of her strong Christian values, she insisted on them being married before they lived together. It was one of the many things he respected about her. And it made him fall in love with her all over again. Several months after the discussion, he'd popped the question. But even with their strong love for one another, life threw curveballs their way. Admittingly, most of the curveballs were as a result of his fear of the future.

She wanted to have children and build a family with him, but he wasn't sure if they were ready. While he'd took great care at keeping it from his wife, Aidan's mind often went back to The Carnations Killer, whether he was active or not. He'd watched interview tapes, read reports, looked over evidence so much that they were embedded in his mind. The victims had become a part of him, and in a way, the killer himself had become a part of him.

On the TV, the news anchor announced that FBI Assistant Special Agent-In-Charge Tara Monroe was going to issue a statement regarding the Maya Gibson murder.

He turned the volume up and watched. Cheyenne entered the room and sat with him on the couch, leaning her body against his.

Tara appeared on the screen with Lieutenant DeLong standing behind her. They both stared straight into the crowd. Tara's posture effected authority and determination while DeLong seemed to be relieved that he didn't have to speak.

"Early this morning," Tara said, "the body of twenty-eight-year-old Maya Gibson was found at Clarks Hill Lake. The last time she was seen alive was last Tuesday night, around six o'clock, leaving her yoga class at Downward Dog. She was discovered at approximately seven o'clock this morning. Mrs. Gibson was tortured, bound, and fatally strangled with a thin wire."

Tara took a deep breath. She scanned the crowd.

"We believe Mrs. Gibson's death was the work of a serial killer who is known as The Carnations Killer."

She discussed what was already public knowledge about the killer. At Aidan's request, she left out that the victim had been tased, and that he'd received a letter from The Carnations Killer. When she finished, she paused again before asking the media if there were questions.

They talked with excitement over one another.

"No, we do not have any persons of interest at this time," she told one reporter. "But the FBI and the Columbia County Sheriff's Office are working closely together, attempting to narrow down the pool of suspects."

Her attention went to another reporter.

"As long as women—particularly blondes—remain in groups, I don't see where there's cause to worry. We're exhausting every bit of enforcement we have. I'm working with an excellent team. It's only a matter of time before The Carnations Killer is caught."

Tara answered a few more questions before ending the press conference. She requested the public contact the sheriff's office or the FBI Resident Agency if they knew anything about Maya's abduction and murder. The numbers flashed at the bottom of the screen. Aidan muted the TV and sank into the couch, his head on the armrest. Cheyenne sat up and pivoted to look at him, her eyes laced with concern.

"Are you okay?" she asked.

He nodded, still staring at the ceiling. He didn't enjoy talking to Cheyenne about his investigations, but she wanted him to set free the frustration that came with the job. She once told him to write things in a journal if he couldn't talk to her. Cheyenne had told him it might help to unleash the evil he saw, rather than holding it inside. She knew him well enough to realize the things he had seen bothered him, and she knew his first year as an agent was a daunting one. He never explained why it haunted him so much.

A part of him wished he could open up to her. But if he did, the parts of the investigation he kept locked in his mind would only make things worse.

The issue was, would it make it worse for him or her?

She lowered her head to his chest and released a sigh.

"I've been chasing him for ten years," Aidan said, his voice sounding rough to his ears. "Every time he'd kill, I'd try to find something—anything—that would lead us to him. But he's always so careful."

"You'll get him," Cheyenne said, stroking his cheek with her hand. "I know you will."

"The sheets are ready for you," Laura said, entering the room.

Cheyenne looked at her sister.

"I really wish you didn't have to go so soon." She frowned.

"I promise when I get back, we'll do something," Laura said. "I'll even take a long vacation. We'll just make the time."

Cheyenne stood to wrap Laura in a tight hug. "Thanks for letting us stay here."

"Well, it works out for me," Laura said, playing with Cheyenne's short ponytail. "Make yourselves at home. *Mi casa es su casa.*"

"Are you guys hungry?" Cheyenne asked when she pulled away. "Supper's ready for whenever."

"Starved," Laura and Aidan said in unison.

They ushered themselves to the kitchen, then afterward while the girls washed the dishes, Aidan turned in early hoping to get some rest.

11

Aidan walked into the building early Saturday morning. He knew Shaun wanted him to take the break; however, Aidan decided his mind would be on the murder, anyway. So, he figured he might as well look into it some more to forget the many dreams that haunted him the night before.

Aidan had nightmares all too often regarding The Carnations Killer murders. They always seemed to seize his mind, keeping him swept in the middle of the visions that would flash before him. The dreams seemed real to him. They always did.

When Aidan would wake from them, he wouldn't be able to fall back asleep. And if he didn't wake, he'd walk around all day feeling restlessness.

Aidan had long ago decided he was living proof that demons didn't come in the form of a little red man with horns and a pitchfork.

They came from the things people see, the terrifying thoughts that seemed to enslave them because there comes a time when a melting point is reached.

And when that time came, it could be too late.

But it wasn't possible to unsee the things in this world. They haunted the mind, so it would be impossible to forget them.

Sometimes the memories of the dreams and the memories of real-life merged, and Aidan would awaken, wondering if it was real; or if he was awake, he'd wonder if he was dreaming.

He rubbed his eyes, trying to force his dreams from his memory.

It didn't work. It never did.

His dreams were always the same. He would feel The Carnations Killer watching every move he made. He'd watch as Aidan investigated the bodies that'd pile up from Sherry Finch, the first victim, to Maya Gibson, the newest. Their faces, their shells—they'd come at him and he couldn't do a thing to stop it.

It made it difficult to breathe, and Aidan wanted it to end.

He would hear the killer taunting him from somewhere in the distance, his voice garbled to hide his identity.

I can kill, and you can't catch me.

His last words to Aidan ten years ago echoed in the halls of his mind.

At some point, the bodies would turn to face him, their eyes dead, blood dripping from the ends of their blonde hair. Their pale faces outlined in the night as each reached out to him, blood dripping from the wounds on their wrists. He'd try to pull away, but they kept drawing him closer.

Magnet to metal.

Calling to him.

Telling him he failed them. And that he'd fail Maya as well.

All the while, The Carnations Killer's laughter resonated in the night.

I can kill, and you can't catch me.

Aidan shook his head, hoping to shake loose the images swimming in his mind. He realized he had stopped walking and was leaning against the wall. A few agents walking by glanced at him, but only nodded their heads in acknowledgment.

Aidan spotted Tara heading to her office, her high heels thudding softly on the thin carpet.

"Good press release last night, boss," he said.

Tara stopped, then turned to make her way toward him. "Agent O'Reilly. You're here early. And on a Saturday. I trust you were able to get some sleep last night?"

Aidan nodded. "Enough."

Aidan had always kept the power of his dreams to himself. He didn't want to be deemed as mentally incapacitated. Those close to him knew he was an insomniac, especially when his mind fixed on a certain subject. But as long as he looked like himself and could do his job, it wasn't an issue, so he didn't like to announce his night troubles.

"Very good," she said stoically. "Before I left last night, I had a few words with Hansford about you. Some end to your vacation, huh?"

Aidan laughed lightly, shaking his head. "Well, I can't seem to stay away for too long."

She smiled. "That's why we chose the career we're in, I suppose. I trust you're finding everything, okay?"

He told her everything was great.

"Very well. If there's anything I can do, my door's always open. I'll let you get to it. I have a mountain of paperwork to go through myself before I meet with Director Zane."

She patted his shoulder as they parted ways.

Aidan noticed Shaun stepping off the elevator, so he waited for him.

"I just got back from the lab," Shaun said.

"Yeah?"

"The only print on the envelope and card was Jordan Blake's and Kent Ory's. And there's no trace of a text message sent to Blake's cell phone."

"Why doesn't that surprise me?" Aidan asked as they continued the short distance to his cubicle.

He lowered himself into his chair and Shaun grabbed another from nearby and rolled it over.

"So, he still wants to cover his tracks." Aidan leaned back into his chair. "We know our killer is most likely a white male. He gets off from torturing people—like many serial killers, he likely started as a young kid torturing and killing animals. Then, when he got bored, he began searching for women of interest. He knows his technology. He uses burners and knows how to remotely delete any trace of a text. The big kicker is that he uses a taser on his victims and leaves the carnations."

"Also, the M.E. called. As you guessed, Maya wasn't sexually assaulted. He killed her around eleven last night," Shaun said.

Aidan nodded thoughtfully as he stared at his desk, littered with files of other victims. It held too many faces.

"And over the last ten years," Aidan said, mostly to himself, "he's killed women from all over the United States. So he likely has a job that travels from state to state."

"Why do you think he chooses women?" Shaun asked. "He never rapes them. He just beats them and then strangles them."

"Maybe a woman—possibly a good-looking blonde—wronged him when he was a kid. Maybe his mother beat him. Or maybe his mother abandoned him." Aidan leaned over his desk, clasping his hands together. "Or he just hates blonde women and feels powerful when he's hurting them. Have you looked over the recent customers for Downward Dog?"

Shaun put the list on the desk and pushed it toward him.

"Ah-ha. Glad you asked." Shaun's eyes gleamed with interest. "Guess who started attending three weeks ago."

Aidan scanned the list of names, using his index finger as a guide. Muttering to himself, he stopped at a name on the second page.

Well.

It seemed they found a person of interest: Jordan Blake.

12

SHAUN AND AIDAN WAITED with patience in the conference room at the WJFX News Station for Thomas Blake to locate his nephew. In the meantime, Aidan reviewed the list, trying to draw out a few other possibilities. But so far, their news reporter friend was the most viable.

He looked up when he heard the creak of the door, and Jordan stepped through the opening, followed by his uncle.

The frown on Jordan's face told Aidan he wasn't happy about being called back to talk to them, but Aidan gave him a satisfied smile, just to annoy him. After all, that was the least he could do.

Jordan crossed his arms, standing in front of the table, but didn't sit.

"I told you all I know. What do you want now? I'm a bit busy."

"Please," Aidan said, gesturing to the chair with a wave of his hand. "Have a seat."

The reporter looked behind him at his uncle, who gave him a sit-down motion with his palm.

Grudgingly, Jordan did as he was told.

"Have you ever met Maya Gibson before?" Aidan asked. "And to clarify, I mean, before you happened on the scene yesterday morning."

Jordan shook his head.

"You sure about that?" Shaun asked. "Because we found out you attended the same yoga studio as Maya—Downward Dog."

"So do hundreds of other people," Jordan said coolly. "I happen to like yoga. It keeps me in shape." Then he smiled. "And I meet a lot of women that way."

"So, Maya wasn't one of the women you met?" Aidan said. "If we were to call the studio and ask around, no one would tell us they saw a young, handsome, arrogant news reporter making conversation with Maya Gibson?"

Jordan looked Aidan in the eyes, a scowl playing on his lips. Aidan held his gaze until the reporter broke contact.

"Fine," he hissed through his teeth. "I've seen her there. I've even talked to her. I only go once a week. Tuesday nights."

"Did you see her last week at all?"

He shook his head. "I skipped."

"How convenient," Aidan said.

Jordan narrowed his eyes and opened his mouth to retort.

Shaun interjected, "How did you hear about the murder so fast?"

"That kid. You know, the one that found the body. He started spreading it around. As soon as I heard, I was there." He scoffed. "C'mon. Do I need to remind you I wasn't the only reporter there? I bet you aren't even bothering to interview them."

"None of the other reporters' names were on the list." Shaun tapped his index finger on the printout.

Jordan rolled his eyes. "Well, knowing some dead woman doesn't make me a killer."

Aidan believed Jordan, but still found it odd he didn't tell them he knew Maya.

"Why did you try to hide that you knew her?"

"I knew how it'd look," Jordan said simply.

"And it doesn't look any better now than it would have had you been straight with us," Shaun said. "In fact, it raises our curiosity even more."

Aidan tilted his head toward his colleague. "He's got a brilliant point."

Jordan frowned. "So what? You going to arrest me for knowing someone? Geez. Talk about police brutality."

"Jordan, calm down," Thomas said. He stepped closer to the table, standing next to his nephew, looking from Aidan to Shaun. "Should I be calling the lawyer?"

Aidan ignored the question. "Yesterday morning, you asked if Maya's death had anything to do with a serial killer. What made you think that?"

"Nothing," he said. "I'm only trying to make a name as a reporter. Covering a serial killer does wonders for my rep."

Aidan's face flared with annoyance, but he couldn't find any reason to detain the young reporter. No matter how badly he wanted to do just that.

"Has The Carnations Killer contacted you again?" Shaun asked.

"Since yesterday afternoon? Nope."

"Okay," Aidan said with a light sigh. "All right. You're free to go. For now."

"Great." Jordan tapped the table with the palm of his hands and jumped to his feet. "Oh, before I go, agents, can I get a statement from either of you?" He held out a recorder.

Aidan narrowed his eyes and told him no statement, although he really wanted to tell him what he could do with the recorder.

Slipping the device back into his shirt pocket, Jordan turned to leave.

"Forgive my nephew," Thomas said. "He's got a lot of ambition, but he forgets to keep his head out of the clouds."

"How does he get along with his colleagues?" Aidan asked.

"I haven't noticed that he's had any problems," Thomas said. "He doesn't have a lot of friends. Only his cameraman, Kent Ory, and Gary Short, our field technician. I mean, you see how he is. He usually spends his time with the ladies, if you know what I mean." Thomas winked.

"Thank you for your time, Mr. Blake," Aidan said, rising from his seat.

Thomas nodded his acknowledgment as they filed out of the conference room.

On their way out, Aidan spotted Jordan talking in the far corner with his cameraman. They looked their way, but after realizing Aidan was also watching them, the two turned to leave in the opposite direction.

"What are you thinking?" Shaun asked.

"I'm not sure," Aidan said as they stepped into the warm morning. The clouds looked as though they were darkening, and Aidan guessed the forecast of rain for this weekend may come true.

"Jordan seems like a great person of interest," Shaun said.

"He does," Aidan said. "As a reporter, he could easily travel across the US murdering women. It'd help make his career."

"Do you remember ever seeing him before?" Shaun asked as they reached the car.

Aidan climbed in the passenger's side and buckled.

Shaun settled into the driver's side and Aidan answered his question: "No. But it doesn't mean he wasn't there."

"Well, it won't be hard finding out," Shaun said.

Shaun turned the key, and the car rumbled to life.

Aidan stared out the window at the news building, deep in thought. There was only one way to find out.

13

He watched his next target as she helped her employee put several large picture frames on the top display. A small owl on another shelf was on the verge of falling, and he knew she wouldn't be able to catch it before it crashed against her skull.

He hurried, and as the owl fell, he caught it, inches from her head.

Quick reflexes had her ducking out of the way. When she realized what had happened, she finished handing the employee the large frame and turned to him. He handed her the small brass object.

"Wow, thank you," she said with a laugh. "That would've hurt."

He smiled. "Right place, right time."

"Daddy!"

His eight-year-old daughter came running toward him, holding a stuffed purple bear.

"Look what I found."

"Wow," he said. "That's really cute, pumpkin."

"Can I have it? Can I please?"

He smiled and regarded his target, whose name tag read *Jane*. "Can't take her anywhere, can I?"

"She's very beautiful." Jane leaned over, her hands on her knees. "What's your name, young lady?"

"Jamie," she answered shyly, hugging the bear against her chest.

"That's a very pretty name." She righted herself and pressed her hand against his shoulder. "You know you can't resist those puppy dog eyes." Jane winked at Jamie.

He looked down at his daughter, who pouted and whimpered, trying her best to pull off the puppy dog eyes without smiling.

"Yeah, and I also know you're just trying to make a sale." He looked back at Jane, putting on a "pretending to be mad" look.

"Who, me?" She tapped an index finger on her chin as Jamie giggled. "Well, now that I think about it, I bet your daughter would love the new line of Disney princess furniture we got in the other day. I'll even throw in a fifteen percent discount, since I'm pretty certain you saved me from a deadly concussion."

"Disney princess furniture? Really?" Jamie's eyes grew as she jumped with excitement. "Can I see? Can I see?"

"I'm afraid not right now, pumpkin," he said. "I've got to get back to work. But I'll buy you the bear if you want him."

She smiled and nodded eagerly that she did want him.

He turned back to Jane. "Well played, Miss Jane. Well played."

"We bear lovers have to stick together. Isn't that right, young lady?"

Jamie giggled enthusiastically, nodding her head.

"All right, come on, pumpkin," he said as he took hold of his daughter's hand.

"I hope you'll come again," Jane said.

He turned and began walking backward. Jamie hurried to the end of a line at the register. "You can count on seeing me again. I did see something I really want, but it's going to have to wait until next week. Can't jump the gun on it, you know."

He gave her a salute and waited until it was his time to pay for the bear.

After the deed was done, Jamie declined a bag, wanting to hold on to her new friend.

"Thank you so much, Daddy," she said, her voice soft as she stared adoringly at the bear. "I really love him."

"You're very welcome, pumpkin. Happy early birthday."

14

Shaun and Aidan spent the next few hours calling around to find out whether Jordan had reported on any of the other murders. They learned he only began reporting six years ago, and he'd covered two other serial murders. However, what interested them was that Jordan was in Michigan five years ago when four people were murdered. Aidan had been on another case during that time, preventing him from joining the investigation.

The local police assumed three of them were part of The Carnations Killer murders because they exhibited the same kinds of torture as all the other women.

One death struck Aidan's interest, and he could tell it did with Shaun as well.

Her name was Keisha Moffett, thirty years old, single with no kids.

And she was African American, which was not part of the killer's usual object of interest.

Aidan had asked why Keisha wasn't in the federal database, and they told him that the agent assigned to the case back then didn't believe she was a victim of the same killer as the other murder. Aidan was told that the agent had claimed it was a state matter and not federal.

A group of hikers found twenty-nine-year-old Brenda Wilkes near the end of a trail in the Porcupine Mountains. While the police were searching the area, they came across the body of Keisha Moffett, approximately two miles away. She had a few scrapes and bruises, multiple lacerations from a knife, and she had bled out from a deep gash across her throat.

The Chief of Police in Ottawa County strongly believed Keisha was a victim of the same man who murdered Brenda. But there was no evidence saying she was, and her murder had never been solved. The FBI claimed she was a target of a copycat, but more likely the victim of abuse.

Based on the police reports, Keisha and Brenda didn't know each other. The day they found the women murdered was the day Keisha's boyfriend, Jamal Foster, had taken her on a day-long hiking date. His family had told the police he'd planned on asking her to marry him during the hike. But she was murdered before it ever happened, and Jamal vanished.

The investigating federal agents suspected the boyfriend and believed he killed Keisha and started a new life somewhere else.

The situation surrounding the murders and Jamal's disappearance baffled the local police and the FBI. Theories passed from mouth to mouth, but nothing made sense of what really happened.

Although Aidan understood why the original agent believed what he did, he couldn't help but wonder if Keisha and Jamal happened upon the killer as he was dumping the body. It was possible. If they did, and the killer saw them, then he'd have to take care of them to ensure he'd remain unidentified.

Taking that into consideration, Aidan decided on a scenario most law enforcement, including the FBI, hadn't believed.

"What are you muttering about?"

Aidan looked across his desk at Shaun, who was busy flipping through paper copies of the FBI and police reports.

"So, the killer's MO is tasing his victims, torturing them, then killing by strangulation," Aidan said, leaning back in his chair. He crossed one leg over the other and began rapping his pen against the edge of his desk. Shaun looked up to give Aidan his undivided attention. "He'd leave them where they'd be found later, right?"

Aidan nodded.

"So, when he killed Brenda Wilkes, he followed his system. Then enter Keisha Moffett and Jamal Foster. They'd planned to spend the entire day in the mountains. Hiking, fishing, camping, whatever. During their hike, maybe they saw something they weren't supposed to see."

"A man tossing a dead body to the side," Shaun said.

"Right," Aidan said. "The killer saw his uninvited guests. Maybe he heard them approach, or they asked if he needed help. But it didn't take much to realize something was wrong, so they'd obviously want to get the heck out of Dodge." Aidan narrowed his eyes. "If it happened to Cheyenne and me, I would tell her to run as fast as she could, then I'd do whatever I could to give her enough of a chance to escape."

Shaun nodded. "According to reports, they thought Keisha was heading down the mountain."

"Yeah, so if Jamal tried to protect her, then it makes sense he'd fight off the killer. And we know the killer had a knife because he used it on Keisha. So, he probably used it on Jamal, chased after Keisha, and caught up with her a couple of miles away."

"So, what happened to Jamal's body?" Shaun asked. "He was never found."

"The wonderful thing about mountains is they are enormous. Plenty of hiding spots. The police and FBI alike weren't thinking of looking for a third body. After finding Keisha, they immediately suspected her boyfriend killed her and took off."

"So," Shaun said, "Jamal Foster's remains could still be somewhere in those mountains."

Aidan swallowed hard. "It's starting to make sense."

"What?" Shaun asked.

Aidan regarded him with hesitation. "I didn't investigate Brenda Wilkes' murder. Or Keisha's and Jamal's. But I was around for the others since I was part of the original killings."

"Okay..." Shaun said.

"The following year, The Carnations Killer started leaving me his notes."

"Oh."

They fell into silence.

Aidan told Shaun that he wanted to get Tara to send out a search party to comb the Porcupine Mountains. He realized she would not like it because it'd take more people and time, but he believed it had to be done.

Aidan rose from his chair, and they made their way to Tara's office. After her muffled voice told them to come on in, they did.

"We may have a break," Aidan said.

Tara looked up from a report she was signing.

"You're kidding."

Aidan sat and crossed his leg over his knee with a despondent sigh. "We don't know how much of a break it is. Could be nothing. But I think we need to follow up and see where it leads."

Shaun and Aidan took turns in telling Tara what they found, and their theories. She listened with intent, but after they finished, her red lips turned to a frown.

"So, you want me to send a search party to look for a body in the middle of the mountains in Michigan, which may or may not be there?"

Aidan nodded.

"I don't know about that," Tara said. "That's going to exhaust a lot of resources we can't afford right now. Especially since we may need them here."

"Tara, please. I realize it's a stretch. And I know there's a fifty-fifty chance I'm wrong. But what if I'm right? It may not get us closer to finding The Carnations Killer, but if we found Jamal Foster somewhere in those mountains, then it'd provide a little closure for his family. And Keisha's. Right now, they're living their lives believing he may have murdered his girlfriend. If we do find him, they'll know that their son, their brother, their friend...isn't a killer."

Aidan told her it wasn't the killer's style to bury the bodies, so he figured while he ran after Keisha, Jamal may have tried to escape the mountains in another direction. He was probably stabbed, so he was bound to lose a lot of blood.

Tara looked from Aidan to Shaun, as if to check on the validity of the claim. Finally, after minutes ticked by, she sighed. She put her hand on the landline.

"Okay," she said. "I'll see what I can do."

"Thank you," Aidan said. "We're going to grab something to eat, then pay Jordan Blake another visit to see what he has to say about his time in Michigan. With any luck, he may remember seeing something."

15

Aidan called Lieutenant DeLong and asked him to bring a few officers with him to the WJFX studio. When he spoke to DeLong over the phone, Aidan relayed everything they found so far, and that they were searching for Jamal Foster's remains in the mountains. DeLong voiced he didn't believe the Michigan police would find anything. Aidan replied they agreed, but had a duty to the families to try.

They were now in Jordan's office, much to the reporter's angst.

Aidan asked him whether he was ever in Michigan on a reporting assignment.

"Yeah, I was in Michigan for a little while," Jordan said. "It was just for a few months."

"Do you remember covering any other Carnations Killer murders?" Aidan asked.

"Kind of, sort of."

"What kind of answer is that?" Shaun said. "I'm sure a brilliant reporter such as yourself would remember. You do realize the more you keep from us, the guiltier you appear."

"I have never hurt another human being." Jordan scoffed, shaking his head. "So I've reported on other Carnations Killer murders. Surprise, surprise. I'm a reporter."

"A reporter with a knack for knowing things beforehand," Aidan said, his arms crossed tightly over his chest. He narrowed his eyes. "I mean, you arrived at the Maya Gibson site shortly after the body was found."

"Told you the kid started running his mouth."

"You knew Maya was the latest Carnations victim."

"He sent me a text saying he was back."

"Which conveniently disappeared."

Jordan opened and closed his mouth, unsure of his next rebuttal.

"And to top it off," Aidan said, "you lied about knowing Maya. You withheld that you were pretty familiar with the other investigations. I'd say that's pretty suspicious."

Jordan frowned. "I had nothing to do with these murders. I love women. Really. And they love me. I have zero interest in kidnapping and whipping them." He winked at Aidan. "Unless, of course, they give me their approval."

"Then, I'm certain you can provide an alibi for last Tuesday night or this Thursday morning." It was DeLong who spoke.

Jordan turned his attention to the lieutenant, squaring his jaw. "No."

"In that case, I'm afraid, we have no choice but to bring you in," Aidan said. "We'll get a warrant to search your home and office."

Jordan released a groan as Lieutenant DeLong motioned for one of his men to read the news reporter his rights. The officer cuffed his wrists behind his back, then guided Jordan out of the news station.

"The guy's a snake," DeLong said.

"That's one way to put it," Aidan said, watching Jordan stroll through the hallway as though he were being escorted to a royal party.

"Advise me of what you find in Michigan," DeLong asked, "if you don't mind."

Aidan told him he would.

After he left to follow his men, Aidan looked at Shaun.

"He looks guilty," he said. "Acts it, too."

"Looking and acting are different from being," Shaun said.

"You don't think Jordan's responsible for Maya's death?"

"You've followed The Carnations Killer investigation for the best part of ten years, right?" Shaun asked. "During all those years, how many times has he let himself be so careless?"

Aidan frowned. "Not enough."

The killer was too detailed to let himself be sloppy. He wouldn't bother framing another man. Not unless the feds were on his tail and he needed an escape.

So what was it?

Coincidence?

Soon enough, once they had the warrant to search Jordan's home and office in their hands, they'd be able to find whether he had anything that may implicate him.

16

Western Upper Peninsula of Michigan
Ottawa National Forest
Six miles to Iron River

Chief Harmon Gillespie watched as his men combed through the vast land in search of the body of a man who'd disappeared five years ago. He remembered the case vividly and had always believed Jamal Foster was not the man responsible for the murder of his girlfriend.

It never sat right with him.

He'd heard of The Carnations Killer from the news before the killer ever struck his first Michigan victim. He knew that he'd killed other women in other states. And he knew the killer had murdered Brenda Wilkes. That much was a given. Even the feds thought so.

But they disagreed with him that the same man who murdered Brenda also killed Keisha Moffett and Jamal. Because Jamal's body was never found, they believed he killed his girlfriend and willingly disappeared.

But Gillespie thought differently.

Until now, he'd never had the resources to search for Jamal's body.

Thanks to Agent O'Reilly, Gillespie could watch as his team, along with the feds, scoured the mountains on foot and by helicopter for the remains of the young man.

Even though it was a strong possibility they were wasting their time, Chief Gillespie scribbled what little evidence they found onto the pad he clutched.

He was thankful that finally, they were trying to understand a five-year mystery.

Daylight was waning, and Gillespie felt a yawn coming, but he refused to call it a night. They'd only been searching for a few hours. He couldn't give in to sleep just yet. They still had a lot of ground to cover.

"Chief!"

A young officer called out to him, and Gillespie hurried to where she stood, kneeling on the ground.

Sergeant Karen Black snapped a photo before reaching into a bed of leaves and pulling out a small, black box. She pushed to her feet so she'd be at the same height as Gillespie, and then opened the box.

Its hinges were rusty, but it creaked open with ease.

Inside was a diamond ring, almost as brand new as it had been when originally bought.

Gillespie exchanged glances with his young sergeant. He knew she knew how important this search was to him. She'd been a part of the investigative team from the beginning. Gillespie knew the sergeant also had reservations about Jamal's guilt.

"Could it be his?" she asked, her voice breathy.

"Over here! I've got something!"

Gillespie's heart leaped to his throat.

With Black hot on his heels, he rushed to where a federal agent was kneeling, looking at something on the ground.

One of his officers carefully stepped to where the agent stooped. When Gillespie arrived, he saw something hidden beneath the leaves and dirt—a pile of bones and a human skull.

"Careful," Gillespie said. "Don't move it."

The agent glared at him but stepped away to allow someone to snap a photo before another carefully brushed away the debris that covered the remains.

Sergeant Black was already on the phone requesting a forensic anthropologist to come to their location right away, as one of Gillespie's men began collecting bugs that crawled around the skull. With the bugs, he'd be able to determine the approximate time of death.

"Hard to believe, isn't it?" Sergeant Black said after she ended her phone call.

Gillespie nodded.

"Want me to contact the family?"

"No," Gillespie said, his eyes still on the skull. "We need to confirm it, then I'll contact his family. It should be me."

GILLESPIE STOOD IN THE medical examiner's office as the forensic anthropologist the FBI sent him ran tests on the remains. She'd already sent fiber samples to the lab and ordered a request for Jamal's dental work.

The testing would take a few hours, and Gillespie realized his presence was annoying her, but he was too eager to be anywhere else. He stood in the far corner of the room, and as he waited for her to finish her analysis, he glanced through the photos his people took of the bones and ring. He'd already emailed the photos to Agent O'Reilly and informed him as soon as he confirmed the remains belonged to Jamal Foster, he'd call him.

The anthropologist's assistant entered the room and handed her a sheet of paper.

"Well?" Gillespie said. He stepped closer to the gray slab of a table and studied the remains. "Is it Jamal Foster?"

"It is," she said. "And gauging from the markings on the cervical and facial bones, his throat was sliced, which caused death. And..." The anthropologist hesitated as she scanned the sheet her assistant handed her. "The bugs collected from the remains match my findings for the estimated time of death. He died around the time Keisha Moffett was murdered."

Gillespie's stomach dived.

"He was likely trying to find help," he said underneath his breath. "He wasn't where the other two victims were."

"I'd say congratulations," the anthropologist said, "but I'm not so sure it is congratulations."

Gillespie stared at the remains that used to be known as Jamal Foster. After five years, they finally learned what happened to him.

"At least his family will know," Gillespie said, breaking the silence. "They can take some comfort in that and now have closure."

Gillespie thanked her and left.

It was time to call the agent in Augusta and tell him the news.

17

Jordan's office had nothing of interest, and so far, neither did his home. He lived alone in a ranch-style house littered with *Playboys*, empty beer cans, and clothing. The wallpaper was peeling off the walls and the bathroom obviously hadn't been properly cleaned in a month.

The way his home looked, Aidan decided that if he could, he'd arrest him for house abuse.

The grass in the backyard needed cutting. There was a doghouse, and a golden retriever stood by the opening near two bowls containing water and food. He was barking, letting them aware they weren't welcome in his home.

Aidan was looking through a stack of Jordan's adult magazines mixed with loose papers of receipts and bills when his phone vibrated against his hip.

Before answering, he glanced at the caller ID and saw it was Chief Gillespie.

"Agent O'Reilly."

"This is Chief Gillespie of Ottawa County in Michigan. I just received the autopsy results from the bones we found."

"And?"

"And it's Jamal Foster."

Aidan sat in the chair at the computer desk, unsure of what to say.

"Forensics confirmed Jamal's throat was cut," Chief Gillespie said. "Before I called you, I went over the original report for Keisha Moffett, and it seems she died shortly before Jamal's estimated time of death. So, I'm guessing after our suspect cut Jamal's throat, he ran after Keisha to take care of her. Jamal may have been disoriented enough to end up where he was and bled to death."

"Why hasn't anyone come across his body?" Aidan asked, as Shaun appeared in the doorway.

"Well, we have experienced heavy storms and inclement weather since then. Over time, he probably sank into the ground and underneath heavy leaf cover."

Aidan nodded. It made sense.

"So now we know Jamal didn't kill Keisha," Aidan said. "Your suspicions all those years ago were correct, Chief."

"Hmm. But that begs the question, who killed Keisha, Jamal, and the others?"

"That's what I intend to find out. Eventually. Thank you, Chief, for everything."

"No, Agent O'Reilly," Gillespie said, "thank *you*. Because of you, I can give Keisha's and Jamal's families some sense of peace knowing he didn't kill her."

"Let's pray we can find the man responsible so we can give all the victims and their families the justice they deserve."

"Will you keep me in the loop?"

"I certainly will, Chief," Aidan said.

"And I'll see if I can't dig up anything on my end. After all, The Carnations Killer struck my city."

"Anything you come across will be a major help," Aidan said.

After they ended the call, Aidan looked at Shaun and reiterated the conversation.

"Why didn't The Carnations Killer use the same means of death on Keisha and Jamal as he did the others?" Shaun asked.

"Well, they weren't his types of victims, so they didn't matter to him. Otherwise, I think he'd probably do to Keisha the same thing he did to the others." Aidan paused. "The Carnations Killer has a particular type for killing. He prefers blondes and whites. Keisha Moffett was neither, and Jamal Foster wasn't either—not to mention he was a male. They were only collateral damage."

Shaun considered what Aidan said and seemed satisfied with the deduction. He looked around the small office and said, "We're about done here. Unless Jordan worked from somewhere else, I'd say he's clean."

Aidan nodded. "That doesn't really surprise me."

"You didn't think he did it?" Shaun picked up a photo of Jordan and his uncle. They stood with fishing poles in front of a large pond, with a house in the background, beaming for the camera. From what Aidan could see, Jordan looked to be fifteen in the photo. His face showed signs of a happy teenager. Aidan couldn't help but wonder what happened over the years to make him the arrogant man he became.

"You don't either," Aidan said.

Shaun shook his head. "What do you want to do about him?"

"Well, he's the only piece of the puzzle we have," Aidan said, looking out the window. "Just because we found nothing here doesn't mean he's not the killer. Despite what you and I feel."

"So, you want to keep him detained?"

"At least over the weekend. It'll give us time to talk with Agent Byers." He was the agent in charge of The Carnations Killer investigation in Michigan. Byers was now retired and living in Canada but had agreed through email to talk to them over the phone the next day at noon, their time. "It'll give me some sense of satisfaction that he's behind bars for a few days."

Shaun laughed at the prospect.

"He'll be out by Monday," Aidan said.

"Why don't we call it a night?" Shaun said. "I think we deserve it. Wanna have dinner and a few beers with me?"

"Sure. I'll call Cheyenne and let her know."

THEY DECIDED ON MELLOW Mushroom, a restaurant Aidan knew Laura loved, but he and Cheyenne had never been.

Inside, it was noisy with chatter and Aidan had to strain to hear the soft-spoken hostess ask how many were in their party.

Shaun told her two and requested the patio.

Cheyenne and Aidan enjoyed dining outside at restaurants during the summer, so he was glad when Shaun said he also preferred it.

There was only one other customer who sat outside, a woman munching on a Greek salad while reading a book. They chose a table away from her since she was smoking, and Aidan hated being around smoke.

"So how long have you been with Cheyenne?" Shaun broke into his thoughts as they scanned the menu.

"About five years," Aidan said. "Seems it's more like five minutes, though."

"Still in the honeymoon stage, huh?"

"Still in the honeymoon stage, and this past week, she's gotten the big idea of renewing our vows." Aidan rolled his eyes. "It's all because we just attended my younger sister's wedding."

Shaun guffawed.

"Leave it to a woman to bring in the romance." He shook his head, still chuckling. "You gonna do it?"

"Isn't one wedding enough?"

Shaun narrowed his eyes, gazing at Aidan with curiosity. "I bet you will. I know you love her. You have that twinkle in your eye. You try to hide that sensitive side with that temper of yours. I bet when your woman wants you to do something, no matter how cheesy, you ain't nuthin' but putty in her hands."

"Guess I should be so lucky that work keeps me busy."

Aidan settled on a Jerk Chicken Hoagie without mushrooms as the waitress approached. They ordered two beers and their food. The waitress took the menus and left them to their conversation.

"Honestly, I'm surprised she's even still with me. I think a part of me is waiting for her to walk. She wants me to take a teaching job they offered me in Quantico. It's safer with better hours. Right now, I'm usually on call. She doesn't like that."

"Ah," Shaun said. "You don't want to go to Virginia?"

"Not really. A field agent is who I am."

The drinks came, and Aidan took a sip from his lager.

"What about you? Do you have someone?"

"I've dated a few times over the years. But mostly, I remain single. The women I meet seem to be afraid of me."

"Maybe it's not *you* they're afraid of," Aidan said. "When Cheyenne and I first met, she wanted nothing to do with me. She knew I was FBI. She thought about how dangerous it was and didn't want to spend her life worrying."

"How did you convince her?"

Aidan lifted the corner of his mouth in a lopsided smile. "By dating her sister."

"Really?" Shaun laughed. "That's classic."

Aidan took another sip of his beer. "It didn't last long, Laura and me. She's always been the flighty type. Plus, I had a major crush on Cheyenne and she knew it. Laura told me I was destined to be a part of her family. So, she convinced Cheyenne to go on one date. That was all it took."

"Some guys have it." Shaun raised his glass at Aidan.

"Just the luck of the Irish, I guess."

Shaun chuckled. "Why don't you send some of that Irish luck my way?"

Their banter subsided as the food came, and then the conversation shifted to favorite movies, things they liked to do on days off, and the places they'd traveled.

It was nine o'clock when they decided to finally pay for their meals and go their separate ways.

Aidan told Shaun he would see him the next day for the call from the retired agent. Because he knew Aidan had promised Cheyenne he'd take at least one day off, Shaun offered to speak with the agent himself, but Aidan declined the offer.

Shaun agreed and told him he'd meet him at Laura's house in the afternoon.

18

Aidan woke early Sunday to the rain pattering against the roof. Every so often, thunder rumbled, and lightning flashed across the sky. He remained under the covers, his arm draped across Cheyenne's body. Her calm breathing made him not want to get out of bed, so he continued to lie there.

Listening to the rain.

Feeling her body rise and fall in slow, steady motions with each breath.

Although Aidan was planning to take most of the day off, he couldn't help but think about the case. He had promised himself he would give Cheyenne and Laura his undivided attention, but his mind never ceased to drift to the search for the killer.

They already found so many things in such a small amount of time, it almost appeared planned.

Jordan Blake was at the Maya Gibson scene, although there were other reporters there as well.

He'd been in Michigan, where The Carnations Killer murdered three women five years ago, along with Keisha Moffett and Jamal Foster. Evidence still didn't point to their murders being connected with The Carnations Killer, but it seemed too coincidental.

Jordan also knew The Carnations Killer had killed Maya, and the text that hinted at the fact mysteriously disappeared without so much as a trace.

And he'd also lied about knowing Maya Gibson.

Aidan rolled to his back and stared at the ceiling. He couldn't help but wonder if The Carnations Killer was playing games with Jordan's life. If he was, then he was doing an excellent job. Although they didn't find evidence in his belongings that may implicate him, it didn't mean they couldn't find some way to charge him.

We've prosecuted people for less, Aidan thought grimly.

He hoped Agent Byers, the former agent in charge five years ago, would shed some light on the matter. Maybe there was information he'd failed to put in the report. Maybe there was a reason he was dead set on believing Jamal had killed Keisha and took off.

"Hmm."

Aidan turned his head to see Cheyenne turn slowly toward him. She kept her eyes closed, but smiled and muttered good morning.

He caressed her face with his finger.

"Morning."

"You're off today." Cheyenne lifted the corner of her lips in a smile.

"I am," Aidan said. "Sort of. I have a call coming in later this afternoon. An agent that was in charge of an investigation a few years ago."

She groaned and sighed. "Aidan, you promised you wouldn't work today."

He rolled over so he could put his arm across her waist and propped up with his other arm to gaze at her. "I know I did, but this is something I *need* to do. It's the only time he's able to talk to us. I promise, after the call, I'm all yours."

"Guess I'll just have to take what I can get."

Aidan leaned in to kiss her.

She parted her lips, welcoming his advances. He felt her hands run through his hair, and Aidan delved deeper into the moment, thankful he had even a minute's worth of thinking of someone other than the killer.

Aidan lifted her nightgown over her head, tossing it to the floor while trailing kisses along her neck. He worked his way down her flawless body, each movement he made slow.

"Mmm. You know what I want you to do for me?" she whispered as he tracked his kisses across her stomach.

"Tell me." His voice grew huskier as he tasted her.

"Make me breakfast."

Aidan stopped what he was doing to look at her.

She smiled at him, her eyes twinkling.

He pretended to scowl. "You're a tease."

"Maybe, but I realized you haven't given me breakfast in bed in years."

"Well, guess I'd better change that," he said. He kissed her again, then rolled out of the bed. Grabbing his robe from the bathroom, he slipped his arms through the sleeves and tied the strings around his body.

Aidan walked into the kitchen, humming to himself as he gathered the bacon and eggs from the fridge. He set them on the counter and grabbed a large pan hanging over the island.

He slapped butter in the pan and waited for it to heat when he heard a knock coming from the front of the house.

At least, he thought he did.

The knock was faint, and he couldn't tell if it came from the thunder or the door. He paused, holding an egg above the edge of the frying pan, and listened.

He set the egg on the spoon rest and made his way through the rooms to peer out the front window. He saw nothing out of the ordinary, but he opened the door. No one was around.

He was about to deem it as his imagination when he saw the note on the ground.

Aidan stooped to retrieve it, his heart skipping a few beats as he inspected the paper.

It was addressed to him, and looked like it was in the same handwriting as the note left on the body of Maya Gibson.

Still hunched on the ground, Aidan scanned the neighborhood, trying to notice if anything appeared out of the ordinary.

No one was around.

With his heart hammering in his ears, he unfolded the note and read what it said.

19

AIDAN READ THE NOTE. He tried to swallow and wet his dry throat, to no avail. He looked around again, then read the note again.

FBI Special Agent Aidan O'Reilly—
How are things faring in your investigation? Have you been able to put the pieces together yet? I know you're good at your job, Agent O'Reilly. But know I am much better at mine. Stay tuned, old friend. I've got wonderful surprises for you. I can hardly wait. I'll keep in touch. Until then, happy investigating.
Your friend,
The Carnations Killer

When his legs were sturdy enough to hold his weight, he rose and went back inside. Aidan pushed the door shut with his foot and returned to the kitchen, where his phone was on the counter.

He tapped the code to unlock the screen and found Shaun's number.

Aidan glanced at the microwave to see that it was almost eight o'clock. He had told him the day before that every morning he tried to run five miles. Aidan wondered whether he would take today off from his routine.

Shaun answered on the second ring.

"Yup."

Aidan could tell Shaun was running at a fast pace, but he didn't appear he was running out of breath as he would be in his place.

"The Carnations Killer left me a note," Aidan said. "A few minutes ago."

"He what?" It sounded as if Shaun had halted. Sucking in a breath, he continued. "What does it say?"

Aidan paraphrased the note as he continued to make breakfast.

"Man," was all Shaun said after he finished. "He knows where you are?"

"It would seem." Aidan grabbed two plates from the cabinet and slipped two pieces of bread into the toaster. When the food was ready, Aidan divided the breakfast onto the plates and retrieved the silverware. He left enough in the pan for when Laura woke.

"Can you have two men stationed outside this house?" Aidan asked. He kept his voice low during the conversation so it wouldn't carry upstairs. "I don't want to say anything to Cheyenne or her sister. I don't want them to worry. Laura will be out-of-town tomorrow. She'll be safe, but I want to make sure Cheyenne is safe."

"I'm on it," Shaun said.

"Thanks." Aidan gathered the breakfast on a tray, poured coffee into two cups, and with the phone placed between his ear and shoulder, he walked up the steps. "Are you still coming over later?"

"Yeah. I'll be there a few minutes before four. I've got to run a few errands first."

"All right. See you then."

He entered the bedroom, balancing the tray in one hand. He set the phone on the dresser.

"Thought you decided to eat without me," Cheyenne said. She sat upright, her back against the headboard. She'd covered her body with the sheets and turned the channel to *The Golden Girls*.

"I thought about it." Aidan forced a smile. "Then decided you should eat, too."

His mind still reeled over the idea that the killer knew his whereabouts, knew he was at Laura's house. It didn't appear Cheyenne noticed a change in him, and Aidan hoped it stayed that way. The last thing he needed was for her to worry more than she already did.

"I'm glad," Cheyenne said, accepting the coffee. She set it on her bedside table. "Because I'm starved."

Aidan bit into his toast.

They fell into silence as she watched the show, and he continued to contemplate the letter.

"So, I know you don't like to talk about it, but how's the investigation going?"

After slipping a forkful of egg into his mouth, he let his shoulders rise and fall.

"Do you have any leads?"

Aidan looked at her. He could see the concern in her blue eyes, and he hated it. He wanted nothing more than for her to feel safe. In this world, she deserved at least that. Especially when she put up with him working in a dangerous job. Aidan wondered if he should take the teaching job at Quantico after all. Train other men and women on how to be good agents. He could protect her better.

"We're doing everything we can."

"I know you are," she whispered. "I'm just—"

She looked back at the television screen. *The Golden Girls* sat around the kitchen table eating cheesecake. It was clear one of the girls were having an issue that needed to be sorted.

"Talk to me," Aidan said.

"I'm worried about you," she said after a pause. "I mean, I hear about how certain cases can ruin agents' lives. They get depressed, they become obsessed. They even shut out the ones they love."

"That won't happen to me, to us," he said.

"How can you be sure? Aidan, you've been after this guy for ten years." She put her empty plate on the tray and twisted in the bed to face him. She blinked back tears. "Every time he kills someone else, some*where* else, you try not to let it bother you. But it does. I know it does. And I understand it does. And you try to hide it. But you don't hide it very well. For the last five years, you've woken up late at night, or you toss and turn so that you don't get a good night's rest. I know you're thinking of him. Of who he might be. You haven't caught him yet, and it's eating you up inside."

Aidan put his hand on her shoulder and squeezed.

"I don't wake up at night dreaming of him," he said. "I wake up because of your loud snoring."

He offered her a smile, but she shook his hand away. Cheyenne climbed out of the bed, pulled on her nightgown, and grabbed the dishes.

"This isn't a joke, Aidan," she said. "I'm being serious."

"I know you are."

"Then why won't you just let us have a serious conversation about it and not make jokes?"

She turned and headed out of the room, leaving him frowning after her.

20

After church, they hung around to speak to a few of the attendees. Aidan's job as an FBI agent always fascinated Laura, and she wanted to show him off. He had lost count of how many times people inquired whether he'd come close to catching The Carnations Killer.

It was quickly apparent that the serial killer's presence in their city had caused fear, especially since the news had told the world. They even said that it seemed The Carnations Killer stepped away from his normal MO to murder Keisha Moffett and Jamal Foster. Any little thing from the media could raise panic these days.

He tried to contain it by assuring everyone that they were working closely with the local police, as well as law enforcement in other states. Some accepted what he said, others—mostly the men—needed further assurance. Understandably, they didn't want anything happening to the women in their lives.

A few of the men asked why he attended the morning service instead of searching for the killer. Aidan replied that even federal agents needed to attend church and listen to God's words. In his choice of career, Aidan needed to hear His words to keep his sanity intact. It reminded him that despite the things he would see on a day-to-day basis, it would work out okay in the end.

But even in church, he always sat on the end of the pew and kept his phone on vibrate in case he was called away. Thankfully, he wasn't this morning, but he drifted from the preacher's sermon to reflect on the note the killer left for him earlier.

He was planning something big, and Aidan tried to presume what it could be.

Shaun had already issued two undercover agents to monitor Cheyenne. It made Aidan feel better knowing she'd be safe.

They ate a quick lunch at a Mexican restaurant before returning home to get out of the Sunday drizzle.

Now, as Cheyenne and Laura watched a movie, Aidan flipped through the dummy files he'd removed from the office. He wanted to make sure he hadn't missed something over the last ten years.

It didn't seem he had.

Aidan pushed out a breath with the sudden desire to hurl the files across the room. Ten years had gone by with at least fifty women murdered and they had nothing. *Nothing!* He kept waiting for the killer to do something—anything—to slip up. But he was always too careful. And that gave the killer enough confidence to contact Aidan, claiming something major was in the works.

Aidan frowned. He couldn't for the life of him imagine what the killer was planning.

Aidan searched his notes for what seemed to be the billionth time, trying to link suspects to the victims. So far, Jordan Blake was at the top of the list, but he didn't think the smug news anchor could pull off such heinous crimes. Then again, when it came right to it, serial killers could be who you'd least expect.

If Jordan really was The Carnations Killer, then maybe he wanted to push his limits. It wouldn't be unusual for a killer to return to the scene of the crime. Jordan's job provided the perfect cover.

"You okay?"

Realizing the living room fell into silence, Aidan eyed Cheyenne. They had paused the film, and two pairs of eyes were gazing at him.

He tried to offer a reassuring smile and claim he was fine, but he could tell Cheyenne knew he was lying—she always could.

"Why don't you take a break? You promised me, remember? Watch the movie with us."

"I'm watching." Aidan looked at the picture on the screen. "I'm just... multitasking."

"You've been focused all weekend on this investigation," she said, folding her arms over her chest. She frowned. "You've been here, but you haven't *been* here."

"It's my *job*, Cheyenne." Aidan swallowed hard as his icy tone flew out of his mouth. But he would not back down. "Unless I cave and accept the position at Quantico, *this* is my job."

For a few seconds, Cheyenne glared at him, then saying nothing further, she un-paused the movie.

Cheyenne narrowed her eyes and leaned back against the couch, crossing her arms tightly against her chest, her lips in a frown.

Laura bit her bottom lip, unsure of what to say.

Even with his mind set on the latest murder, Aidan couldn't let it rest at that. With a sigh, he closed the files and set them on the table next to him. Leaving his recliner, Aidan moved to sit on Cheyenne's left side. He draped his arm over her shoulder. "You know I love you, right?"

"I guess," she said.

Aidan rolled his eyes toward Laura. "Your big sister's going to kill me one of these days."

Laura giggled and rose. "I better finish packing for tomorrow. You guys need privacy to talk." She pointed her index finger at Aidan. "You'd better be good to my sister, buddy."

After she was out of earshot, Aidan pivoted on the couch to see Cheyenne better. "Look, honey, I understand this isn't easy for you. You know, me working this type of job. But I want to do everything possible to be sure you live in a safe world. And these victims..." He looked the window at the rain. "I owe it to these women to find out who took them away from their families. They don't have anyone else to speak for them."

"Yeah, I get it," she said. "I don't want to worry about you every day. I don't want you to be shot, and I don't want these memories of cases you haven't been able to explain to destroy you."

Aidan put a hand on the back of her head and stroked.

"I won't get shot at," he promised. "And my memories won't destroy me."

She remained silent.

"Look." Aidan pointed to his files resting on the table. "Until Shaun comes over, I promise that will stay right there. Until he comes, I'm all yours. Promise." He held his hand in a scout's honor.

Cheyenne looked sidelong at Aidan. He could see her eyes glistening with tears. With a small smile, she kissed him before resting her head on his shoulder.

They'd had the same discussion several times before in the five years of dating and chances were, they'd have it again. Aidan couldn't help but wonder how many more discussions and arguments over his obsession with his job they'd have before she finally gave up and left.

Aidan sighed and tightened his hold on Cheyenne, then kissed the top of her head, which still rested on his shoulder.

For her sake—and his—he tried to push The Carnations Killer out of his mind.

But it wasn't easy.

21

IT WAS STILL RAINING when Shaun arrived at four o'clock. They sat in the living room talking while Cheyenne and Laura stayed upstairs. Although Cheyenne and Aidan had made amends earlier, he was still concerned about the choices he was making regarding her in terms of his career.

So, he confided in Shaun, to see what he thought. In the short time since they met, Aidan had begun to think of him as a friend and figured it couldn't hurt to hear an unbiased opinion.

"I understand where she's coming from," Shaun said after Aidan finished unloading on him, taking a sip from his beer.

"So can I," Aidan said. "But this is who I am, you know? She knew that when we started going out. Actually, I think in truth, it's what she liked most about me, although she will never admit it."

"Well, when you're young, being with someone that's a federal agent is highly impressive and alluring." He leaned over to set his bottle on a coaster on the coffee table. "But when you really start developing feelings, while it may be impressive, it's not so alluring anymore."

"So, I guess this is why you prefer to be single, huh?" Aidan asked. "No one to tell you it's too dangerous."

Shaun frowned. "No, not exactly."

Aidan noticed the hint of sadness in his words.

"What exactly is it, then?"

He looked at Aidan, but instead of directly answering, he said, "Sometimes you have to make a choice. The love of your woman or the love of your job. If you accept the position in Virginia, you will still be in the FBI. You just won't be investigating, and you won't be in the line of fire."

It was Aidan's turn to frown. "So, what you're saying is I should take the job?"

"I can't tell you what to do, Aidan. If that's what prompted you to talk to me, then I'm sorry I can't be of more help. There will always be consequences. Someone always loses something."

He picked his bottle up, took another swig, then set it back down.

"Let me tell you a story about a friend of mine."

Aidan stared at the floor as he listened.

"Years ago, my friend married a woman. She was beautiful, and they were very much in love. He'd already been in law enforcement for some time. But one day, an opportunity came that would force him to choose between the job he loved and the job that would allow him to keep the woman he loved."

Shaun took another sip. Aidan stared at him.

"What did he decide?"

"Well, after weeks of fighting and decision-making, he chose the job over his woman. So she took his children and left." Shaun lowered his eyes to focus on his bottle.

Aidan wondered if Cheyenne would really leave him if he refused the job at Quantico. He had tried, but he couldn't imagine being anything other than a field agent. Even after fighting his demons, the job was ingrained in him. However, he didn't want to lose her.

They fell into a long silence before Aidan spoke again.

"Do you ever get to see your kids?"

Shaun hesitated with a sigh. "I get them for a week once a year and we Skype sometimes. But rarely enough. She moved them back to North Carolina, where her parents live."

Aidan's cell phone interrupted their conversation. The caller ID told him it was the retired agent. He answered and put it on speakerphone so Shaun could listen in.

"This is O'Reilly."

"Good afternoon, this is Jeff Byers. How are you doing today?"

Aidan glanced out the living room window. "Trying to remain dry. It's raining."

Byers grunted. "Same here."

"Thank you for taking the time to call," Aidan said. "I'm here with Agent Henderson. We'll try not to take up too much of your time."

"Very well," Byers said. "What can I do you for?"

"We're investigating The Carnations Killer," Aidan said. "A lead brought us to Michigan, where I believe you headed the investigation five years ago."

"Yes, I remember it clearly."

"Do you remember the murders of Keisha Moffett and her boyfriend Jamal Foster?"

"Uh-huh," Byers said. "Foster murdered Keisha and vanished."

"Actually, Agent Byers," Shaun said, "Foster didn't kill Keisha. We recently found his remains by Iron River."

"Oh, really?" Byers sounded surprised.

"Yes," Aidan said. "Was there any reason you didn't believe Keisha and Jamal were victims of The Carnations Killer?"

"She didn't fit the profile. And Foster was never found. It made sense that he took off."

"Did you investigate to see if there was a link between the cases?"

"Why would I?"

Shaun and Aidan exchanged glances.

"Because it was your job," Shaun said, narrowing his eyes.

"My job was to investigate The Carnations Killer. Not the murder of a woman and the disappearance of her boyfriend. Keisha Moffett and Jamal Foster were African American. That's not the killer's MO. He prefers good-looking white, blonde women."

Aidan pushed out a heavy breath, fighting the urge to curse the retired agent's ineptitude.

"Do you remember a reporter named Jordan Blake?"

"No," Byers said.

"Did you have any suspects at all in any of the murders?" Aidan asked.

"The scenes were too clean," Byers said. "The victims didn't know one another, neither did their families. We spent two years searching for answers. But it was always the same: no DNA, no prints, no nothing. So the investigation went cold."

Aidan was glad this agent wasn't part of the FBI anymore. He also wondered if the bureau forced him to retire. Men like him were what gave agents a bad name.

Aidan asked a few more questions, and when satisfied that they wasted an hour of their Sunday, he thanked the agent for his time and pressed *end call*.

"What a jerk," Shaun said.

"Yeah."

"I get that there was no evidence hinting at who The Carnations Killer was," Shaun said. "I mean, you couldn't find leads ten years ago. But to not give Keisha and Jamal a second glance? That makes me angry."

Aidan said nothing. He had hoped talking with Byers would have helped shed some light in the right direction, but it appeared they were grasping at straws in the dark.

Shaun and Aidan spent the rest of the afternoon trying to piece together the puzzle, but the only conclusion they came to was that Jordan Blake was the primary suspect. Neither of them believed it was him. However, the little bit of evidence they had stated otherwise.

And that was all the jury needed to make a conviction.

When Shaun left, Aidan searched for Cheyenne, making himself a promise to pretend he was just an ordinary guy, working an ordinary job, spending his Sunday off with his extraordinary wife.

22

EARLY MONDAY MORNING AFTER Cheyenne hugged Laura goodbye and instructed her to be safe, Aidan drove his sister-in-law to the airport and then continued to the office.

One agent informed him that Jordan's lawyer got him out on bail. Aidan already prepared himself for it to happen, but was now discouraged that they were back at square one. Of course, Aidan had requested for Lieutenant DeLong to have some of his men monitor the young reporter.

Although Shaun and Aidan believed in his innocence, he didn't trust him as far as he could throw him. The reporter was trouble waiting to happen and Aidan knew he needed to be there to either protect Jordan or arrest him.

"Have you heard anything more from the killer?" Shaun asked when he spotted Aidan. He held a coffee thermos in one hand and a huge blueberry muffin in the other as he left a conversation with another agent.

Aidan shook his head.

"What about you and Cheyenne?" He bit into the muffin, and with his mouth full, he added, "Everything okay?"

"Yeah."

"And?"

"And I think we should go into Tara's office and tell her about the note."

"Fair enough," Shaun said as he followed Aidan to the assistant special agent-in-charge's office.

Aidan knocked on the door, and a second later, it opened.

In the doorframe stood a man with black hair and a goatee. His hair was lightly grayed. His face was set in a business manner, and he had a pair of reading glasses sitting on the top of his head. He was about two inches taller than Aidan.

"Agents O'Reilly and Henderson," Tara called from inside the office. "This is Director Zane. He recently came in from Atlanta."

Aidan recognized the name. They recently hired him to his division, but since Aidan had been on vacation, he hadn't had the chance to meet him. In preparing for his arrival, Aidan had heard about him from Hansford. He was told Zane was all business and no play. Hansford didn't seem to care much for him.

Aidan shook hands with Zane.

"It's nice to meet you, sir," he said as they filed into the office. "I'm also in the Atlanta division."

"Ah, yes," Zane said, sizing Aidan up. "You're the agent who The Carnations Killer keeps contacting?"

"Yes, sir," Aidan said.

"Do you have any reason he's singling you out?"

"No, sir," he said. "Except I first investigated him ten years ago. He seemed to be taken by me. It's unclear why."

Zane nodded once.

"Have you had any other contact with The Carnations Killer?"

Aidan glanced toward Shaun, then back at Zane. "Actually, I have. Which is unusual."

"When?" Tara asked, narrowing her eyes. She leaned against her desk, crossing her arms and legs.

"Yesterday morning. I found this at my door."

Aidan passed the note to Zane. Aidan tried but failed to read his expression as Zane gazed at the written letter.

"What surprise do you believe he has in store for you, Agent O'Reilly?" Zane passed the note to Tara.

"I haven't figured that out yet," Aidan said.

"And you do not know why he's choosing you? You, out of all the other agents? Other than you've investigated him in the past?"

His tone sounded accusatory, and Aidan didn't appreciate it. But instead of saying so, he told him he had no idea what prompted The Carnations Killer's interest.

"The only lead you have is that reporter? The one Tara informed me was released this morning?"

"That's correct," Aidan said. "He has reported on previous Carnations Killer investigations in the past. He lied about knowing the latest victim and somehow, he knew it's all connected to The Carnations Killer. However, other than withholding truths and having a knack for being in the right place at the wrong time, he seems innocent."

"I see," Zane said. "What's your profile on the killer?"

"White male, mid-thirties to early forties," Aidan began. "It's likely he has a job that allows him the freedom of traveling. The killer subdues his victims by tasing. He doesn't seem interested in sex, however, he re-dresses his victims. He gets off seeing them in pain. He probably harmed animals as a child, and thinks of it as a game."

"What else can you surmise about him?"

"His victims are usually white women between the ages of twenty-eight and thirty-three. Blonde hair. Usually long, but not always."

Zane nodded thoughtfully. "Sounds credible from what I've studied. Where do you believe is his home base?"

"He's very meticulous," Aidan said. "I don't believe the killer would take his victims where he lives. Especially if he has a family, as do a lot of serial killers. So, I'm thinking he has a place that doesn't stand out in a crowd but provides him with privacy."

"You seem to know him well," Zane said.

"Well, I have been trying to stop him for many years." Aidan cleared his throat. "Too many."

"Hansford has told me a great deal about you, and I've read your file. He was your first," Zane said. "Wasn't he?"

"Not the best way to be welcomed to the FBI."

For the first time since Aidan met him, Zane offered a smile. "No, it's not. I've heard good things about you, Agent O'Reilly. Hansford thinks highly of you. As does Tara. You're dedicated. You're thorough. And you care about the people and the victims." He stepped behind Aidan and reached for the doorknob. "I hear you have a teaching opportunity at Quantico?"

"Yes, sir."

"Are you going to accept?"

"I haven't decided yet."

"Hmm."

Aidan couldn't tell whether he liked the idea of him going to Quantico.

Zane opened the door. "I wish you the best of luck. I'll be in touch." He left the room, shutting the door behind him.

"Now I know why Agent Henderson requested the agents to watch your house," Tara said as she scanned the letter. She looked back at Aidan. "Maybe you should tell your wife to go home."

Aidan shook his head. "She doesn't know about the note. I'd like to keep it that way. And anyway, she's too stubborn to go home. Besides, I want her where I can keep an eye on her."

Tara hesitated, then nodded. "I understand. Do you have anything else to report?"

After Shaun and Aidan briefed her about their conversation with former Agent Byers, they left her office to continue searching for the serial killer.

23

THE NEXT FEW DAYS were quiet.

Aidan didn't receive any messages from The Carnations Killer, and there were no reports of another victim found anywhere in the city.

It was quiet. Too quiet.

He found that unsettling.

Aidan spent his days and nights reviewing the information in the file, willing for vital information to appear.

Shaun and Aidan, along with a few other agents, spent a good deal of their time calling the families of the victims, asking questions they'd already answered in years past. Aidan wasn't sure about the families Shaun and the others talked to, but the ones he dealt with seemed to want to move on from the nightmare they'd suffered.

A part of them wanted to forget they'd ever lost their loved ones. Others pleaded for him to tell them there had been some fresh development.

Aidan couldn't decide which was worse—the ones that wanted to give up, or the ones holding onto the glimmer of hope that they would finally receive justice.

It was for this reason he couldn't stand talking to the families. He was never good at it. He was afraid he'd become too emotional, and the families were emotional enough without adding his own feelings.

Aidan stopped by Shaun's cubical to see if he was getting anywhere. Shaun busied himself consoling someone over the phone, promising he was doing everything he could to find the man who took away their loved one. He offered a small smile to the phone, which told Aidan he'd done what he'd set out to do.

After hanging up, he typed something into the computer.

"How do you do it?"

"Do what?" Shaun kept his focus on the screen.

"You talk to the grieving families, but by the time you've finished the conversation, it seems they feel better than they did minutes before."

"I guess people feel like they can confide in me. Most people know the tears and fears don't help. They just want somebody to understand. They want somebody to listen."

"I guess that's my weak point," Aidan said. "I never know what to say to them."

"You don't have to say anything. You listen," Shaun said, the corner of his lips turning upward. He looked at Aidan, studied him. "Why did you want to become an agent?"

Aidan widened his eyes at the unexpected question. "What?"

Shaun repeated himself.

"Because I wanted to be in law enforcement," Aidan said.

Shaun contemplated the statement before responding. Aidan tried to guess what he was thinking, but came up empty.

"If you wanted to be in law enforcement," Shaun said, "then you could have been a beat cop. It's less demanding. Instead, you chose to be a federal agent. You investigate serial killings, terrorism, or things of that nature."

"I guess I believed I could do better as an agent than a regular cop. Or even a detective."

Shaun nodded. "So basically you want to help people in a bigger way. Bring down a serial killer who's been killing for ten years." He put his hands behind his head. "What will happen if you never catch this guy?"

"I've got to." Aidan put his hands on the edge of the desk and leaned over, his voice in a harsh whisper. He squared his jaw. "He has to be caught, Shaun. I *need* to catch him. If I don't, then—"

"Then what, Aidan? If you don't catch him, what?"

Aidan's breath rose and fell in quick motions. He realized the edge of the desk was digging into the palms of his hands. Shaun watched him with curious eyes but remained calm and silent as he waited for an answer.

Aidan wanted to scream that if he didn't catch this guy, then he'd continue to kill. Aidan wanted to shout that if the killer kept killing, everything he had worked for in his career would be for nothing.

But Aidan didn't say any of that.

He righted himself and ran a hand through his hair. As he realized it was happening, he calmed his breathing. He was becoming obsessive.

Or maybe he already had.

Aidan had promised Cheyenne it wouldn't happen to him. He promised he wouldn't lose himself in The Carnations Killer investigation.

Not this time.

Not again.

Aidan looked at Shaun, who was still watching him. His curious gaze turning to concern.

"I want the families to have justice," Aidan said quietly. "That's all I want."

"It's okay to feel close to this," Shaun said. "But even the best agents need to take a break. All you've ever done is try to catch him. It will not be whether you take the job at Quantico that'll cost your relationship with Cheyenne. If she sees you going off the deep end, that's when she will leave. Because a wild-eyed, obsessive federal agent isn't any woman's fantasy."

Aidan hated to admit it, but Shaun was right. He had lived and breathed the investigation for ten years. And now that the killer had returned, it was all Aidan thought about. He'd left him messages. The man was taunting him. He was hinting at the things he planned on doing. But he was a ghost. He had Aidan pulled into a game of cat and mouse, and Aidan couldn't tell whether he was the cat chasing the mouse, or if he was the mouse running from the cat.

"You're right," Aidan said, finally.

Shaun smiled. "Of course I am."

Aidan looked at his wristwatch and said, "You know what? I'm going to take today off. I think it'd do me good."

Shaun nodded. "I agree."

Aidan returned to his desk to finish his paperwork, then logged out of the computer and gathered his things.

He left the office to go home to Cheyenne.

24

It was Friday evening, and he watched as the lights of HomeGoods went dark, blending the store in with the night. A few minutes later, he watched as a group of employees walked out of the store. The young girls chatted amongst each other as they headed for their cars in the vacant parking lot. An older woman with a scowl on her face climbed into her Buick in the handicapped parking spot and pulled away.

His target, named Jane, was one of the last to leave.

Only one employee remained as she made her way to the car, the clicking of her heels echoing into the night.

He straightened his cap on his head and walked in his target's direction as the male employee slid into the driver's seat of his car.

"Excuse me, ma'am."

She looked at him. He could tell she was tired from a busy day of labor. She worked eight hours nonstop. It was enjoyable watching her work. He hoped for her sake it was a good day because, though she didn't realize it yet, he knew it would be one of her last.

"I'm sorry to bother you," he said. "I'm afraid I made it back too late before you closed. What time do you open in the mornings?"

Despite her weary eyes, she smiled at him. "Eight o'clock."

She didn't seem to remember him from last week.

"Okay, great," he said. "I was in there earlier and saw a beautiful wooden trunk you have on clearance. I forgot my credit card, so I had to run home and get it. But then my daughter needed me for some school project."

"Oh, that antique trunk with the elephant lining the top?" she said. "Yes, that is very beautiful."

She used her key fob to unlock her car.

She waved at the last vehicle, which pulled away from the lot.

They were now alone.

"It's going to be an anniversary present for my wife. She loves antiques and elephants."

"Then I'm sure she'll love the trunk. You've got excellent taste."

"I only hope it'll still be there when I return tomorrow." He inched toward her.

Another smile as she opened the car door. "Our clearance has been going fast. It's not usually busy in the morning, so if you're able to make it shortly after we open, you'll be in luck."

He now stood close to her and smiled. He could smell her strong perfume clinging to her body. "Thank you so much."

"You're more than welcome. Have a good night, sir."

She turned to face her door. Reaching for the taser in the back of his jeans, he pulled it out. As she climbed into the car, he zapped her. Her body convulsed, and she only whimpered from the shock before slumping to the side, falling onto the black tar.

He popped the trunk. After double-checking that there were no prying eyes, he used the fishing wire to bind her arms and feet together. After securing her so she couldn't get away, he carried her to the trunk.

She whimpered.

"I'm sure I'll have a wonderful night," he said. He touched the skin underneath her clothes. Her flesh warmed his hand. She reeled in disgust. "Unfortunately, you won't be having too much fun. My women never seem to."

"Please," she said, almost inaudibly. Her green eyes blinked at him and a tear slid down her face.

"I'm sorry. What was that?"

He leaned in, cupping his ear as if to hear her better.

"Please," she said. "Please don't hurt me. I'll give you anything."

"Sorry, dear," he said with a mock frown. "I'm afraid I can't understand you."

He taped her mouth, closed the trunk, and climbed into her car.

The night was still as he pulled out of the store's parking lot to take her to the last place she'd ever see before she died.

25

He watched as she slowly crawled away from him.

He'd already been at work on her for an hour and the shrilling that came from her was ecstasy. He had an urge to jump as if he were a kid opening a major birthday present.

She begged him to stop.

So, he did after a while.

He sat on the floor, watching her squirm and sob and beg.

"You're beautiful when you're like this, Jane from HomeGoods," he said. He crawled to her side and stroked her cheeks.

She was ice cold, but that was because he'd set the thermostat to run the cool air. He liked it when the goosebumps appeared on her skin.

"What's that?" He leaned close to her lips. "You're having fun?"

He pulled back, pushed to his feet, all the while keeping his eyes on her.

"I'm glad, Jane. I'm also having a pretty good time, if I do say so myself."

"You—" Jane slurred as her words trembled, "You're i-inane. I-i-insane."

"But I thought you were having fun," he said with a mock sympathetic frown. "We're going to be here all week."

"Please." She tried to look at him, but her head wouldn't cooperate.

He looked at his watch. He'd have to leave soon if he was going to make it home in time to read Jamie her favorite bedtime story.

"Okay," he said. He removed his glasses and set them on the dresser.

He turned her to her stomach, stepped on her head to hold her in place, and gripped the tire iron.

"It's about time for me to go, Jane from HomeGoods," he told her. "But I'll come for a visit tomorrow."

He made contact with her lower back, her cries muffled against his foot. He swung the weapon in the air again, slamming it against her leg.

The pain she must have felt.

Just like ecstasy.

After he'd finished with her for the night, he chained her to a table leg.

He touched her again to make sure she was still breathing. She was, but only slightly. He decided to give her a break tomorrow.

Give her time to heal.

Of course, he'd stop by to feed her three times a day. After all, he wasn't a monster, right?

Smiling, he leaned close to her ear. Her body shivered slightly. Whether it was from the cold or their closeness, he wasn't sure.

He whispered goodbye and left.

HE PULLED UP THE driveway of his house, turned off the car, and entered through the front door.

"Honey! I'm home from work!"

"Daddy!" Jamie's feet pounded the stairs, and he kneeled to catch her in his arms. She was already dressed for bed in a Princess nightgown. "Read me a bedtime story?"

"Of course, pumpkin," he said, kissing her cheek.

He carried her up the stairs and read her the story of her choice. After Jamie slipped into dreamland, he went into the master bedroom.

His wife lay in bed, thumbing through a magazine.

"How was work, honey?" She closed the magazine and smiled at him.

"Exhilarating," he said. He undressed and climbed into the bed. "Sorry I'm late."

"Yeah, about that. I'm going to have to—"

He crushed her lips with his.

She kissed him back, hungry for him.

"Oh, I love it when you come home like this." She moaned as he bit into her neck.

He said nothing as he prepared to release himself with his wife, something he could never do with his targets, as it would only leave traces of evidence.

His mind echoed with the screams from Jane from HomeGoods when the tire iron slammed against her stomach.

He never left evidence he didn't want to leave.

He saw the blood from the one the media called Maya Gibson trickle down her neck.

The erotic pleasure surged through him as he heard the satisfying moans from his wife.

No, he was much too careful about that.

26

IT WAS NEARING THREE in the morning when Aidan's eyes flew open. He was lying on his side, staring at the bright red numbers of the alarm clock. He had gotten four hours of rest, which was more than he'd received in a long while.

Cheyenne snored softly next to him, hunched in a tight ball, the sheets pulled to her chin.

It was then Aidan realized he'd tossed the sheets off his body and was covered with sweat. Despite not wearing clothing, the temperature rose through his body as though he was lying in the middle of a blazing furnace.

Running a hand through his hair, he found it was also very damp.

Aidan rolled to a sitting position.

Something in the corner of the dark room caught his attention. He looked over, then blinked his eyes to try and get the reflection of Maya standing there out of his head.

She reached out to him, mouthing something, but no sound came out. Blood flowed from her eye sockets and the ends of her hair.

In several jerking movements, she crawled into the bed with Aidan. The mattress bounced ever so slightly. He glanced over at Cheyenne to see she was still asleep, undisturbed.

Maya inched closer, closer.

It was only a dream, right?

It had to be.

Aidan wanted to move, to get away. But it was impossible.

Soon, Maya's face was close enough to touch. He could feel her cold, cold breath on him.

"You're not real," Aidan said, his words almost inaudible to even his ears. "You're not."

Only Cheyenne's peaceful snoring, in tune with the pulsating veins in his ears, filled the room. The blood dripping from Maya was thick and warm, despite the draftiness. Sweat poured down his face.

"No," Aidan said. "Get away from me. You're not real. You're not."

He shook his head with fervor. It appeared his blood would seep out of his skin until the veins burst.

Aidan closed his eyes tight, telling himself he was only dreaming.

That Maya wasn't really there. She wasn't. She couldn't be.

Chills crawled across his back.

Aidan reopened his eyes.

Maya had vanished.

He scanned the room for any remnant of her, but she was gone. Using the light of the moon, Aidan looked to see that there was no blood, only sweat, which continued to run down his face.

His feet wobbly, he inched out of the bed to feel his way to the bathroom. Intending to take a long, cool shower, he turned on the water.

Aidan stepped under the cold water spewing from the showerhead and placed his palms against the wall, leaning his head forward. He closed his eyes and shuddered.

He tried to shake the image of Maya out of his head, but she seemed to have embedded herself into his consciousness.

The dreams were too real, too vivid.

The image of Maya etched in his mind, just like the faces of the other victims.

They continued to flash before his eyes until they merged, and Aidan couldn't tell one from another.

"Please, God," he said, his words just above a whisper, "Please make it stop."

He remained in the shower until the temperature of the water turned lukewarm.

When he got out, he dried himself off, his mind whirling.

After pulling on a tank and shorts, he slipped out of the bedroom, went down the stairs, and left the house for an early morning jog to clear his mind.

27

Ben Ridgeway stepped into the police station, wondering where he should go. There was no one around to help him. He needed to find someone *now*. His wife was missing—she had been missing for two days. He'd tried to call the police on the phone, but of course, they were of no help. They wouldn't help him unless Jane had been missing for forty-eight hours.

Well, now it's been forty-eight hours, and someone had to help him.

He hurried to the glass window where he figured somebody should be. Banging on the glass, he cried out, "Hello? Anybody there? Please, I need someone to help."

"Can I help you, sir?"

The tone from the short, dark-skinned woman sounded annoyed with him, but Ben didn't care. She sat between the security alarm and the conveyer belt.

"My wife," he said through his tears. "She's missing. I heard—I-I heard..."

He fell to his knees as the feeling in the pit of his stomach told him the man the media referred to as The Carnations Killer took his wife.

"Please help me," he begged. "My wife didn't come home from work the other night. I'm worried something might have happened to her."

With her irritable tone, the woman told him she'd find an officer to help.

Ben stayed on the floor, not caring if people saw him. He wasn't sure if he'd be able to stand, anyway.

Finally, a tall man came his way.

"Sir, I'm Lieutenant Davis. You say your wife's missing?"

Ben told him yes, that she didn't return home after work like she was supposed to.

The lieutenant nodded slightly and instructed him to follow, so Ben did. He led Ben to a private room and was instructed to sit in a chair.

Ben followed his orders.

"What's your name, sir?"

"Ben Ridgeway. My wife is Jane."

"When was the last time you saw or spoke to her?" Davis was scribbling in his pad as he spoke.

"Two days ago," Ben said. "I got home from work in time for her to leave. She's an assistant manager at HomeGoods and was working nights every day this week."

"I see," the lieutenant said, distractedly. "Have you contacted her friends? Other members of her family?"

"Yes. No one has heard from her."

"Is everything going okay in your marriage?"

"Yes, sir," Ben said. "We're still honeymooners. I heard on the news that someone is killing blonde women. My wife is a blonde."

"Do you have a photo of her?"

Ben pulled one from his wallet and passed it over. "Please help me find her."

"I'll let the FBI know about this, okay? Just to be on the safe side. But right now, I need you to calm yourself. Go home, and we'll contact you as soon as we know something. All right?"

"You'll find her?"

The lieutenant stared across the table at Ben. "We'll do everything we can, sir."

Ben hesitated before rising from his seat. But he realized there was little to do except wait. He left the police station to go to his empty house. He didn't want to, but he had nowhere else to go.

28

The next week went by slowly. They were at a standstill where the investigation went. They heard a report about a woman named Jane Ridgeway vanishing, and since she fit closely with The Carnations Killer's MO, Aidan wanted to monitor her case.

Jane was born on January 30, 1983. She worked as an assistant manager at HomeGoods. She was married with no children. There was no sign of her vehicle at the store, no trace of her, period. The police interviewed the employees that saw her last, but no one could offer any leads.

Ever since the night Aidan had the waking nightmare of Maya Gibson coming toward him in his room ... the night he felt her blood and the coldness of her breath ... he didn't want to sleep. He had never had something so real happen to him like that, and it unsettled him.

He did what he could to avoid Cheyenne. She wouldn't understand. There was nothing he could tell her that would make her understand. And Aidan wasn't sure he wanted her to, after all.

Shaun was another story.

Aidan could feel his probing stare throughout the days.

Aidan knew Shaun wanted to bring it up, but at the same time, he knew Shaun understood what was wearing him down.

Aidan was on the phone giving Hansford an update when Shaun strolled toward his desk. He waited patiently until he slipped his cell on its hook attached to his slacks.

"Come with me," Shaun said.

Aidan arched an eyebrow.

"Where are we going?"

Shaun tilted his head in the door's direction. "Just come with me. I want to show you something."

Curious, Aidan followed him into the humid afternoon.

They climbed into his car, and Shaun began driving.

"I understand this investigation is difficult for you," he said, his eyes on the road. "It's hard for me as well, knowing Maya's death was at the hands of someone who has murdered fifty women in ten years."

Aidan looked sidelong at him to see him frowning.

"I mean, fifty's a lot of women, don't you think?"

"Well," Aidan said, "Ted Bundy killed at least thirty women in four years. Patrick Wayne Kearney killed about thirty-two homosexuals in two years."

"It's a lot to deal with," Shaun continued before Aidan could go on listing other serial murders.

"What are you getting at?" Aidan asked as Shaun turned onto a new street.

"When I was first at Quantico," Shaun said, "there was this instructor who told us that sometimes we see things we wish we didn't have to. It comes with the job. But if you let it fester, you'll end up going stir-crazy."

He parked the car, and Aidan realized they were at a boxing gym.

Without a word, Shaun turned the ignition off and climbed out, so Aidan followed him.

"Remember when I told you I liked to hit things when I'm stressed?"

"Yeah."

"Well ... when I have to deal with something I can't handle—whether it's personal or work—I come here."

He opened the door, and they entered the building. Punches and karate shouts reverberated in the building, and he could smell the sweat.

A few men and some women called Shaun out by name. He introduced Aidan and told them he was a friend, and they had better be nice. They pretended to fear his empty threat, and then either shook Aidan's hand or slapped him hard on the back, welcoming him to their humble abode.

Shaun led Aidan to an empty punching bag. He motioned toward it with his hand.

"What?" Aidan asked sheepishly.

"Go on," he urged. "Hit it."

He did.

A burst of deep, amused laughter erupted within his friend. Once he composed himself, Shaun said, "Do it again. This time, like you mean it."

Rolling his eyes, Aidan set one foot in front of the other, bent his knees in a fighting stance, and held his fists in front of his face. He threw another cross punch as hard as he could muster.

"Again."

Aidan followed his instructions, knocking the bag with a jab.

"Again."

Aidan did, then slammed his fist against the bag once more.

Then again.

And again.

By the time he stopped, minutes had flown by and his hair stuck to his scalp, his face drenched with sweat. Aidan's fists throbbed, his breath heaved. He put his hands on his knees, hunching over, trying to slow his heart rate.

Shaun slapped a monstrous hand on Aidan's back, almost knocking him unsteadily to his knees.

"Feel better?"

Aidan looked at him, trying hard to catch his breath, and told him he did.

In fact, he felt a whole lot better.

Aidan returned home after work and found Cheyenne sitting on the deck out back. There was a bottle of red wine on the table next to her. She turned the page in the book she was reading, then reached for the wine glass. She took a sip and set it on the table.

Aidan shut the door, careful not to make a sound, then leaned forward to kiss her neck.

Her first reaction was a gasp, then she let out a contented sigh.

"You seem to be in a good mood tonight," she said.

"I am," he said. Aidan took the book from her hand, set it on the table, and pulled her to her feet. "In fact, I'm in a very good mood."

He swept her off her feet, and Cheyenne let out a shrieking giggle. Opening the door, Aidan carried her inside and up the stairs to the master bedroom. He tossed her on the bed and climbed on top of her.

"You're sweaty," Cheyenne said as he lifted her shirt over her head.

"Yeah, Shaun and I went to a boxing gym," he said. "Worked up a sweat."

Aidan peered into her eyes as he worked to undo her shorts.

"Want me to take a shower first?"

"Yes." She propped herself with her elbows and planted a kiss on his lips. "But I'll join you."

Aidan's lips curved in a smile and released a low growl.

He peeled off his sweaty shirt as Cheyenne started the shower. As Aidan continued to undress, his cell phone rang.

He grabbed it from the dresser. The caller ID read *unavailable*.

"O'Reilly."

"Oh, good, I caught you."

Aidan heard a scream in the background.

The hairs on the back of his neck stood at attention and chills rolled up his back. His throat closed, and he couldn't swallow.

"Who is this?"

Cheyenne appeared in the doorway from the bathroom. Her expression told him she knew something was wrong.

"Please," a weak voice said in the background.

A sound like a baseball bat splintering against a fence echoed through the phone line, then came cries of pain.

"Stop it!" Aidan gripped the cell phone tightly. "Let her go."

"I just wanted you to know we're having a marvelous time. Are you?"

His heart hammered in his chest as he stood in Laura's bedroom, helpless to stop him from hurting the woman. Aidan heard the cracking sounds and cries a few more times before the call ended.

Aidan's hands shook, and his knees became weak. It was then gravity failed him and he fell to the carpet. Cheyenne rushed to his side.

"Aidan!"

He couldn't speak. He couldn't move. The sounds of pain echoed in the air.

Cheyenne, teary-eyed, consoled him for a few minutes until he found his voice.

"I need to call Shaun."

29

Aidan woke Saturday morning to the smell of pancakes and the crackling of thunder. Climbing out of bed, he made a beeline for the window and parted the curtains to see the rain coming down in torrents. It was light out, but the sun remained hidden behind thick, dark clouds. Lightning struck the starless heavens in one long bolt.

He still wasn't able to get the phone call from the night before out of his mind. Aidan had a feeling that soon they would inform Ben Ridgeway his wife, Jane, was dead.

Aidan had spoken to Shaun for two hours last night, discussing the phone call. The conversation didn't need to be long. There wasn't much to do about it except have the lab guys trace it, only to find the killer used a burner. Although minutes seemed to stretch into hours, the phone call from the killer only lasted thirty-five seconds.

Aidan took a quick shower, dressed, and headed down the stairs.

"Something smells good," he said.

"Good morning," Cheyenne said.

Although he couldn't see her face, Aidan could hear the worry in her words.

He wrapped his hands around her body and she sank into him.

"I wish you could stay home with me today."

"I do, too."

"Are you okay?" she asked.

"Yeah." He kissed her temple and moved toward the coffeepot.

The thunder resonated through the morning.

"Were you able to sleep last night?" Cheyenne asked as she turned the pancakes over.

Aidan poured himself a cup of coffee and leaned against the counter.

"A little."

As they spoke, his mind drifted to what he needed to do at work.

His first order of business would be to find out if they'd been able to trace the call to his cell.

After breakfast was made, Cheyenne and Aidan sat at the kitchen table and blessed their food and the day. He chewed his first bite when his cell phone rang.

It was Shaun calling.

Stuffing another thick square of pancake into his mouth, Aidan answered.

"Are you sitting?" he said.

"Yeah." Something in his words snagged Aidan's attention. He swallowed the pancakes with a big, uneasy gulp.

Shaun hesitated, then sighed. "We've got another one."

The fork slipped through Aidan's fingers and clattered to his plate.

"Where?"

Shaun said it was the woman they reported missing earlier in the week: Jane Ridgeway. She had been killed in the same manner as the others and dumped at the Keystone Grounds Park. An elderly couple had found the body.

Aidan closed his eyes tight, drawing in a shaky breath. After pushing it out, he released a soft curse, which was drowned by the rumbling thunder.

The killer called Aidan as he was killing her.

A chill crawled down his spine.

"Here's the interesting part," Shaun said. As Aidan listened, he pushed his chair back and rose. "The female witness claims to have seen a man leaving the scene."

Aidan had poured the remaining of his coffee in a thermos, but Shaun's words gave him pause.

"She did?"

Shaun confirmed, but said the woman seemed confused, so he wasn't sure if she'd be a valid eyewitness. Aidan told him it was at least something to go on.

It may be the break they needed.

The break that would end the search for a ruthless serial killer that had been terrorizing the states over the past ten years.

Once he ended the call, Aidan grabbed his keys and turned to Cheyenne.

"Sorry, love," he said. "But I've got to run."

"I know," she whispered. "Be careful."

As he kissed her on the cheek, he promised her he would, and then rushed out the door.

◈

THE POLICE HAD SECTIONED the Keystone Grounds Park off when Aidan arrived. Lieutenant DeLong saw him in the distance and made a beeline toward him.

"It's a mess," he said.

The rain was still falling hard, the thunder sounding as though it was moving closer.

"Shaun said an elderly couple found the body? What were they doing out in the storm?" Aidan asked.

DeLong shrugged. "It wasn't raining like this when they arrived."

Aidan followed him to where the body was. They had covered the remains with a tent to preserve the crime scene. Federal agents and the police were combing the area for evidence that was likely not there.

"The husband—" DeLong glanced in his notepad, "—Mr. Gibbs has health problems, and his doctor suggested walking a little more, so they've been walking around the track. Before they were going to leave, they went to the restroom. It had started to rain right after we got the call."

They reached the tent, and Aidan opened the flap to peer inside. The medical examiner was inspecting the body as Shaun watched.

"What do we have?" Aidan asked.

"I guesstimate TOD was last night around eleven. Same as the last victim."

Jane Ridgeway's body was white amidst the cuts and purplish bruises. Aidan could tell she'd suffered broken bones, probably more so than Maya. The killer's mistreatments usually became worse after each victim. Aidan imagined the first was always his warm-up.

Jane had two markings on the side of her neck, showing the killer tased her.

She wore a black dress, and her hands held a bouquet of white carnations over her chest.

This time, he didn't leave a note. But, then again, he called the previous night, so Aidan presumed it was a note of sorts.

"I don't know if the killer got lucky, or if he planned on leaving her in the middle of a storm," Shaun said over the thunder.

Lightning flashed across the sky, illuminating the premises.

"Luck," Aidan said. "It wasn't supposed to rain today. I'm going to go talk to the couple that found her."

Aidan crawled out of the tent and headed toward the restrooms, where an elderly couple stood underneath the awning. Shaun followed behind.

As they walked, Aidan silently cursed the rain for disturbing his crime scene.

"Mr. and Mrs. Gibbs?" he said as he approached them. "I'm Special Agent Aidan O'Reilly."

"How do you do, young man?" Mr. Gibbs' voice trembled and betrayed his age, as did his white hair and walker. His wife looked a few years younger, her hair bright red. She wore a large pair of bifocals. She squinted at Aidan, and he could tell she wouldn't have been able to see anything much. Not from a distance, anyway.

"I'm doing well, considering. Thank you," Aidan said. "I understand you found the body?"

"Yes," Mr. Gibbs said. "My wife said she saw someone carrying something over his shoulder. He set it down."

"Next thing I knew," Mrs. Gibbs said, her voice wavering slightly, "he was leaving."

"At first, I thought it was her imagination," Mr. Gibbs said. "She has trouble seeing. But she was insistent, so I went to look and—" he frowned as he glanced in the police's direction and agents, "—and I found that poor young girl's body. I checked for her pulse, but she was already dead."

"You didn't see anyone yourself?" Shaun asked.

"No, young man," he said. "I was in the restroom."

"Ma'am." Aidan directed his attention to Mrs. Gibbs. "Do you remember what he looked like? Do you know if he was short, tall...?"

"I don't know." Tears filled her eyes. "I don't see too well these days."

"And it was only one man leaving?"

She nodded.

"Do you think he may have seen you?" Aidan asked.

"I don't know," she said, her voice trembling. "I've heard about the serial murders on the news. I was afraid it might be him, so I hid in the bathroom. I'm sorry, I'm so sorry."

Her lips trembled, and Aidan put a hand on her shoulder.

"You did the right thing, ma'am. There was nothing you could have done. Your safety is more important than anything else."

"You don't think we're in danger, do you, young man?" Mr. Gibbs asked.

Mrs. Gibbs sniffled, and her husband took her hand in his.

"No, sir. He likely didn't notice you." Aidan opted not to mention the Gibbs more than likely wouldn't be alive had the killer realized they had seen him. "But I'll have an officer escort you home," Aidan said. "If we need anything else, we'll contact you. And if you remember seeing something that may help, call us anytime. Day or night."

Aidan passed Mr. Gibbs his card. He accepted it with a quick nod and thanked them, then guided his wife toward the parking lot.

As Aidan watched them, he noticed reporters had begun to arrive, filming the crime scene. The police were holding their arms out to the side as if to keep them from getting through.

"Well, look who we have here," Shaun said.

Aidan scanned the crowd and when a tall officer moved to the end of the police tape, he saw Jordan Blake among them.

30

Jordan wore a gray raincoat, its hood slipped over his ball cap. He spotted Aidan and Shaun, then motioned for his cameraman to point in their direction. Kent did as he was told until the coroner loaded the body, then the focus moved back to the murder.

Aidan began walking toward the crowd.

"Don't," Shaun warned, following close behind.

"Don't what?" Aidan asked. "I only want to have a chat with our friend."

Shaun said nothing more as they approached. Police officers were telling the reporters they could say nothing about the crime scene, and the reporters needed to stay behind the police tape.

"Agent O'Reilly," Jordan said. Kent pointed his camera in their direction.

"Mr. Blake," Aidan said matter-of-factly. "Here you are again." He glanced to where Jane Ridgeway's body rested. "At my crime scene."

"Here I am," Jordan echoed, a smile playing on his lips. "Every good reporter knows when a high-profile crime has taken place."

"Really?" Aidan said. "This was an actual human being, Blake. How can you make light of this?"

Instead of answering, the reporter turned to face the camera. "This is Jordan Blake reporting live at the Keystone Grounds Park. The Carnations Killer has struck our city yet again, and I'm standing here at the scene of the crime with Agents O'Reilly and Henderson." He turned to face them. "Agent O'Reilly, can we get a statement from you?"

Aidan considered telling Jordan exactly what he could do with himself, but he thought better of it—not only because Shaun had his bear-like hand on his shoulder in a silent warning. Instead, Aidan replied he didn't have a comment and once the team finished compiling what they'd found, they would be happy to share.

"So, you did find something?" Jordan said.

Man, this guy is irritating, Aidan thought with silent infuriation.

Aidan tried ignoring the reporter as he walked away, but not before he heard Jordan speak to the camera: "Well, viewers of WJFX, you saw it for yourselves—the Federal Bureau of Investigation is yet again keeping us citizens in the dark."

"Shaun, I'm about three seconds away from using *him* as a punching bag," Aidan hissed, jabbing an index finger in the reporter's direction.

"I hear you," was the reply. They stopped at their cars. Shaun looked toward where the reporters were trying to get answers from the nearby agents and police officers.

"A part of me wishes we'd find something to implicate him, so I'd have the pleasure of locking him up." Aidan crossed his arms. "Actually, you know something? I don't think prison would do well for him. A padded room and a strait jacket might do the trick."

Shaun snickered. "Just let it go. I'll see you back at the office."

With a frown, Aidan nodded and climbed into the car.

As he sat behind the wheel, he noticed something on the floor on the passenger side. Aidan leaned over and retrieved the object.

His heart drummed along with the pouring rain against his ribcage.

It was a taser.

Aidan stared at the device and then looked out his window, scanning his surroundings. No one was around. Shaun had already pulled out of the parking lot, and the reporters were still standing with the officers, trying to get their statements.

Jordan glanced at Aidan, but he couldn't read his face.

Aidan wondered whether he really knew something about the killings.

He'd lied before, he seemed to know where the victims were before they announced it, and he knew about The Carnations Killer connection.

He was also acting irritatingly smug—something Aidan imagined the killer would do if he were in Jordan's shoes.

And now someone left a taser on the floorboard of his car.

Whoever The Carnations Killer was—whether or not it was Jordan Blake—he was here.

And he was watching.

31

Using a newspaper Aidan found in the car's backseat, he carefully wrapped the taser and carried it into the building.

He found Shaun at his desk, gnawing on a blueberry muffin.

Aidan set the folded paper in front of him.

Shaun stared at it and arched an eyebrow. "If you're going to give me a paper to read, I'd rather have the current edition."

"Open it," Aidan said. He grabbed a nearby chair and rolled it over.

Shaun did, and when he revealed the taser, he sat back in his seat. "Where'd you get this?"

"Someone put that in my car. On the floorboard."

"And I'm assuming you didn't see who?"

Shaking his head, Aidan said, "Whoever it was, was there. At the scene. I would assume he watched as we checked out the body, questioned the witnesses. There's no telling how long he was there. He could have been there for a few minutes, or even long after I left."

Shaun frowned at Aidan. "Why would he want to leave you the taser?"

"I don't know."

"You're the profiler," he said.

"Well..." Aidan leaned close to the desk to inspect the device. "Maybe he's trying to frame me. Maybe that's the 'surprise' he has in store." He shook his head. "But I don't think that's it. He's proud of what he's done. He wants to take the credit." Aidan considered what he knew about the killer. "He was there while we were."

I can kill, and you can't catch me.

The last words the killer said to him ten years ago found their way to the forefront of Aidan's mind.

He looked at Shaun, whose eyes clouded over as he considered what Aidan was saying.

"He wants to be sure we know he's watching. He wants us to know he's close, but we can't touch him."

"Profound," Shaun said. "I'll send it on to the lab and see if there's a chance of fingerprints."

"I touched it at first," Aidan said. "I wasn't thinking."

"No prob." Using a napkin, Shaun picked the device up and studied it. "Looks like this is handmade. A very good handmade one at that."

As he rose, Shaun jammed a hunk of his muffin into his mouth. Crumbs fell to the desk, and he swiped them on the floor with his hand. "Wanna walk with me?"

"Yeah, I'll go."

They made their way in silence to the elevator and once inside, Shaun jammed his index finger on the number that would take them to the crime lab.

"By the way," Shaun said as the doors closed, "we got nothing from the call you got last night."

"Kinda figured that." Aidan turned to give Shaun his attention. "If I ask you something, will you keep it between us?"

Shaun said he would. He eyed Aidan curiously.

Aidan sighed and rested his head against the metal elevator wall.

"Do you ever have dreams?" he asked. "Not normal dreams. But of the things you see at work. Murders."

"Sometimes," Shaun said.

"Do they affect you?"

Shaun shrugged. "Nightmares are common. And this job can get to you. That's why I go to the gym and beat the heck out of the bag. It helps me with the anger and frustration."

"I have dreams," Aidan said. His words lowered an octave. "Of the victims. They're so vivid. I wake up and have to tell myself it was only a dream. But a part of me doesn't believe that. Part of me believes they are real. Makes it difficult to get back to sleep."

"Hmm," Shaun said. "Well, you know, dreams are our subconscious' way of speaking to us. Maybe your subconscious is giving you information you don't immediately see about the murders. Information you might realize you've never noticed before when you log into the database."

"How does waking up feeling Maya's icy breath and the heat of her blood encourage my subconscious to help me solve her murder?" Aidan asked.

Rather than answering, Shaun asked, "Have you told Cheyenne about your dreams?"

The elevator jerked to a stop, and the doors slid open.

"No," Aidan said as they stepped off. "She already worries enough about me. I don't want to add more to it. I try to keep work and personal life separate."

"I don't want to tell you what to do with your relationship," Shaun said as they walked down the hall and turned a corner, "but that rarely works. Keeping everything bottled inside never does anyone good."

They paused outside the door of their destination. Shaun looked at Aidan, his face downcast. "Remember, all Cheyenne knows is what she hears on the news. She doesn't know what it's like to see the victim's skull beaten in, and the bruises on their skin. She may never understand it. But you can do your part by confiding in her. At least about the dreams. It may help you, in the long run, to talk about it."

Shaun placed a meaty hand on Aidan's shoulder and gave him a soft, reassuring squeeze before pushing the door open.

"Hey, Jackson," Shaun said, announcing their arrival.

"What up?" Jackson was in his early twenties and had yellow highlights in his dark brown hair. Though he wore long sleeves, Aidan noticed a tattoo of a dragon tail peeking out.

"Need a favor," Shaun said. When Jackson lifted his head from the microscope, Shaun handed him the taser. "See if you can get prints off this. At least one set will be Aidan's."

"You got it."

Jackson went to work, and Shaun turned to face Aidan.

"Think our guy has a family?"

Aidan shrugged. "It's not uncommon for serial killers to have a family. He has excellent people skills. He's able to get close enough to his victims to throw them off guard and tase them."

"So, he could be like Ted Bundy, a good-looking, smooth-talking serial killer?"

Aidan shrugged.

"That's scary," Shaun said.

Aidan silently agreed.

"Okay," Jackson said, mumbling underneath his breath. "Now running the prints in the program..." He trailed off and began singing a song underneath his breath. "The only print," Jackson announced a few minutes later, "is yours, Agent O'Reilly."

"Why doesn't that surprise me?" Aidan asked. He retrieved the taser.

"Sorry, wish I could add a 'but' to that statement and work my magic, but..."

Aidan offered Jackson a smile. "You're good, man. Thanks for checking on it."

"Anytime."

Shaun shook his hand, and they turned to leave.

"I've been meaning to tell you since we questioned the elderly couple," Shaun said as they exited the crime lab, heading for the elevator. "Your compassion skills are better than you think."

"Thanks," Aidan said. When they stepped into the lift, he heard a low rumbling coming from his stomach. "I'm going to run to the cafeteria. I didn't get to finish my breakfast, and I'm starving. Want to come?"

"Always."

32

SHAUN AND AIDAN PULLED into the parking lot of HomeGoods and climbed out of the car. The rain had subsided, leaving behind the fresh scent of dew. It was humid, which was normal in the south. Although it was nearing eleven o'clock, the sun hid behind a small dark cloud, begging to come out. But according to the weather report on the radio as they drove to the store, it would rain again around noon.

After Shaun parked his car, they made their way into the building.

There were only a few shoppers by the registers, and one employee.

They made a beeline to the employee, and as she rang up her customer's sale, Shaun requested to speak with the manager on duty. Skillfully multi-tasking, the employee continued to scan as she spoke into the phone.

"MOD to the front, MOD to the front registers." Her voice echoed through the loudspeakers.

Shaun thanked her and received an "mm-mmm" in response.

It took a few minutes for a stocky man with a well-trimmed beard to arrive. The girl at the register pointed to the agents as she made herself look busy at the already-neat end cap.

"Good morning, I'm Brad. How can I help you folks today?"

"I'm Special Agent O'Reilly, this is Special Agent Henderson. Is there a place where we can talk in private?"

Brad nodded and looked over at the girl, who pretended not to eavesdrop.

"Will you be okay on your own for a few minutes, Sharon?"

"I think so," she said.

Brad turned back to his guests. "Right this way."

They followed him to the back of the store and through a door marked "employees only."

"As I'm sure you've guessed," Shaun said as they settled into his office, "We're here about your assistant manager, Jane Ridgeway."

Brad folded his hands on his desk. "I saw it on the news this morning. Such a tragedy."

"When did you last see her?" Aidan asked.

Brad pushed out a heavy sigh. "Last week. Tuesday night. She was supposed to come in the following morning. She didn't show. I knew something was wrong the minute one of my supervisors called me. It wasn't like Jane at all."

"Do you know if Jane has had problems with anyone in the past? A customer, an employee? Anyone that didn't seem to like her?"

Brad shook his head.

"No. Jane is—was—very much a people person. We'll certainly miss her around here."

"Did you see her leave with anyone that night?" Shaun asked.

Brad shook his head. "I left around nine. She closed up shop about ten-thirty."

"Who closed with her?" Aidan asked. Before finding Jane's body, the police had already questioned the employees, but he wanted to double check to make sure no one was missed.

Brad glanced at his board on the wall, which must have the names of employees working for the month. He read off the names, and Aidan wrote them in his pad. He requested their addresses and phone numbers, and Brad looked on the computer and handed over a printout of the requested information.

After concluding the interview, Aidan thanked him for his time.

"Was it The Carnations Killer?" he asked as he walked them out.

"It would seem," Shaun said.

"I hate it for her husband. They got married only a few months ago."

They thanked Brad again, told him they were sorry for his loss, then left the store.

As they ambled to the car, Aidan called Lieutenant DeLong and told him the names and addresses of the employees that worked the night of Jane's disappearance. After listening to the information, DeLong said the husband was distraught and didn't know of anyone who would want to hurt his wife.

The lieutenant said he would get with Aidan later once his men interviewed the other employees.

Aidan told him he was going to schedule a briefing for two o'clock in the afternoon. DeLong replied he'd like to attend if circumstances allowed—apparently, an accidental shooting had happened. Thankfully, there were no fatalities, but he needed to assess the situation.

The life of law enforcement officers.

Shaun and Aidan stopped by McDonald's for lunch and brought it back to the office.

Now they sat at his desk, reviewing the recent murder.

The downside was they still didn't have evidence on the body. The upside was they now had a witness—though she didn't see very well—and a handmade taser the killer had placed in Aidan's car.

Two new things they never had before.

At least that was something.

The lab was examining the taser to see if anything of interest could provide some clue as to where the parts came from. They hoped to come across a trail of breadcrumbs.

As it neared two o'clock, Aidan's desk phone rang.

"O'Reilly."

It was DeLong.

"I'm not going to make it to the briefing today after all," he said. His voice sounded tired. "But one employee that night—Devon Richards—said he saw someone in the shadows as he left. Then the guy walked up to our vic and started talking. The suspect wore a cap and Devon didn't see his face."

"Did we question him before? Why didn't he mention it when we were trying to find Jane?" Aidan asked.

"He said he didn't remember it until now. He was too tired to pay much attention, but his window was down, and he heard part of the conversation. Our suspect was asking what time the store opened because he wanted to buy a chest that was on clearance."

"So, he'd been in the store," Aidan said. "This Richards guy didn't remember seeing him before?"

DeLong cleared his throat. "All he said was that he sees too many people every time he's working to remember faces."

"What time did this occur?"

"He said they left the store around ten forty-five."

"Okay, thanks, Lieutenant."

As Aidan gathered everything he wanted for the briefing that was happening in ten minutes, he paraphrased what was said.

"Sounds to me like the killer is getting careless," Shaun said. "We know he doesn't leave witnesses."

"Let's hope he is," Aidan said. He looked at his colleague and rose. "Because we sure could use a break."

33

After the briefing, Shaun and Aidan went back to the beginning, where Maya Gibson was found three weeks ago. They agreed to take on a fresh approach—viewing the scene through the eyes of a killer.

Thankfully, it hadn't rained again as the news had predicted, but the sky was still dark, so Aidan was guessing their luck would eventually run out. It was only a matter of time.

Until then, Shaun and Aidan stood outside of the car at Clarks Hill Lake, brainstorming what they knew with what they presumed.

It appeared years had passed since they first found Maya's body. Standing before the scene where she was found brought an emptiness to Aidan.

He flipped through his case files and read.

"Maya's husband said she'd gone missing the week before she was found," Aidan said. "After she didn't return home, and he hadn't heard from her for a few hours, he called the police. Dispatch took the information but told him their hands were tied until forty-eight hours had passed."

Shaun released a low curse. "That's a long time to wait when you know it's out of character for someone to disappear without a word."

Aidan agreed, but didn't voice it.

"TOD was said to be around eleven the night before she was found," Aidan said. "It's about the same time frame for all the other victims, give or take an hour. So, he'd kidnap them and hold his victims captive for a week. But he never sexually assaulted them. We know he hit them repeatedly with a heavy object."

"Like a baseball bat?"

Aidan considered the sounds he heard when the killer called him. He had come to the same conclusion. Before answering, Aidan looked at the autopsy photos and studied the cuts and bruises.

"I don't think so. Whatever it was, it was metal. Slimmer than a bat."

"So, what? Tire iron, golf club..." Shaun stared at the scene.

"Could be one of those." Aidan continued to scan the reports. "So after he gets bored with the victim, he kills her, redresses her, then dumps the body here. He did the same last night with Jane at the Keystone Grounds Park."

Deep in thought, Aidan lowered himself to the ground so he could get to the other side of the police tape. They ambled to the scene.

"Maya's body was found early in the morning by the teenagers." Aidan looked at the file. "Around six-thirty. They didn't see anything out of the ordinary. The girl tripped over Maya's feet."

They looked around the scene. Although the police tape was still protecting the area, Aidan saw the crime scene unit had cleaned it up.

"Her personal items aren't on her. What does he do with her phone and her wallet? Her car is found where she last was seen. How does he transport her?"

"I think that's the million-dollar question," Shaun said. He looked sideways at Aidan. "Did Devon Richards notice any other vehicle around the night Jane went missing?"

"No. He said someone was 'standing in the shadows.'"

"So, when he selects his victims, he does so on foot." Shaun narrowed his eyes as he worked out a theory. "Considering he doesn't use a car, he'd need a way to take them to his home base. He can't exactly carry them, right? And he wouldn't have a shopping cart or anything because if someone spotted him, they'd become suspicious, and he'd have more unintended murders on his hands."

Aidan saw where he was going.

"When he grabbed Jane Ridgeway, according to Devon, she was at her car. Which means her keys would be nearby. So, if I'm following you correctly, he could have driven Jane's car to his home base. Later, he'd return the car where he'd originally found them. Either he has another car stashed somewhere waiting for him, he steals another car or he simply uses some public transportation system to get around."

"You think he did the same with Maya?"

"Our guy is habitual. He has a routine and sticks with it."

"Agreed," Shaun said. "We need to take another look at Jane's and Maya's cars. We need to see the mileage."

34

"So, WHAT DID YOUR uncle say?" Kent asked.

Jordan eyed the basketball goal, tucked his arms to his side, and shot the ball into the air. It went in without hitting the backboard.

"He thought about it for a while and now that there's a second murder, he wants me to lie low. Maybe take a vacation somewhere," Jordan answered. He grabbed a beer from the cooler as Kent scooped the ball in his hands to swing it toward the goal.

He missed.

Kent jogged to the cooler, grabbed his can, and popped it open.

"Sorry, man."

Gary Short was quick to snatch the ball before it rolled further away, then jogged toward his colleagues.

Jordan shook his head. "It's crazy! I didn't do anything, and Thomas is looking at me like I did."

"I'm sure he doesn't think that," Gary said, tucking the ball under his arm. "He just needs to think about the reputation of the station."

Jordan scoffed. "Really? That's what you think he's worried about? I *am* the reputation." He jabbed a finger toward his chest. "I made the station what it is. I report the news and people tune in to watch *me* report the news."

"Wow," Kent said. He sipped his beer. "I never knew what Thomas meant by you having your head stuck in the clouds. Now I see it."

Jordan glared at him but didn't respond while Gary held back a snicker.

"I told you not to go on camera the first time," Kent said. "Remember? When you got that card, I told you to go to the cops. You didn't listen. And you're the one who lied about knowing Maya. You didn't even tell *me* you knew her."

Gary arched an eyebrow at the statement.

"So, what?" Jordan snapped, glaring at his friends. He returned his focus to Kent. "Now *you* think I'm killing these women?"

Kent closed his eyes and took a deep breath. "No, I am not saying that at all. Come on, man, give me some credit. I'm only saying you should have been more forward about your involvement with both Maya and reporting the other cases. You thought the cops really wouldn't find out?"

Jordan cursed under his breath.

"And another thing," Kent said, "Stop acting like you're king of the world. You're not. Thomas is right—others can do your job. You *are* replaceable. Just because he's your uncle doesn't mean you're invincible. You're lucky to be walking around now and not rotting in jail."

Kent set his beer down, retrieved the ball from Gary, and began dribbling. He tossed it in the air. The ball bounced off the rim and rolled back toward Jordan, who snatched the ball from the ground. He spun it on the tip of his index finger with a sneer.

"Man, you're a terrible basketball player," he said with a shake of his head.

"No kidding," Gary chuckled.

"I'm a cameraman," Kent said with a shrug. "Not a ballplayer."

Jordan shot it in the air. It hit the rim, slowly falling into the net. He turned to his friends with a sigh.

"You really think I have my head in the clouds?"

"Maybe not the clouds," Kent said. "More like the trees."

Jordan laughed at him.

"I'm going to go," Kent said. "Unlike you, I do have work in the morning. So this is where Kent Ory signs off."

Kent bowed his head with a smile and Jordan shook his hand.

"Thanks, man. I'll call you. I'll probably take Thomas' advice and take a trip out of town. I want to stay under that Agent O'Reilly's radar for at least a few days."

"See you later, then."

"Yeah, I should go too," Gary said. "The wife's having company later and I need to clean up a bit."

He slapped Jordan on the shoulder and headed toward the cars.

As Jordan watched his friends walk away, he thought about what they had said. Maybe everyone was right. Maybe he did put himself on a pedestal. However, he was one of the top reporters in the southeastern states.

And why was that?

Because he was good-looking, young, and he did whatever it took to report the news.

Was he disheartened because a hot woman he knew personally was dead?

Sure.

He liked her and it surprised him when he learned the victim was Maya. But did that mean he needed to change his ways?

Not for a second.

Jordan dribbled the basketball as he ran across the court. He jumped in the air and slammed the ball into the hoop.

35

While Shaun checked Maya's vehicle, Aidan examined Jane's. The total number of miles on Jane's odometer read a hundred and eight thousand. Pressing the trip button, he saw it was set at fifty-six miles.

Aidan wrote the figures in his pad and made a mental note to ask her husband when Jane usually set her trip odometer.

He was thinking it was possible to guesstimate where the car had been since last night. If they were lucky, conferring their victim's vehicles, they may narrow down probable locations of the killer's home base.

When Aidan finished, he climbed out of the car and shut the door.

"What did you find?" he asked Shaun.

He recited the numbers, which were slightly higher than what Aidan had come up with. But now they both had something more to work with.

Something Aidan was sure the killer hadn't even considered.

On the way back to the office, Shaun called Maya's husband, then Jane's. After Aidan pulled into the parking lot of the federal office, Shaun said Maya would reset the trip after she had an oil change, which she did a week before she was murdered. Jane had gotten gas two days ago, and she'd reset it then. Both husbands also relayed the places they knew their wives had driven.

It was getting late, so after they informed Tara of what they'd found, Shaun and Aidan finished and went their separate ways.

When Aidan pulled into the garage, he went into the house and found Cheyenne pulling a roast out of the oven.

"Hey," she said. "How was your day?"

"Well, we may have found something useful for finding where the killer's been operating."

"That's good," she said.

Cheyenne stirred the green beans and asked Aidan to get two plates from the cabinet.

As he did so, he observed her. She took in a deep breath and pushed it out as she dumped the beans in a container and brought it over to the table.

"What did you do today?" Aidan set the silverware next to the plates.

She shrugged as she finished gathering their supper. "Not much. Laura called today."

"How is she?"

"Good," Cheyenne said as they ate. Then she laughed. "She met a guy at the hospital."

Aidan raised his eyebrow. Laura picked up men and threw herself into a serious relationship. Her longest romances usually lasted less than two months. It was enough time for her to have her usual fling while in Florida.

"Really?"

"His name's Michael and he's a heart surgeon."

"Wow," Aidan said. "Very prestigious."

Cheyenne gathered a forkful of mashed potatoes and stuffed it in her mouth. Aidan finished his green beans before taking two sips of his drink.

"She says he may be 'the one,'" she said, using air quotes.

"Well, you never know," Aidan said, "Your sister's at the age where she might want to settle down."

Cheyenne rolled her eyes. "Oh, please. She's got too much of our mother in her. At least she doesn't marry so she can get divorced five times—yet."

Aidan finished his roast and potatoes as she stabbed the rest of her beans with her fork.

"Give your sister some credit." He rose and pushed the chair under the table. He began clearing the table as she stood and helped pack the leftovers.

"Want to make a bet?" Cheyenne challenged.

"A bet?" Aidan considered it as he waited for the faucet to shoot out hot water. "Name the stake."

"How about..." He washed a large pot as she thought. "... If she ends the relationship before she leaves Florida, the loser is the winner's slave for a month. Back rubs, breakfast in bed, whatever."

"You've got yourself a deal, little lady."

They shook on it, then Aidan used the water sprayer to wet her.

"Oh no, you didn't!" Cheyenne laughed.

She attempted to grab the sprayer, but her laughter weakened her, and he could pin her arms to her side. He leaned toward her neck and kissed her.

"Give?" Aidan asked.

"Yes," she said with a sigh.

Aidan released her, and she quickly grabbed the sprayer and squirted him.

"Oh, you're gonna pay for that," he said. "I'd sleep with one eye open tonight."

To end the water feud, she leaned in for a kiss. They enjoyed each other in silence for a few minutes, then he told her he was going to take a shower to wash the day away.

36

AGAIN, THE CARNATIONS KILLER invaded his sleep. The victims, new and old, reached out their hands, yearning to touch him. They would tell him how he failed them. Blood would run from the ends of their hair and their skin always appeared pale.

Aidan would feel the coldness surrounding his body. His breath rose and evaporated into the stagnant air.

He saw Jane Ridgeway and Maya Gibson being beaten by a heavy object. They pleaded for the hands to just *stop*.

But the hands that held the object wouldn't.

The crunch as the object contacted their skulls sounded like booming thunder.

Crunch. Crunch.

Aidan stood on the sidelines watching, desperately wanting to help them, but he couldn't. He stood, frozen in place.

Crunch.

Powerless to stop The Carnations Killer from bludgeoning them.

From murdering them.

Tears of dark blood ran down their faces until they lay in a pool of thick red liquid.

And the laughter echoed in the darkness. The deep laughter that just wouldn't stop surrounded Aidan.

Crunch.

Then Maya ripped her head off the ground. Her eyes blackened, and a ghost of a smile crawled across her pale face. Her mouth moved, but it wasn't her voice that spoke.

It was her killer's: *I can kill, and you can't catch me.*

And at that moment, Jane appeared next to Maya.

They began chanting the killer's words.

Their bodies made quick, jerking moves as they inched closer, ever closer.

Aidan wanted to back away, but he still couldn't move.

His legs appeared they stood in hardened cement.

The black night was prominent against their pale gray faces.

Next, the scenery changed, and he saw the killer dumping Maya's limp body at Clarks Hill Lake. Aidan saw the silver moon gleaming against the water, creating a hazy aura across the surface. The trees outlined the sky.

Then he stood at the Keystone Grounds Park watching the killer toss Jane away as though she were nothing but trash.

The sounds of the night mocked him. The birds, the wind, everything laughed.

It was growing colder, but he felt the heat rise in him.

The killer climbed back in the car, hands bloodied. Looking into the rearview mirror, Aidan saw his face for the first time.

But it wasn't The Carnations Killer.

It was his own.

Blood stained Aidan's skin and his normally blue eyes were black.

He couldn't recognize himself, but there was some sense of familiarity, and he knew it was him. The image of the mirror slowly swirled until the blood began dripping.

Drip.

Drip.

He wanted to cry out, but his voice seemed to be lost in his throat.

Then Jane appeared in the backseat of the car. The smile stretched across her face made the hair on the back of his neck stand at attention. His body shook, and he wasn't sure whether it was from the cold or seeing the dead woman's lifeless face.

She didn't say anything.

She only smiled.

Aidan's eyes were on her. She moved her mouth as though she was trying to speak, but no sound came forth.

He only heard the whistle of the wind outside the car.

Then, out of nowhere, hands grabbed his shoulders and pulled him back into the darkness.

37

Aidan's eyes flew open.

His breathing rose and fell in quick, heavy motions, his skin hot and clammy.

He remained gazing across the dark room, into the bathroom, trying to control his emotions.

Slowly, he turned onto his back and looked to where Cheyenne was sleeping. The moonlight glistened through the curtains, revealing the outline of her body. One of her legs hung out of the covers, over the side of the bed.

She snored softly as her breath entered and exited her body.

Aidan sat up slowly and crawled out of bed, careful not to wake her. The clock on the table told him it was only three in the morning, but he knew he wouldn't be able to fall asleep even if he wanted to. So he grabbed his robe and crept downstairs.

He made a pot of coffee and leaned against the counter until it finished brewing a few minutes later. Pouring himself a mug, he sat at the kitchen table with the dummy files.

Aidan stared at his and Shaun's notes on the mileage. He knew the agents over the weekend would attempt to triangulate likely locations for the killer's home base.

They'd call him if they found anything.

But because he couldn't sleep, and because he couldn't stop thinking about the killer, with the help of a map, Aidan used the mileage of Jane's and Maya's vehicles to mark where their cars may have been on the nights of their murders.

He heard the stairs creak from footsteps. A second later, Cheyenne appeared in the kitchen, rubbing her eyes as she yawned.

"What are you doing up?"

"Sorry, honey, I didn't mean to wake you."

"It's late," she said, eyes half-closed. "Come back to bed."

Aidan shook his head. "I can't sleep."

She frowned but didn't press the subject further as she pulled a glass from the cabinet. Cheyenne filled it with water from the refrigerator door.

"Hey," Aidan said, setting his pen on the table.

She glanced at him, her face tired.

"Come here."

She came, and he grabbed her hand to pull her into his lap. He stroked her cheek with his thumb.

"I'm fine, okay?" He rubbed his eyes as he looked at the map on the table. "I just woke up and had an idea where we might find the killer."

"Did you find him?" Her words were soft and full of sleep.

"Almost," he said softly. Aidan kissed her cheek. "Go back to bed, okay? I'll be up shortly."

She kissed him and left the room.

Aidan rubbed his eyes before resuming the work he was doing.

Soon, he had found a handful of possibilities within a fifty-mile radius. He made a note to contact the agent on duty in the morning so he could check into it and try to narrow the search even more.

After he finished, Aidan followed through on his promise and went back to bed.

But instead of trying to sleep, he climbed under the covers and draped his arm across Cheyenne's body to keep watch over her as she slept.

38

Aidan promised himself and Cheyenne he would give her his undivided attention the rest of the weekend. No more thinking about The Carnations Killer murders. Not until the following morning, anyway.

Agent Douglas Miller, who was in charge when Shaun and Aidan weren't, excelled at what he did. So Aidan figured he would allow himself to have a day or two to refresh him mind.

It proved to be no easy task. Douglas sent him a few texts, at which time Aidan would make an excuse to be out of earshot of Cheyenne.

The last he heard from Douglas was that a tip had come through to the Columbia County Sheriff's Department that a dog walker spotted a vehicle matching Jane Ridgeway's blue Honda at a house on Mike Padgett Highway.

Aidan didn't hear anything more from Douglas, which made it difficult for him to concentrate as the day went on.

When Cheyenne suggested they make a date for dinner and a movie, Aidan agreed. He took her out for an early dinner at their favorite restaurant before the movie.

Aidan realized they had hardly seen each other for almost two months because of his sister's wedding and the resurfacing of The Carnations Killer.

Making a promise to himself, Aidan was determined to be present for his wife. That thought in mind, Aidan wrapped his arms around her as they watched the movie on the large screen, and she laid her head on his shoulder. When Aidan's phone vibrated in its hook on the side of his pants, he tried not to be conspicuous when he checked to see who was calling. Aidan could feel Cheyenne's glare as her attention moved from the projector screen to him.

The caller was Agent Douglas.

"I have to ... get something to drink," Aidan whispered in her ear.

Aidan ignored her wondering eyes as he left the vast, dark room. By the time he exited, the vibration had stopped, so Aidan called Douglas back.

"We've found something," Douglas said when he answered.

"Tell me," Aidan said, keeping his voice low.

"The witness panned out. The information on the mileage you sent this morning coincided with a house on Mike Padgett Highway," he said. "We found tire tracks matching Jane Ridgeway's car. The house is perfect for taking his victims. It's secluded, surrounded by trees, and has more than eighty acres of land." He paused. "And you'll never guess who owns it."

"Who?"

"Thomas Blake."

Aidan's heart beat against his chest, and he leaned against the wall.

"You're kidding. Jordan Blake's uncle?" Aidan paced, rubbing the nape of his neck. "You get a warrant yet?"

"Got it two seconds before I called you. I have my guys running a check on both the house and Thomas Blake. In the meantime, we're on our way to give him a proper hello," Douglas said. "Care to join us?"

Aidan glanced at the closed door of the theater, thinking of Cheyenne. If he left her here, she wouldn't be happy. But then again, they may have caught up with The Carnations Killer. And he wanted to be there when they slapped cuffs on his wrists.

Aidan told Douglas where he was and asked if he could have someone swing by for him so Cheyenne could take her car home.

"I'll do it myself," Douglas said. "I'm minutes out."

"Thanks," Aidan said. "Notify Shaun. He'll want to come along."

After he ended the call, Aidan slipped into the dark room. It had become silent on the screen and a girl was slowly creeping through the house.

Aidan returned to his seat to whisper in Cheyenne's ear.

"I've got to go," he said.

Her eyes burned with fire. "What?"

"Someone's picking me up, so you'll have the car. I'll see you later, okay?"

She nodded her head once, but he could tell it wasn't okay. Aidan kissed her cheek. She continued to glare at the enlarged screen, her arms crossed tightly against her chest. Her lips curled into a scowl.

Aidan never liked it when Cheyenne was mad at him, but right now, catching the one responsible for the deaths of over fifty women took precedence. He'd have to deal with Cheyenne's wrath later.

39

THOMAS BLAKE'S HOUSE STOOD in the middle of his land, a few trees scattering the area. It was a two-story brick house, with four white columns holding the roof of the porch intact. The upkeep told Aidan that he—or someone at the least—kept it clean. The grass was freshly cut, the flowers recently watered.

There was a large pond in the front, and a tackle box sitting next to a small deck.

Aidan recognized the house immediately as the one in the photo in Jordan Blake's home office.

According to the real estate archives, the house on Mike Padgett Highway had been in the Blake family for at least three generations. On the drive over, Douglas informed him that Thomas didn't live in the house—he had bought another one in North Augusta with his wife. He'd been renting it out for a few years.

Looking around the area, Aidan agreed with Douglas that it seemed to be the perfect spot to take victims and murder them. No neighbors to hear the screams, and it looked normal enough for passersby to not give it a second glance.

If Aidan were a killer, he decided he'd want to operate at a place just like this.

With that thought in mind, he slipped on a vest and held his weapon at the ready.

Douglas and Aidan were stationed at the front door, along with four other agents. Douglas signaled for a few of the men to survey the backyard to be sure there wouldn't be a chance for the killer to escape.

Two agents held a battering ram at the ready, preparing to rush the door when ordered. The other two held their weapons in front of them.

Douglas nodded his head twice at Aidan to signal him to take charge.

Aidan rapped on the doorframe. "FBI! We have a search warrant!"

He tried one more time, to no avail.

Aidan gripped his weapon.

Took a breath.

Standing on the side of the doorframe, he looked behind him and nodded to the men holding the ram.

On that note, they crashed through the door and the agents entered the premises.

"FBI!"

They scattered throughout the house, looking through every room on both floors. The silence was deafening, and after Aidan cleared his part of downstairs, he regrouped with Douglas in the kitchen.

Upstairs, an agent said, "All clear!"

"All clear," Shaun said as he entered the kitchen behind him.

"Want to bring Thomas in for questioning?" Douglas asked.

"Yeah." Aidan looked out the window across the vast backyard. "I don't think it's a coincidence we found this place."

Douglas nodded. "I agree."

Aidan waited as he got on the phone to put in a request for someone to bring Thomas in for questioning. Shaun rummaged through a stack of papers on the counter.

"Looks like someone named Ron lives here," Shaun said. Without looking away from the pile, he passed Aidan a note.

Ron—

Let me know if there's anything you need. Here's my address to send your first month's rent.

They didn't see any other mail for Ron or a last name for him.

As Douglas spoke into the phone, the radio on Aidan's shoulder came alive and someone announced they had found something in the back room.

Exchanging glances with Douglas, they made their way to the back of the house.

Entering the room, Aidan saw that someone had pulled back the red rectangle rug, revealing a trap door.

"It was like this when we came in," an agent said.

Interesting.

Aidan kneeled and steadied the hatch, and Shaun followed suit.

Putting a finger to his lips to show to be as quiet as possible, he wrapped his fingers around the latch and pulled open the door. It made a soft creak as it revealed stairs leading into the darkened cellar.

There were no other sounds, and Aidan grabbed his flashlight and shined it below. Motioning for the other agents to stand guard, he silently told Shaun to follow.

Using the beam as a guide, Aidan slowly descended, trying to reduce the number of creaks as possible.

40

He was preparing for his next victim when he first heard the footsteps above him. He slipped on his hat, turning the bill downward so it'd cover his eyes. Next, he switched the lights off in the cellar.

He didn't know how they'd found him so soon, but that didn't matter now. He needed to take care that he didn't get caught.

His heart thrummed in his chest as he stood in the shadows, remaining quiet hoping the agents wouldn't find the hatch in the back room of the house.

He held a knife in one hand and a taser in the other.

His mind raced as he tried to figure out a way to escape without being caught. There were no windows, nor was there a door in the cellar—the only way out was the stairs. And now the trap door slowly opened, revealing light from above.

He moved behind a nearby chifforobe and peered over the edge, taking in his surroundings.

There was a fuse box on the opposite side of the room.

Next to it was a table that held a few homemade gadgets, including a smoke bomb.

Yes, that should do the trick.

He only had to get over there and turn off the lights for the rest of the house.

From there, he could figure out a way to get past the agents he was sure kept watch outside the house.

He watched feet slowly appear onto the top rung of the pull-down ladder.

It was Agent O'Reilly who first appeared, then Henderson after him.

Agent Henderson was a big man, so he was hoping he wouldn't be the one heading his way. It'd take some doing to overpower him.

The flashlight beam swept across the room, and he ducked deeper into the shadows.

AIDAN LOOKED AROUND THE room to see only a cellar full of old furniture. There was a large stained tarp in the middle of the floor. A tire iron rested against the dresser, which also held a container of duct tape and fishing wires.

Aidan glanced at Shaun, who motioned with his eyes that he was going to look near the antique chifforobe.

Aidan tilted his head in the opposite direction, and they separated.

HENDERSON HEADED HIS WAY, as The Carnations Killer gripped the taser in his hand.

AIDAN CREPT NEAR THE other side of the cellar, keeping an eye out for a light switch. He saw nothing except a fuse box and more fishing wires, as well as a box of tasers and smoke bombs. They continued to move slowly to hear better, but Aidan only heard the blood pulsating in his ears.

HENDERSON STOPPED AT THE chifforobe and glanced behind it. The agent's eyes grew wide when he saw him. By instinct, Henderson raised his weapon.

"Over—"

The killer expertly knocked the hand gripping the gun and swept his foot against Henderson's. He swung a left hook to the agent's side, resulting in a soft grunt.

Working quickly, he jammed the taser against the agent's upper arm, so he'd earn the momentum to get away. Henderson shouted with surprise as his body convulsed and he dropped both his weapon and the flashlight. The beam from the light sent rays across the cellar floor before it blinked out after banging against the floor.

He grabbed the weapon.

Agent O'Reilly had spun around but didn't shoot—he guessed it was in case his friend was in the line of fire.

He fired a shot at O'Reilly, who ducked behind a large desk to keep from being hit.

Agents descended the stairs, so the killer fired a few more rounds to buy himself time. The results were what he'd hoped. The agents took cover, providing him enough of a chance to make his way toward the fuse box.

A second later, he flicked off the lights in the house.

Someone grabbed his neck from behind.

He swung his chin toward the ceiling so his head would knock against the agent's, then spun to connect his fist to O'Reilly's temple.

He sent a forceful low kick to the agent's leg, and O'Reilly cried out as his knees buckled underneath him. He pulled off the helmet and wrapped his arms around his neck. O'Reilly tried grabbing some part of him to loosen the hold, only managing to knock off the cap. Soon, the agent went limp in his arms.

"Not today, Agent O'Reilly," he whispered, lowering him to the floor. He dragged the unconscious agent behind the dresser and quickly removed the FBI vest. He slipped it on, tucking his hat inside. He fitted O'Reilly's cap and pulled in a heavy breath, pushing it out.

Agents had begun to descend the stairs again, their strides slow and cautious, weapons and flashlights filling the room.

He held Henderson's weapon in front of him and quickly, but quietly, slunk to the table with the smoke bombs. He grabbed two.

The flashlight beam mowed in his direction, so he tossed the bomb on the ground. Immediately chaos erupted amongst the agents as they scurried to exit the cellar.

He used his shirt to protect his nose and mouth and made his way out, blending in as best as he could.

With the aid of O'Reilly's cap, he kept his head lowered and exited the hatch. He tossed his second smoke bomb at the agents standing guard nearby.

They began coughing, shouting for each other to get out. One agent decided to tough it out. He squinted his eyes, tears filling the corners. The agent held his gun at the ready.

"FBI, freeze!" His voice sounded muffled behind his shirt.

Without a second thought, he held the gun to the agent's head. For half a second, he saw the fear in the agent's eyes.

But he didn't shoot. Instead, he knocked the agent hard on the side of his head and hurried out the back door to safety.

41

"Aidan?" Shaun's voice called to his friend.

Aidan couldn't open his eyes. The pain still exploded in his head, and his knees throbbed, making it difficult to focus. He also felt his eyes burning.

"You okay, man?"

Now it was Douglas' voice.

Everything sounded garbled and far away. Aidan tried to bring himself to the present, but it wasn't easy.

The buzzing in his ears was loud.

Aidan slowly forced his eyes to open. The light was blinding, but after a few blinks, he made out Shaun's concerned expression, then Douglas'.

"What happened?" Aidan said.

Looking around the room he was in, he remembered.

They were in the cellar at Thomas Blake's house. One of the team found a trap door and Shaun and Aidan went inside. Then everything that followed happened fast.

He remembered hearing Shaun cry out.

As Aidan turned, he had seen Shaun falling hard to the ground.

Through his foggy mind, he remembered the killer rushing for the fuse box. Aidan had grabbed him from behind. The killer banged the back of his head against Aidan's before flipping the switches. That was the last thing he remembered before hearing Shaun's voice.

Aidan tried to sit up too quickly. The pain sliced through his head, forcing him to groan and lay back down.

"You're okay, buddy," Shaun said. He put a large hand on Aidan's shoulder. "Just stay down. A bus is on the way. We'll get you fixed up."

"What about you? He attacked you."

Aidan looked at him through his eyelashes and saw Shaun glance toward his arm. "The killer tased me. Hurt like a mother. But I'll be fine."

"Did we manage—?"

"Smoke bombs. He got away through all the confusion," Douglas said. "Agent Hensley cornered him but froze when the killer held the gun to his head."

"Is he—"

"Nah, he's a tough cookie. Other than the knot on the side of his head, he'll be fine."

"Did he get a good look at him?"

"Couldn't see with all the smoke."

Aidan tried to sit up again. Shaun attempted to prevent him from rising, but when he insisted he was fine, Shaun helped him to his feet.

Aidan realized he was going to get an earful from Cheyenne later when she found out he got himself injured in the line of duty on his day off. He was glad he was still alive for her to yell at him.

Aidan's ears perked to the sounds of sirens blaring outside, announcing the ambulance and backup.

His eyes scanned the cellar. Now that the lights were on and the smoke had subsided, he saw the large blue tarp in the middle of the floor. Dark red stains splattered against it.. The killer left behind several containers of duct tape and fishing wires. The bloodied tire iron rested against the dresser.

With Douglas's help, Aidan followed Shaun up the stairs so the EMTs wouldn't disturb the crime scene.

Aidan sank into the chair against the wall and noticed Shaun holding his shoulder. The tased area must bother him.

Douglas was cussing out Agent Hensley for failing to apprehend the killer while Shaun tried to calm him. Though Aidan was just as upset, it wasn't at the agent. He was sure Douglas felt the same way. He only needed to blow some steam.

Aidan hoped the agent realized that. He wasn't familiar with him. Hensley looked to be in his early twenties. He frowned as he released several shaky apologies. He made a mental note to commend him after the excitement died down.

Aidan watched, his mind reeling, as the crime scene unit went down below to process the scene while the EMT checked him out.

They were right that Thomas Blake's house was the killer's home base. The question now was, who was Ron?

The EMT wanted Aidan to go to the hospital for a complete check-up, but Aidan assured him he was fine. All he wanted to do was go home.

Frowning, the EMT wrapped Aidan's knee tightly in a bandage. He was then ordered to go home, ice his knee and try to stay off it as much as possible.

So that was what he did.

42

After his near confrontation with the FBI, he went home to finish putting up the decorations for Jamie's eighth birthday party later in the evening.

Though she had turned eight a few days ago, they had chosen today for her party to stretch her special day to last just a little longer. Plus, it was a better time for her best friend, Alice, to attend.

"She *has* to be able to come," Jamie had told her parents.

Who could refuse that?

Now, with everything party-ready, he grabbed two beers from the refrigerator and joined his wife in the living room.

She was watching the latest development of the FBI's search for The Carnations Killer.

The search for him.

He handed her a bottle and sat on the couch, wrapping an arm around her slender shoulders.

"This is so awful." She set her beer on the table. "They almost caught him, too. But he got away. We're just not safe anymore, are we?"

He squeezed her shoulders and kissed her cheek.

"I promise nothing will happen to you, babe."

She gazed at him and offered a weak smile.

"I just feel sorry for the victims' families. I can't imagine what they're going through."

"It's terrible." He kept his voice soft. He'd mastered compassion over the years, and his lovely wife was fooled. She believed he took these cases to heart.

She'd always remained in the dark about his secret hobby. It never even occurred to her the man she slept next to was the same man everybody was talking about.

The same man everyone, her included, feared.

It was only a matter of being sure that she stayed fooled. They'd known each other for almost eleven years. All she knew was his good side. They went to church most Sundays and even volunteered at the soup kitchen during Christmastime.

Sure, they had arguments—every couple does, don't they?

He never wanted to have to kill her, but he'd do it if the situation called for it. Then he'd make himself be just another face on the news to lose his beautiful young blonde wife to a crazed serial killer.

He smiled at her and stroked her cheek.

"I love you," he said. "Very much."

"I know." She leaned in and kissed him. He cupped his hands underneath her chin and brought her deeper into the moment.

"Eww!"

He looked to see Jamie appearing in the room holding her new purple stuffed bear. She hadn't let go of the stupid thing since the day he bought it for her.

"Eww?" he echoed. "Don't tell me 'eww.' The Daddy Monster's going to get you for that, little birthday girl!" He threw her a crazed laugh and hopped off the couch.

Jamie's eyes widened in fake shock, and she darted out of the family room. He began chasing his daughter throughout the house.

He laughed at her shrieks and caught up with her in her bedroom.

He swept Jamie off her feet, and she squealed and shouted, "Mommy, Mommy, help me!"

"No one's going to save you from the Daddy Monster," he said, tickling her stomach.

They paused when his wife called up the stairs to announce some kids for Jamie's birthday party had arrived.

"They're here!" Jamie's eyes shined with excitement.

He widened his eyes in mock surprise and gasped. "Then you'd better hurry!"

Jumping out of his arms, Jamie rushed down the stairs.

He stood in his daughter's rainbow-colored room, drawing in a deep breath.

During the altercation he had with the FBI agent, he had strained his side. He still hadn't been able to figure out how they found his "office", but now he needed to find another location. It was best for him to lie low for a few weeks. He would use the time to find somewhere else, find another victim, then the surprise he had for Agent O'Reilly would come in effect.

Over the next few days, he would observe the agents before returning to the house. There was something he needed to retrieve. Something special he planned on giving Agent O'Reilly. He wasn't worried, though. There was no way the agents would find the album. He hid it somewhere they wouldn't even think to look.

Pushing the pain from his side out of his mind, he made a beeline for the living room. He saw a small group of kids, including Alice, had arrived and were playing in the backyard. The parents were hanging around in the family room.

"Hey, how are you doing?" he said, slapping a few of the men on their backs. He leaned in to hug the women in their lives. "It's so wonderful to see you again. Thank you for coming."

He listened in on their chatter. As the party of people grew in attendance, he overheard some of the women talk amongst themselves about the recent murders.

He frowned as he joined in the conversation by the party table.

"I really hope they catch this guy soon," he said. "I hate knowing my wife could be in danger." He glanced at his wife, who went to answer the door for more arrivals. "And with work, I can't always be here to protect her."

He dished out a ladle full of red punch she had made earlier while he was at the other house and sipped it.

"Oh, I know it," one woman said. She put a consoling hand on his elbow and patted him. "It's scary knowing the killer can be standing right next to you, and you don't even know."

He took another sip.

Yes, it was quite scary, wasn't it?

He continued making his rounds amongst the guests, and when it was time, he put eight candles on the cake and lit them.

He brought it to the picnic table outside. They joined in chorus, singing "Happy Birthday."

"Now make a wish, pumpkin."

He watched as his daughter closed her eyes and blew the candles out with one breath.

43

AFTER THEY BRIEFED TARA, she insisted both Shaun and Aidan go home for the night. Aidan resisted because he wanted to get back to work and find the killer now more than ever.

It didn't matter to Aidan that the pain in his knee was taking its vengeance, but in the end, he caved.

He was spending the rest of the night with his leg iced and propped on pillows as the EMT originally ordered. Cheyenne had said nothing about his injuries, but he was sure the time would soon come—he could see it in her eyes.

Aidan had received a text an hour and a half ago from Douglas saying they had brought Thomas Blake in for questioning. According to him, he'd rented the house to a man named Ron Heady.

Thomas claimed to have never met Heady personally—only over the phone.

Heady had wanted to rent the place off the books, and because Thomas loved money more than background or credit checks, he went along with it.

Douglas ran the background check and learned Heady was an eighty-three-year-old man who had died of pneumonia two years prior.

At that point, Aidan suggested for Douglas to go after Jordan Blake for more questioning.

It was making sense to him that his instinct was wrong, and Jordan Blake could easily be The Carnations Killer. After all, he lied many times. It didn't take much to believe he could easily use his uncle's house to murder the women.

Aidan used his newfound free time to watch various news stations, but primarily WJFX. Surprisingly, the young Blake hadn't reported on anything the past few days.

He had texted Douglas to see whether they'd contacted him. The answer came that Jordan seemed to have vanished. His uncle wasn't being helpful with his nephew's whereabouts, which made Aidan even more suspicious.

Thomas had gone from being helpful to silent. Did he think Jordan killed these women? Was he trying to protect his nephew?

"Do you need anything?"

Cheyenne stepped in front of the couch where Aidan lay and looked at him. He grasped her hand and brought it to his lips for a kiss.

"Yes," he said. "I need you to sit."

She frowned. "Aidan, we've got to talk."

The doorbell interrupted them, and Aidan let out a soft curse, resulting in the famous Cheyenne glare.

"Why does it seem like every day I need to tell you not to talk that way?"

"Sorry," he said.

Her arms crossed, she went to answer the door, and he heard her scold Shaun for not keeping himself and Aidan safe.

Shaun said, "We're alive, aren't we?"

Cheyenne asked which shoulder was the sore one so she could punch the other. Aidan's lips curved in a small smile as she and Shaun entered the living room.

Cheyenne appeared in the doorway to announce she was going to run to the store and pick up a frozen pizza for supper. Then she asked Shaun if he'd like to stay for dinner.

After he answered that, of course, he would, she said her goodbyes and left.

"How are you feeling?" Shaun asked.

"Like I've been kicked and had the breath knocked out of me," Aidan said. Sitting up, he said, "What about you?"

"Like I've been tased." Shaun sat in the recliner. "But I'll live. Tara wants us to take tomorrow off to recuperate."

"Fat chance," Aidan said. "I'm going to find this guy, whether or not I'm on the clock."

Shaun nodded. "I told her you'd say that. She agreed, and that's why she's not going to make us take the day off."

Aidan narrowed his eyes. "What's the catch?"

"You noticed that, huh?"

Aidan frowned. "Please don't say she wants to put us behind the desk."

"Okay," Shaun said. "I won't say that." He rose, and Aidan watched him step into the kitchen. A second later, he returned and passed over a beer.

"We can't do too much behind a desk," Aidan said.

"It's that or nothing," Shaun said. He popped open his can and took a sip. "We're lucky it's something. My pride and I got tased, he knocked you out. We're kinda damaged goods right now."

Aidan frowned as this afternoon replayed itself.

"Who are we dealing with?" he asked.

"I don't know," Shaun said. "But we're going to figure it out."

44

After they ate dinner and Shaun left, Cheyenne cleaned the kitchen and Aidan hobbled up the steps with his bag of ice. He stretched out on the bed, his two pillows propping the injured leg above his heart.

Cheyenne entered the bedroom, eyes tired, but she stood in the doorway, frowning at him.

"We need to talk."

Aidan had hoped she'd forget about wanting to talk. A lump formed in his throat as he prepared himself for what she wanted to say to him.

"Okay," he said, mentally trying to settle his racing heart. He didn't want to have this conversation.

"I can't do this anymore."

Aidan narrowed his eyes. Although it worried him that one day he'd hear those words, it didn't prevent the lump from forming in his throat.

He'd hunted serial killers. He'd been in shootouts resulting in severe tragedy—but one of the worst things he could think of to happen in five years seemed to come to light.

Swallowing, Aidan asked, "What are you talking about?"

"You know, I've almost forgotten what you look like," Cheyenne said. It seemed she was on the verge of tears. "I haven't seen you for ages."

"I know," Aidan said, his voice low. "I'm sorry. I've just been focused on this investigation."

"Yeah," she said with a scoff. "I've noticed. Look at your leg. And the bruising on your neck. You could have died today."

"But I'm fine," he said.

She shook her head firmly. "No. You are not fine. *We* are not fine."

"Cheyenne, I'm only trying to do my job," Aidan snapped. "I've gotten hurt before. This isn't anything different. We came out all right then. We'll be fine now."

"This has nothing to do with you getting hurt, and you *know* it," Cheyenne hissed. "You think I don't realize you've been sneaking out of bed to look at your files in the kitchen? You do that every single night, and I can't take it any longer."

"I know it's been tough. But I promise I'm managing it."

"That's what you said last time. But you're obsessed. This investigation? It's going to destroy you."

"Come on, Cheyenne," Aidan said. "What am I going to have to do to show you I'm fine?"

She hesitated. He couldn't tell whether she was going to answer.

Finally, she said, "Leave your files at work."

Aidan gaped at her, but soon realized she wasn't kidding.

"What?"

"You heard me," she said. "I don't want to see it in your hands. When you're not at the office or with Shaun on duty, I don't want you to even glance at the folders."

"Listen—"

"No, *you* listen," she said, jabbing her finger at him. Her eyes clouded with a mixture of fury and worry. "I cannot watch you waste away. At least if I know a part of what's hurting you isn't near us, I can control it."

Aidan considered protesting again, but thought against it.

"Fine," he said. "I'll leave it at the office from now on. I don't care. I want you to be happy."

She swallowed and then pushed out a heavy breath before turning to leave the room.

Aidan wasn't fine with her giving an ultimatum. But he knew he didn't really have much of a choice. She was coming close to asking him to choose her or his career. Aidan realized he needed to show her he really loved her.

But he had a nagging feeling this wasn't the end.

He thought about Shaun and his wife, how he chose his career over the woman he loved.

Aidan couldn't help but wonder, would he do the same thing?

Or would he choose Cheyenne?

Aidan closed his eyes in hopes of sleep allowing his concerns to fall away.

As usual, The Carnations Killer's victims occupied his dreams, and this time, he heard Cheyenne's pained voice in the distance.

45

THE NEXT MORNING, AIDAN walked into the office and sat at his desk. He didn't immediately log into the database as was his normal habit. He sat in his chair, his head resting in his hands.

"Everything okay?" Shaun asked.

Aidan looked at him with a sigh. "Yeah, I'm great."

He scoffed, looking Aidan over. "You look great. Bloodshot eyes, you didn't shave this morning. And I saw you trying not to hobble on your leg."

"So my knee's bothering me. It's not like we're going to be able to go on a chase anyway. What does it matter?"

Shaun's eyebrow lifted.

"Sorry," Aidan said. "Cheyenne and I had a disagreement after you left."

"Because you got hurt?" he asked.

Aidan shook his head. "Because I don't want to worry her about my nightmares and she knows I've been waking up in the middle of the night to stare at dead women's photos."

"You should tell her," Shaun said. "It might not make anything better, but at least she'll see why you're affected by all of this."

"No offense, Shaun," Aidan snapped, "but you don't know the half of it. And I won't be taking relationship advice from a divorced man who chose his career over his family."

Shaun frowned, but instead of replying to the insult, he said he had work to do.

As he walked away, Aidan's landline rang.

"Yeah, O'Reilly," he said dryly.

"Good morning," Jackson from the lab chirped. "I wanted to confirm with you that the blood on the tarp was positive for Maya Gibson's and

Jane Ridgeway's blood. The fingerprints you guys lifted belonged to the victims as well."

"That all?"

"Yeah, sorry I don't have more, man."

"All right, thanks."

Aidan replaced the phone on the hook and released a curse. An agent passing by glanced his way. When he locked eyes with Aidan, he scampered away.

Aidan pushed his chair back and hobbled to where Shaun kept himself focused on the computer screen.

"Hey," he said.

Shaun looked up.

"Look, man," Aidan said. He wasn't sure of what to say. Thankfully, Shaun waved his beefy hand as if he was wiping off a clean slate.

"Already forgotten. We're cool."

Leaning against his desk, Aidan scoffed. "You know, I'd like you a whole lot better if you'd lose your temper every once in a while."

As an intern came near them, Shaun shouted out a curse, slapped a large hand against his desk, then shouted, "I didn't get my muffin this morning!"

The intern froze, eyes wide. She held a slip of paper in her hand, unsure of whether to approach.

Aidan smiled at her. "He loves his muffins."

She giggled warily, and handed Shaun the paper and stepped away. Slipping it in one of his boxes, he rose from his chair.

"Speaking of which," he said, stretching his limbs, "I'm going to go grab that muffin. Wanna come with?"

"Sure."

As they walked, Aidan relayed what Jackson said.

"So, he must use gloves," Shaun said. "This guy doesn't miss a step."

"Told you," Aidan said. "He's thorough. Plans things before he even does them. He knows the process."

As they took the elevator to the cafeteria, they discussed the suspects: Jordan Blake, who seemed to disappear into thin air although it was obvious he was still under suspicion, and his uncle, whose house the killer used and his sudden unwillingness to help locate his nephew.

Aidan couldn't help but think they were missing some vital piece of information.

◈

AFTER REVIEWING COUNTLESS NUMBERS of files, Aidan and Shaun agreed to call it a night. However, Aidan didn't go straight home. Instead, he went to the boxing gym Shaun took him to a while back.

If it helped him feel better that first time, he figured it might do the trick now.

They had come so close to catching the killer. He fought him, but he still slipped by undetected. He had a lot of pent-up resentment rising in him as the minutes ticked by, and he wanted to unleash as much as possible. He had already taken it out on Shaun once and it concerned him that he was building toward taking it out on Cheyenne, and that was one thing he couldn't allow.

Aidan found an empty punching bag and began knocking it around. The noise of the gym soon drowned out with each punch, and his bare knuckles grew sore.

But he felt better.

That was the important thing.

Shaun was right about the gym.

He made a mental note to thank him later. But for now, Aidan decided to go home, put his knuckles on ice. As he left the gym, he decided he'd buy a pair of boxing gloves the next day. He could see himself as a regular.

46

When he saw it was finally safe to return to the house, he went around the back to grab a shovel from the shed. He didn't need to break inside. That wasn't where he hid what he wanted.

He jammed the shovel into the ground by the back pond and lifted the dirt, little by little.

He whistled as he did.

He may have lost his point of operation, but he was close to finding a new one. It didn't matter one way or another. The police hadn't seen him. He'd even spoken to Agent O'Reilly once at the grocery store when he was shopping with his wife.

If he had an inkling of an idea, he was sure he'd be in jail now instead of digging through the dirt.

But, no.

He was here, and he was free.

Free to do what he wanted.

He'd already chosen his next target. She was a teller at a bank. He'd gone to her with the pretense of opening a savings account. During their conversation, he found out she liked to write—he did, too. He urged her to submit her romance tales, but she had smiled shyly and said she wasn't good enough. He reminded her that she wouldn't ever know until she tried. Her eyes shined as though he'd given her the courage to do just that.

It was a shame she wasn't going to have a lot of opportunities to do her writing. He considered letting her slide since he held a soft spot for writers. But he decided against it.

Halfway through the ground, his shovel hit the top of what he was searching for.

It wouldn't be long now.

A few more dirt tosses aside, he revealed the brown album. Brushing off the soil, he smiled. A few weeks ago, he had decided to give it to O'Reilly as part of the surprise he had in store. He thought the agent might appreciate a gift from the heart. But first, he needed to duplicate it. He didn't want to give him the original copy.

As he refilled the hole, his cell phone rang.

"Hello?"

"Hey, honey." It was his wife. "Are you stopping at home anytime soon?"

"I can, sure."

"I need a few things from the store if you don't mind going for me. I can text you the list."

"Of course, babe," he said.

"What are you doing? You sound out of breath."

"I'm working out. I've got to look my best if I'm going to keep you, right?"

Her laughter sounded self-conscious. He pictured her blushing. "Oh, I didn't intend on bothering you, babe."

He finished filling the hole and returned the shovel to the shed.

"You never bother me," he said. "So don't ever think that. You know, I don't have a lot left to do at work. Why don't you send Jamie to a friend's house and we can have a little champagne, create a bit of romance..."

"Really?"

"I want to show you how much I really love you, baby."

"Then hurry home."

"Yes, ma'am."

Now at his car, he tossed the album in the trunk, burying it under the early Christmas gifts he and his wife bought.

He climbed in as the text came with the grocery list. He also decided to buy his lovely wife a bouquet of red roses—her favorite.

47

A SOUND IN AIDAN'S dreams jarred him awake. For the first time, he couldn't remember the specifics of what he dreamt, and he was glad. Considering his heart drummed against his chest as though he'd run five miles at top speed, he didn't want to remember.

Aidan sat upright in his bed and swung his feet over the edge.

It had been a few weeks since their close encounter with The Carnations Killer, and they hadn't found enough helpful leads to catch up with him. It was wearing and tearing him down. Aidan could feel it, and he could see in Cheyenne's eyes that she was still troubled by it—although she stopped bringing it up. That worried him. Cheyenne not saying whatever was on her mind was never a good thing.

The crime scene unit confirmed Thomas Blake's house was used as the killer's home base. They assumed the duct tape was used to cover the victims' mouths and the fishing wire matched the gashes on the bodies.

One of the crime scene units found a broken fingernail in the corner of the cellar. They were able to confirm it came from Maya—it appeared that she may have been attempting to dig her way out of the basement.

The cellar didn't have noticeable fingerprints other than the victims, so they weren't sure whether or not Jordan had ever been there.

However, Aidan realized even if his prints were there, it wouldn't have been surprising, considering his uncle owned the house. Any lawyer would claim it as inconclusive evidence.

And they'd be right.

When they finally caught up with the reporter, they learned Jordan had taken a vacation to New York with a couple of girls, so there was no way he would have been on the premises at the same time as the FBI.

They were back to square zero and the days were creeping along with no word from the killer. Maybe his last encounter with them had scared him off and he decided to go on his usual sabbatical.

Did they really lose him again?

Aidan hoped not.

He'd begun to find himself staying at work late. Cheyenne seemed okay with the late hours. At first, Aidan decided it was probable that she preferred he spent his time obsessing at a distance.

When they were together, however, the tension between him and Cheyenne grew thicker and thicker.

He wasn't entirely convinced the killer was gone for good. So how could he stop searching for him? Especially since he claimed to have a surprise for Aidan.

Aidan figured that unless he missed it, the killer hadn't done anything remotely like a surprise.

And now, Aidan rested his back against the headboard after having another series of nightmares.

His throat parched, he headed for the kitchen to get himself a glass of water. He closed his eyes as the iced liquid wet his throat.

When Aidan reopened them, an image flashed in front of his eyes.

Aidan gasped and jumped backward, knocking into the kitchen chair. He fell back, his glass of water falling out of his hands, almost in slow motion, to the tiles. Water and glass spewed across the floor. His head snapped back, and he let out a sharp cry.

White circles swam in front of his eyes as he tried to refocus. Sharp pain throbbed in his head as he rubbed his temples.

Aidan heard Cheyenne's frantic cries from the bedroom and footsteps thumping down the stairs.

"Aidan!"

She flew into the kitchen wild-eyed. Seeing him on the floor, she rushed to his side.

"Are you okay? What happened? Are you hurt? Do I need to call an ambulance?"

Her constant chattering was making Aidan's head pound more. She helped him sit up and then took his head in her hands.

"Talk to me!"

"I'm fine," Aidan said. He shook his head. "I don't know what happened. I saw...I thought..." Aidan heard his voice tremble, and he couldn't shake the awful image he'd just witnessed out of his mind.

Cheyenne put his head against her chest.

"I'm fine, honey," he said, although he didn't sound convincing even to his ears.

Aidan heard her soft whimper as she said a quiet prayer. He couldn't understand what she was saying, but he held her tighter. He didn't want to let go.

He blinked, trying to erase images of the blank faces of Maya and Jane leaping in front of him. Their skin pale gray, their eyes darkened.

Their movements were so sudden, he'd fallen backward, trying to get away from their angry spirits which seemed to rush into his soul.

48

AIDAN WOKE AGAIN WITH the sun shining through the window.

He turned his head to see Cheyenne, lying on her side, facing him. Her breathing was soft, and she seemed to be studying him. For a few minutes, they looked into each other's eyes. Hers were so mesmerizing, the sea of blue bearing deep in him.

Aidan reached over to stroke her cheek.

"I'm sorry I scared you last night," he said, his voice hoarse. He cleared his throat and turned to stare at the ceiling.

Cheyenne leaned on her elbows.

"You scare me every day, Aidan. More and more."

"I scare myself sometimes," he said. "It's just—"

She cut him short by putting her finger over his lips. "Don't. No more excuses. No more of 'this is my job.' You need help. If you won't talk to me, then talk to someone. Anyone."

Aidan sat up in bed to rest against the headboard with a sigh. He reminded himself of what Shaun had suggested he do. He didn't want her worrying about him, but Shaun was right—her not knowing was worse.

"Do you really want to know?"

She raised her body and gave him her full attention with an affirming nod.

"Okay. If I tell you, you cannot repeat me."

"I won't."

Aidan looked away from her, drawing in several long, shaky breaths. He wanted to tell her, but at the same time, he didn't want to.

"Then I'll tell you. About ten years ago, around the time I first joined the FBI, my sister had a friend. She was beautiful, you know? Long blonde hair, a smile that would melt your heart. I was infatuated with her. She was also a wonderful person. Never met a stranger."

Aidan looked at Cheyenne, who watched him with worry and wonder clouding her eyes.

"Candace had a boyfriend, so I never had a chance with her. But then one night, she went to visit my sister because she and the boyfriend had a major argument. She wanted to talk to Mairead. You know how girls get. Candace wanted her opinion on how to proceed. Should she break up with him, take a few days to herself, or go back and try to talk to him? She had told Mairead she would go back to him. But when she left my sister's house, it was the last time anyone saw her until..."

Aidan closed his eyes, drawing in a long, deep breath. It'd been so long since he'd said the words out loud, and he wasn't sure he'd be able to, even to his wife.

"No!" Cheyenne whispered. Her voice was laced with tears.

"I got called to a crime scene." Aidan looked at Cheyenne and watched as her eyes brimmed with tears. His voice became so low, he wasn't even sure if he'd spoken them. "Candace was the third victim of The Carnations Killer. Everything was the same as the other girls prior. She wore a black dress, had a bouquet of white carnations. She was beaten so badly, I almost couldn't recognize her. The worst part was that I had to tell my sister."

"I'm so sorry," Cheyenne said. She put her head on Aidan's shoulder and wrapped her arms around him. "Mairead mentioned a friend named Candace, but never mentioned what happened to her. And I never thought to ask. I just assumed she was a childhood friend and they drifted apart."

Aidan nodded. "She was Mairead's best friend. They were like sisters. I swore to her I'd find the killer. Since then, when I see each woman this guy murdered, I see Candace. Each face I saw was hers. It followed me everywhere. It's why I left Boston. I just...couldn't. Mairead rarely mentions her because she doesn't want to upset me."

Aidan closed his eyes. He remembered the tearful admission Mairead had told him on the day of her wedding.

I wish Candace could have been here. I could use her support right now, Aidan. I'm so scared of this new life I'm going to have. She would have comforted me.

Aidan told Cheyenne about his dreams, about the reasons he couldn't sleep. He told her how vivid, how real they seemed.

"And for four years, he's left me notes. Ever since the Michigan murders, he started leaving me the notes. Just to make sure I was still searching for him. Still playing his game."

Cheyenne listened with intent, finally getting a glimpse of understanding of what he'd been living with over the years, particularly the last few months.

Aidan couldn't decide whether he was better having told her everything, or worse.

"I have to find him, Cheyenne." His voice went from soft to determined. He balled his hands into tight fists as he thought of all the women who were killed. "I have to."

Cheyenne remained silent for the longest time. Finally, she said, "Just don't lose yourself to him, okay? Please. I can't lose you to him."

Aidan kept silent as the seconds ticked by.

"It'll be okay," Aidan said. He wrapped his arms around her and hugged her tight. "As long as you're here with me, everything will be okay. You've become my rock."

He held her for a few minutes before pulling away and climbing out of the bed.

"I'm going to go on into work."

Before he could turn to walk away, Cheyenne grabbed his wrist. She pulled herself up for a kiss and told him she loved him.

After telling her he loved her too, he took a shower. With every drop of water running down his body, he tried to convince himself that telling Cheyenne everything was the right thing to do.

49

WHEN SHAUN FIRST SAW Aidan, he questioned his appearance. Aidan knew he had black circles around his bloodshot eyes. His hair was also half combed. Aidan admitted he couldn't sleep. He was too tired to care how he looked.

Aidan didn't want to bring up the dream—or vision—or waking nightmare, or whatever it was that caused him to fall in the kitchen. He didn't ever want to think of it again.

It fell quiet again over the next few weeks. Aidan hadn't received additional notes or phone calls from the killer. He remained in Augusta working with Shaun and Douglas on finding links to Jane and Maya or anything they may have missed.

They had two briefings, one of which Zane and Hansford attended.

Douglas suggested the killer might have gone underground. Aidan disagreed. Something in him convinced him the killer wasn't finished. After evading capture for ten years, whoever was kidnapping and killing these women believed he was invincible. He had a process and never failed to stick with it.

The Carnations Killer wasn't finished yet.

"Agent O'Reilly?" He looked away from the computer to see one of the new interns standing in front of his desk. She bit her lower lip. "Sorry to bother you. I was trying to get your attention."

Aidan shook his head to clear it.

"I'm sorry, I was lost in my thoughts. Allison, right?"

"Ashlee," she said, her voice soft.

"Right." Aidan offered her a smile. "What can I do for you?"

She reached her hand toward him, passing over an envelope. "Someone asked me to give this to you."

Aidan accepted the item and opened the letter.

It was handwritten, just like the other letters he'd received from the killer.

Aidan looked at the intern. "Who gave this to you?"

"He was wearing a hat and sunglasses," she said. "Maybe a little taller than you?"

"Okay, thank you," he said. "That'll be all." He waited until Ashlee turned and disappeared around the corner before reading the letter.

FBI Special Agent O'Reilly—

It was a close call last time, wasn't it? I assure you it won't happen again. How did you find me, anyway? That was very good investigative work if I do say so myself. Well, I wanted to drop by and say I'm still here. I didn't want you to think I'd forgotten your surprise. Keep an eye and ear out. It's going to be magnificent! But first things first...

Your friend,
The Carnations Killer

Rereading the letter, Aidan rose from his chair and made his way to Shaun's cubical.

He found him rummaging through his desk. Aidan dropped the letter in front of Shaun and leaned against the edge.

"He's still here."

Shaun stopped what he was doing and read the letter. After he finished, he muttered a curse.

"Have you told Tara yet?"

Aidan shook his head. "One of the interns brought it over a second ago. I came straight here."

"'First things first,'" Shaun recited. He frowned. "I don't have a very good feeling about this."

"Me either."

"Let's go talk to Tara."

Shaun and Aidan headed for Tara's office and met her as she stepped out with Zane.

"Agents O'Reilly and Henderson," he said.

Shaun and Aidan nodded their heads in acknowledgment. Aidan glanced at Tara, who folded her arms across her chest.

"The Carnations Killer contacted me again."

Zane raised his eyebrow. "He did? How?"

Aidan informed him how he received the letter, then showed it to him. His eyes widened with surprise.

"Curious," he said. He looked away from the letter. "You still have no clue what he means by 'surprise?'"

"No, sir," Aidan said.

"Well," Zane said as he handed back the letter. He lifted his reading glasses to the top of his head. "Looks like you're going to find out."

50

He watched as she stared at her tire by the gated dumpsters at the end of the cluster of townhouses. The daylight was quickly waning, and the bulbs from the street lamps were out. He made sure of that. He couldn't risk anyone happening by and him not notice.

It was time to bring his new target to her final home.

She shouted out a curse and kicked the front tire twice.

He'd disguised himself with a gray wig and beard. When he checked himself in a mirror before leaving home, a smile crept along his lips. His own mother wouldn't recognize him.

He made a beeline toward her, holding a grocery bag that held his supplies in one hand.

"Are you having car trouble, ma'am?"

She frowned but didn't look at him. "Yeah. As if my day couldn't get any worse. I only came to take the trash out so my husband wouldn't have to do it. When I came back, it was flat. Of course, it had to happen to me. When it rains, it pours, right?"

She punished the tire with another kick.

He smiled at her. "Well, I'm no expert or anything, but I don't think kicking the tire will put air in it. Do you have a donut?"

She looked at him dubiously.

"A spare," he said.

"Oh," she said with an embarrassed giggle. "I think so."

She popped the trunk and moved a few things aside, then lifted the board that hid the spare tire and jack.

"My husband insisted I keep it, but I'm sorry to say I haven't a clue how to change this thing."

"Don't worry about it," he said. "I'll take care of it."

He lifted the tire from the trunk and tossed it on the ground, then used the jack to remove the tire he'd stabbed the knife into a few minutes ago.

"Thank you for helping me," she said.

"Oh, it's not a problem at all. I'm John."

"Carol."

After he finished, he pushed to his feet and placed the old tire and the jack in the trunk.

"Tire looks as though it was cut," he said. "Maybe you ran over a thick piece of glass, or a nail or something. Anyway, that should get you to work. Then tomorrow, I'd suggest you go get a new tire."

"Thank you again so much," she said. "You're a lifesaver. What do I owe you?"

"Nothing," he said simply. "Well..." he looked around to be sure no one was nearby. "Except your life."

Before she had a chance to respond, he tased her and watched as she squealed before slumping to the ground.

He opened his bag, tied her arms and legs with the wire, and taped her mouth. After she was secured, he gathered her and tossed her in the still-open trunk.

"Where are your keys?" he asked. He felt around her waist, finding her keys in her pockets. "Ah-ha. Thanks, my girl."

He slammed the trunk shut, glancing around to make sure all was clear.

He climbed into the car. He turned the key in the ignition, bringing the vehicle to life.

He took the thirty-minute ride downtown to his new point of operation. It was an old warehouse that was used to store electronics. But the store recently went bankrupt, so he was lucky enough to snatch the building off the market. As he did when he rented a new location, he called the owner, told them a fake name, and offered double the asking price if they could keep it off the books.

Thankfully, the owner agreed. If they didn't, he would have been in search of another location until he found someone that agreed to his terms and money.

After he parked the new target's car by the old warehouse, he unloaded her. She was now awake, her eyes wide with fear. As he carried her inside, she thrashed in his arms, trying to get away.

Of course, even if she got him to drop her, she wouldn't get too far. Not with her hands and feet tied, anyway.

"Stop it," he said as he set her on the ground.

She tried to say something through the tape, but it was hard to make out the words.

He opened the door leading to another room and slipped on his clip-on sunglasses. Grabbing his target and throwing her over his shoulder, he expertly held her while flipping the light switch. It was bright, but his sunglasses helped protect his pupils. It was something new he was trying. He'd installed four hundred watt lights to see how she'd react. Would it cause her more pain? Would she just lay still, afraid to move?

Whatever her reaction, he was sure he'd get a thrill out of it.

He set her on the ground.

She squirmed, just like the others did, but he ignored her.

Her eyes were closed tight, trying to keep out the light. She began crying through the duct tape.

Rolling his eyes, he ripped the tape from her mouth.

The target screamed, a bloodcurdling sound.

Though it made his head hurt, he waited until she got it out of her system. After a few minutes passed, he slapped her hard.

"Shut up," he said, cursing her. "I've got a headache. Don't make me put the tape on you again."

"What do you want from me?" she said, her voice harsh from all the screaming she shouldn't have done.

He remained silent as he cut through the wires that bound her arms and legs. After all, it was no fun unless she was free to *try* to escape.

He removed his disguise—it had begun to itch—and set it on the table.

"Please," she said. "I'll do anything you want. Just let me go."

He let out a hesitant sigh and kneeled next to her so he could tap the cool metal of his knife against her cheek. "You're right. I really should just let you go, shouldn't I? This has gone on far enough. I mean, I've been killing women like you since..." He paused as though to think. "...I can't even say. Let's just say a long, long time." He sighed again and slid the knife underneath her chin. He smiled when she shivered. "I'll let you go. But you have to promise you won't tell anyone, okay?"

She shook her head with fervor. "I promise. I won't say anything. I won't—" he cut her words off with the taser.

Her shrill echoed through the room.

"You women are too gullible," he said with a light laugh.

Grabbing a new tire iron he'd found in a junkyard, he swung it toward her stomach.

The girl whose name was Carol gasped for breath upon its impact.

He hit her again, this time connecting with her temple. She cried out in pain, but he wasn't worried. He never worried. He wouldn't choose a point of operation unless he was sure he could be alone with his women.

He'd blared music in this little room so he could be sure nothing would be heard outside the warehouse walls.

He only barely heard it, and it was so much louder than the screams.

It was nine o'clock at night and they could be there for hours.

No one would hear her cries.

No one would come.

So he continued to hit her.

After his arms grew tired, he'd let her rest for a little while. He'd watch as she let the tears fall from her eyes. He'd watch as her body jerked in sharp pain.

He'd chat with her about life.

He'd ask her questions about her pain. How it made her feel.

She would only whimper, plead with him.

But he ignored her.

Then he picked up the tire iron and started all over again.

51

Carol Rider remained in a tight ball on the floor.

Her abductor stepped out a few minutes ago to answer a phone call. She'd been crying out, begging for someone to help her. But if they hadn't by now, she knew they wouldn't.

Every nerve ending cried out in sheer pain.

She remembered when she'd accidentally tripped over the cat and burnt her hand on a hot stove, trying to catch herself.

This was like being burned alive in comparison.

And the room was so bright. She hadn't had the chance to adjust her eyes yet.

Slowly, Carol straightened her legs. Her bones popped as she did so, and she moaned as scorching pain exploded through her body.

After she found she'd be able to move her legs, she worked on sitting up. Her head sent sharp knives through her eyes.

She wiped her tears still streaming from her face and slowly opened her eyes. It wasn't easy. The brightness added to her growing migraine, but if she was going to have a fighting chance, she'd need to do whatever it took.

Looking through her eyelashes, she saw her hands were covered in blood.

Her blood.

Carol scanned the room, trying to find something she could use to defend herself with once her captor returned.

There was a reel of fishing wire and duct tape on top of the table, a bloodied tire iron leaning against it. Thick globs of blood slowly dripped to the ground.

When she saw the weapon he'd obviously used on her, she sobbed. Carol forced herself to remain strong, but how could she?

She was in so much pain, and she was the captive of a man who seemed aroused by hitting her.

She only wanted to go home. Why wouldn't he just let her go home?

Stop it, Carol! Thinking it won't make it happen. You've got to fight him.

She sniffled, trying to inch her way to the table.

She worked on lifting the tire iron, but it seemed too heavy for her. She'd become too weak since she'd met the man who kidnapped her...how long ago had it been? She had no idea. It was as if she'd been there...wherever *there* was...for days.

She didn't normally pray, but she did now. If there was a higher power out there like her mother insisted, she begged for Him to listen.

Carol struggled to put her hand on the edge of the table and lifted her body. When she did, she shook as her legs fought to support her weight.

After she began believing she was hopeless, she noticed something in the middle of the wide table.

She reached for it.

There was a button on the side.

She pressed it, and it made a hissing noise.

A taser.

She remembered he'd used it on her twice. Once when he'd first abducted her and again when he told her he'd free her.

Well.

Maybe now she could turn the table on him.

The more she flexed her muscles, the easier it became to move. She ran her hands along the wall, still blinded by the bright light until she found the knob on the door. She flattened herself against the wall, waiting for the abductor to return.

As her eyes slowly adjusted to the bright light, she tried to remember what he looked like so she could tell the police if she managed to escape.

No, not *if*. *When*.

She knew he had gray hair and a beard. But was it a disguise?

When she was brought into this room, she thought he had removed something from his face, but couldn't be sure. The light hurt her eyes and she still hadn't been able to adjust.

When she heard the click of the knob turning, she gripped the taser.

Her heart pulsed in her ears.

It's okay, Carol. You can do it. You're strong.

"I am terribly sorry about that," he said as he opened the door. "That was my—"

She jammed the taser somewhere on his body. She wasn't sure where and she didn't care.

His piercing scream of surprise rang into her already excruciating headache, but the most important sound was the soft thud of his body hitting the floor.

Carol dropped the taser when he fell and flew over his body, leaving the light to enter the darkness. She didn't know where she was going, but she knew she had to work fast.

After she crashed into the wall, Carol ran her hands along the side, moving frantically, in search of a door knob.

"Hey!" she heard him call from behind.

She saw a hazy aura from a flashlight behind her.

She finally found the knob.

"Get back here!"

She swung open the door.

"No!"

Forcing herself to be blind to the pain in her body, Carol flew from the building, running as fast as her legs would carry her.

He stood outside the warehouse and watched as she ran off into the distance. The tingling sensation from the taser still lingered in his nerves.

Kicking the door hard, he released an angry curse. Now he'd have to gather his things and find another location.

Again.

He wasn't too worried about her fingering him. The light in the little room was bright enough for her to not see his face, and he could tell by the way she was running into signs that she was still having trouble seeing in front of her.

Still, he couldn't take the chance she remembered where she was being held.

He hurried inside, grabbed everything he'd brought, and threw it in the trunk of her car.

He knew he'd need to ditch it soon, but first, he wanted to see if he could find the girl before she ran her mouth about him and his point of operation.

52

Aidan woke to his phone vibrating on the bedside table. Looking at it, he saw it was Shaun calling. It was almost midnight.

He answered as Cheyenne stirred in the bed next to him.

"This better be good," he said into the phone.

"We've got a live one," Shaun said excitedly.

Aidan frowned into the phone, attempting to figure out what he'd heard. "What?"

Shaun informed him a possible Carnations Killer victim had escaped, but they didn't know other specifics at this time.

The room started spinning after Aidan sprung upright in his bed.

"She's alive?" he repeated, unable to believe the news.

Shaun told him she was taken to the Georgia Regents Medical Center. After scribbling on a pad where to go in the hospital, Aidan said he was on the way.

Throwing on clothes in the dark, he began buttoning his pants as he ran down the stairs.

There was no telling if he'd be back before Cheyenne woke to find he had left, so Aidan wrote a quick note telling her he was called out, and he would touch base with her later.

Grabbing his keys from the counter, then the floor after dropping them, Aidan hurled himself into the car, waiting impatiently for the garage door to open, then left the house.

Careful not to go too far over the speed limit, he went downtown to the hospital and parked in the parking deck.

Shaun had arrived at the same time, and they found the victim together. Aidan introduced himself and Shaun to the Richmond County police lieutenant and learned his name was Dirk Powell.

The victim lay on the bed wearing a hospital gown. Her eyes were covered with white patches and her body held deep gashes and bruises. Aidan made notice of the taser marks on the side of her neck.

They were told that along with broken ribs and bones, her corneas were damaged. However, they were confident she'd heal with little to no loss of her eyesight. The doctors kept her hooked up with tubes, and the room was filled with the rhythmic beeping of machines.

"Has she said anything?" Shaun asked Lieutenant Powell.

The bald older man shook his head. He crossed his arms over his chest, puffed his stomach out, and put a scowl on his lips.

The look on his face as he glanced between Shawn and Aidan said that he didn't like federal agents at all.

Aidan walked to the side of the bed and leaned in.

"She won't answer."

Aidan eyed the lieutenant and said, "Maybe not, but I'm going to try."

He looked at the victim.

"Ma'am." Aidan waited. "I'm Special Agent Aidan O'Reilly. Can you hear me?"

A few minutes crawled by and he suspected she was unconscious—either from the pain or the drugs the doctors had given her. But soon, her head moved slightly, and she released a weak moan. Her hands jerked on the bed.

From the corner of Aidan's eye, he noticed Lieutenant Powell taking a step forward. Aidan held out his hand, a silent gesture for him to stop.

"Ma'am?" he repeated in a low voice. "Can you hear me?"

She parted her mouth to speak, but her words were almost inaudible. He leaned in closer.

Getting nothing valid from her, he decided the medicine the doctors gave her put her into a deep sleep.

The doctor came in to inform them they needed to leave and allow his patient to rest. Aidan handed him his card and requested that he call as soon as she was able to answer questions.

In the hallway, Aidan told Lieutenant Powell that under no circumstances should the public know the victim was still alive. He still wasn't sure of the circumstances, so Aidan didn't want to risk that the killer would come to the hospital and finish her off.

After much prodding and threatening to speak with the lieutenant's superior, he finally agreed to say nothing until the Bureau authorized him.

After he stalked away, Shaun asked Aidan what the girl had said.

"I couldn't make it out."

"How did she manage to escape?"

Without answering, Aidan looked over at the closed door, where their victim rested.

"We need to have men stationed outside this door," he said. "I don't want her to be alone for even a second. Maybe he let her escape for reasons we don't know, maybe she was lucky. But until we find him, that woman's life's in danger."

"I'll call it in," Shaun said, grabbing his phone from its holder clipped on the side of his jeans.

After the call was made, they made their way to the waiting room, where the witnesses who brought Carol to the emergency room sat. Although the police already questioned them, Aidan wanted to be certain nothing was overlooked.

The woman, possibly in her early forties, sat in the corner of the room, her arms wrapped around a little girl. Aidan guessed her to be close to ten. She blinked repeatedly like she was trying to stay awake.

Aidan introduced himself and asked, "Can you tell us what happened?"

The woman—Sheila Grayson—told them she and her daughter were passing through town. The girl, Kayla, saw someone running wildly through the streets, screaming "somebody help." She'd brought it to her mother's attention. The woman tripped but didn't get up. They saw she was sobbing and didn't seem to be able to move. Sheila told her daughter to stay in the car as she went to see what was going on.

The only thing the woman would tell her was that a man was trying to kill her.

She begged Sheila to help her, so she assisted her to the car and rushed her to the hospital. By the time they'd arrived, the woman was hardly breathing.

After Aidan finished writing his notes, he thanked Sheila, then kneeled to be at eye level with Kayla. Putting a hand on her shoulder, he offered her a smile.

"You're a hero, Kayla. You saved someone's life tonight."

She smiled sleepily, and Aidan rose to his feet. He told Sheila she and her daughter were free to leave and if they were needed for anything else, they'd contact her.

"I'm going to stay here for a while," he told Shaun as the witnesses left the waiting room. "I have all the information I need with me, and I want to be here when she wakes up."

Shaun said he wanted to wait around as well, and when the guards Shaun had requested arrived, they informed them they'd be in the waiting room if the victim awoke.

53

A FEW HOURS LATER, Aidan woke to the neck pain he'd earned from sleeping in the uncomfortable waiting room chairs. Shaun was next to him, sipping a cup of coffee. Aidan realized his head was resting on his shoulder.

"Good morning, sleeping beauty," Shaun said.

Aidan sat up and flexed his neck and arms, bones popping as he did.

"You make an awful pillow," he said. "Any news on our live one?"

Shaun shook his head.

Aidan glanced at his phone to see that Cheyenne had called five different times.

Great.

He was in trouble now.

As Aidan went to pour himself a cup of coffee, he called her back.

When she answered, she began spewing angry words at him, demanding to know why didn't he come home, and did he know how worried she was when she woke in the middle of the night to find only a note saying he'd touch base with her later.

Once he was able to get a word in edgewise, Aidan apologized for his haste and explained the reason he ran out.

She stuttered as though she wanted to remain angry, but ended by saying, "Well, as long as you're safe."

A doctor entered the waiting room, and Aidan recognized him from the night before, so he told Cheyenne he was sorry for his disappearing act, and he'd talk to her later.

The doctor acknowledged them and informed them that the victim's name was Carol Rider, and she was now alert. He'd allow them to question her but warned them not to stay with her for long.

Shaun thanked him and Aidan followed him into the room where a nurse was checking Carol's vitals. Seeing the agents, she offered a friendly smile and reminded them of the doctor's orders.

"She's got to rest. She has a long road of recovery ahead of her."

"We understand," Aidan said.

Again, she smiled and left the room.

Aidan stepped over to Carol's bedside. "I'm Agent O'Reilly, and my partner is Agent Henderson."

"How are you feeling, Mrs. Rider?" Shaun asked.

She coughed. She put her fingers over the eye patches and said, "Like I've been through Hell and back."

"You're very brave," Aidan said. "And very lucky."

Carol shook her head. "I don't feel very lucky." Her voice was scratchy.

"Do you remember anything?" Aidan knew it was best not to press her. Memory can be very fragile, especially during a traumatic experience.

"I had a flat tire," she said. "A man came to help. He said his name was..." She hesitated, then said, "John."

"Do you remember if you've seen him before?" Shaun asked.

"I don't know," Carol said. "Maybe."

Aidan wrote the name in his pad but knew the killer most likely made it up. He asked Carol what he looked like, and she said she wasn't sure.

"My mind's fuzzy. I can't remember him much. I think his hair and beard were gray, but I'm not positive." She let out a series of coughs and again put her hand over her eye patches. Aidan assumed it made her feel uneasy.

She went on to say he used a taser on her and she passed out from the pain.

"It felt like I was being electrocuted."

"Then what happened?"

"I woke up and could tell I was moving. But it was dark where I was. Then we stopped moving and a second later, I saw him standing over me. I couldn't move or talk. He'd taped my mouth, and my hands and feet were tied. He picked me up and carried me."

"Do you know where you were?"

She whimpered slightly, and a single tear escaped from underneath her eye patch. "I don't know. He opened a door. He carried me through a dark room. Then he opened another door and turned on the lights. It was so bright. I couldn't see. It was like I was looking in the sun."

That'd explain the extensive damage to her eyes.

She paused as she tried to think, but was interrupted when one of the men stationed outside the door peeked his head in.

"I'm sorry to interrupt, sir, but there's a man outside. He says he's her husband? A Staff Sergeant Rider."

"Frankie? Frankie, where is he?" Carol said, her words tearful.

"Let him in," Aidan said.

A second later, a man wearing an army uniform pushed his way into the room.

"Baby," he said. "What did he do to you, baby?" Frankie let out a curse as he sat on the edge of the bed and leaned down to wrap his wife in a hug. "I was so worried when you weren't home. Are you okay?"

Through her tears and scratchy voice, Carol told him she was.

Aidan introduced himself and promised they would do their best to find the man who hurt his wife, and that they only had a few more questions.

He refocused his attention on Carol.

"What happened after he took you to the bright room?"

"He cut me loose. He said he was going to let me go." She whimpered again, her words catching in her throat. "But he tased me, then hit me. He hit me so much, I just wanted him to stop. I begged him."

"How did you escape?" Shaun asked.

She hesitated. Her husband lifted her hand to his lips and kissed her.

"He had a phone call," she said. "I heard him step out of the room. I was hurting so much. But I found his taser. I don't know how. And when he came back, I used it on him, and then took off. I heard him come after me, but I kept going."

Well.

That's a fighter.

"You have no idea where he took you?" Aidan said.

Carol shook her head. "Wait."

Aidan and Shaun watched her closely as she reflected on what Aidan imagined to be the worst few hours of her life.

"I saw a sign...I saw...Broad Street. I came out of a large building. The smell inside was like sawdust. Then I saw colorful windows." Her head wavered around the room as though she wasn't sure where to look. "That's all I can remember."

"Colorful?" Shaun echoed. "Like stained? Maybe a church?"

"Maybe," Carol said. "I'm sorry, everything's jumbled. All I kept thinking was 'I've got to get away.'"

Shaun looked at Aidan. "The St. Mary's Cathedral is on Broad Street. There's an old warehouse across the street from it."

"That's good," Aidan told Carol. He put a hand on her shoulder. "You did real good."

"When I noticed she was missing," her husband said. He seemed to be in a daze. "I called around, trying to find her. I was told a serial killer had been killing women around town. A buddy of mine said all the victims were blonde." He glanced from Shaun to Aidan. "It was him, wasn't it?"

Aidan looked into his eyes and saw the worry. He empathized with him and nodded, informing the staff sergeant they were posting a few men outside the room for Carol's protection. He assured him that because of his wife, they could be closer to finding him.

The doctor would take a look at her eyes later, and if he could, he'd remove the patches. Then Carol may be able to speak to a forensic artist. Even if he had worn a disguise, it would give them something to work with. Maybe he wore the same disguise at work. Maybe someone had seen him hanging around.

54

So far, there hadn't been any news report regarding the abduction of the girl that had gotten away.

But that didn't mean he was in the clear.

The police were tricky.

They seemed to enjoy hiding details to draw them out.

Over the last few days, he'd been watching as Jordan Blake reported Good Samaritan stories, now that he was back at WJFX. It made him laugh that a talent like Jordan's was being used in such a feeble way.

He'd been watching Jordan, and he could tell the reporter was aching for actual news.

And the people of Augusta didn't know that he, the renowned Carnations Killer, remained in town. They went about their business as carefree as they did before he entered the picture.

That needed to change.

"Daddy." Jamie interrupted his thoughts. "What are you sitting all alone in the dark for?"

He looked at his daughter, who peeked into the room. She wasn't supposed to enter his office, ever. But he didn't yell at her. Instead, he smiled at his daughter and set her on his lap.

She put her right arm around his neck.

"Well," he said with a sigh, "Daddy's just trying to work out an issue he's been having."

"Like what?" Her eyes twinkled as only a child of eight would.

"Some bad men are trying to keep a secret. Something everybody needs to know."

Jamie frowned. "The bad men?"

He nodded slowly. "The police and the FBI." He positioned her on his lap so he could see her face better, using the glow of the hall light. "You see, people do things in this world. Things some people believe are wrong. It's the police's job to tell us about those things."

"But they don't?"

"No," he said. "They don't. They keep it a secret. And secrets are a killer. So, I'm trying to figure out how I am going to stop them."

"Oh," she said.

He knew she didn't understand.

But she would.

As she got older, she would understand it all. He'd make sure.

He kissed her cheek and told her to go find Mommy and see what she was up to. Before she jumped off his lap, he asked her to not tell her mother about what they discussed.

"We don't want her to worry, right?" he asked.

Jamie dutifully shook her head.

"That's my girl."

As his daughter skipped out of the room, closing the door behind her, he turned on the desk lamp, then removed a new burner phone from the drawer to send Jordan Blake a quick text.

It wasn't right the public didn't know about the girl that had gotten away.

So he decided to help the good reporter out.

In the process, he might even manage to help himself. It might help him find the woman. Then he could finish what he started.

In the meantime, he called around for a new point of operation.

After an hour, he'd finally found the perfect place. The owners were subletting while on vacation in Europe, so they didn't need to meet with him or anything. He promised to wire the money to their account this afternoon.

He'd requested for someone to leave the key under a rock for him.

The house was in the heart of the West Lake subdivision and had a basement.

Talk about hiding in plain sight.

55

The warehouse on Broad Street was formerly an electronics store. It had gone out of business six months before and sat empty until two months ago—shortly after the killer went off the grid.

According to the lessors, they needed to rent it out, so when a man contacted them, offering double the asking price to remain off the books, they jumped at it.

The man in question went by the name Harlan Groves. After running a system check, they found the real Harlan Groves had died nine years ago.

As Aidan prepared to enter the building, he found his heart was lodged in his throat. His hands sweat even more than was normal for a raid. He worked on steadying his breathing.

"You okay?" Shaun asked as he checked his weapon.

Aidan did the same, although he'd done so five minutes ago. He nodded, unsure he'd be able to speak. His mind replayed the last encounter with the killer and his mind continued replaying the dreams.

Aidan had lived with this investigation for so long, he'd begun to wonder if he'd ever escape the nightmares.

He felt strong hands grip his left shoulder.

"I'm right behind you," Shaun said.

"I'm fine," Aidan said. "Okay?"

"Okay," Shaun echoed.

Aidan glanced at him and saw in his eyes that Shaun knew he wasn't but chose not to press the issue.

Aidan chambered his weapon. "Let's do this."

Shaun motioned for a few agents to slink around the back.

It had a chained lock, so it made sense no one was inside, but still, they were prepared for anything. After all, they thought Thomas Blake's house was empty.

Using the battering ram, the agents rushed the door, splintering it open. Daylight peered through, showing just enough of the space.

There was nothing but old boxes and dusty shelves. Some shelves still hung in place, others leaned against the walls. The agents used flashlights to scan the room until they spotted another door.

The blood pulsed in Aidan's ear as he and Shaun stood at either side.

Once they crashed through the door, they entered a smaller room.

It was empty.

"Here's a light switch," Shaun said.

Carol had said when her abductor turned on the lights, it had blinded her eyes. Aidan prepared himself for what may happen when Shaun switched it.

The light poured over the room. Aidan shielded his eyes.

Shaun flicked it off with a curse. White and black circles swam in front of Aidan's eyes. He blinked, trying to adjust to the sudden change in his vision.

"It's a wonder he didn't completely blind her," Aidan said.

"Nothing's here," Shaun said.

"Agent O'Reilly. Over here."

Aidan moved toward the agent that had called for his attention. He pointed to the table, his flashlight glaring off the surface.

Aidan looked at what the agent wanted to show him.

"Not nothing," Aidan said.

When Shaun appeared by Aidan's side, he cursed again.

Carved in the table was a message.

FBI Special Agent O'Reilly—
Sorry, we missed each other. But don't worry, I'll catch you soon.
Your friend,
The Carnations Killer

56

When Jordan finished reporting his story about an event the Humane Society would be running next month, he tossed his microphone onto the table and scowled at Kent.

"I'm sick of running these stupid stories," he said. "I can't believe my uncle's punishing me like this."

Kent began breaking down his camera so he could place the pieces in the case. "I don't see it as punishing. Not much seems to be newsworthy around here these days."

"When did The Carnations Killer stop being newsworthy?" Jordan snapped.

Kent raised his eyebrow. "You know something about him I don't? Please share."

The reporter frowned. "I want cutting-edge stories. Not...cutesy."

"Well," Kent said as he snapped his case shut, "just be thankful your uncle is letting you report anything."

"I'm not a Good Samaritan reporter," Jordan said.

"Haven't we gone over this?" Kent asked. "You're worse than a woman. You change your mind from it's okay to lay low to wanting to be on the cutting edge. Let's go over this again—you went on the air before you were authorize—"

"The FBI was hiding that we had a serial killer roaming around. The people had a right to know."

"And you lied to the feds," Kent said.

"How do you think it'd look if I told them I knew Maya Gibson?"

"And you baited Agent O'Reilly," Kent said. He heaved his camera case from the table and began carting it toward the van.

"He baited me first," Jordan said, trailing after him.

"He was doing his job," Kent said.

Jordan frowned. "And I was doing mine. I'm a reporter. I report the news as I see fit. I'm sorry if no one likes it." He jabbed his index finger at Kent's shoulder. "You went along with me, by the way."

"Because you point and I shoot. I need a job and don't want you having me fired over my unwillingness to help you on your way to glorified fame."

Jordan rolled his eyes.

"You have nothing to prove," Kent said.

"I'm not trying to *prove* anything," Jordan spat as he fished his cell phone from the passenger's seat.

"Hello?" Kent said, waving his hand in the air. "All you've been trying to do is prove..."

Jordan tuned the cameraman out as he stared with interest at his phone. He'd received another text message.

It's time for you to report real news again. Get in front of the camera and tell them The Carnations Killer kidnapped a woman. She was a lucky one. She'd managed to escape. But tell them it's not going to stop me from going after another.

"...Are you even listening to me?"

Kent shook Jordan's shoulder.

"You okay, man? You look like you've seen a ghost."

"Look." Jordan showed Kent the message. "Have you heard anything about another woman being kidnapped?"

Frowning, Kent said he hadn't. "But he says she got away, right? So that's good."

"But he's going to go after someone else."

"I think you should tell the FBI and be done with it," Kent said.

Jordan considered his options. If he went on the air, he could inform the people The Carnations Killer was still lurking around the city. In the process, it may boost his career as a reporter, showing the people that he wanted nothing more but to share the truth. But it'd make the FBI and his uncle angry that he went with it. He'd already been threatened once by O'Reilly that he'd be detained if he went over the agent's head again.

On the other hand, if he told the FBI about the text, they'd force him to keep quiet. And the public had the right to know a serial killer was still in town.

Right?

He looked at Kent, sitting on the hood of the news van.

"Get your camera."

57

AIDAN OPTED TO GO home for a late lunch to attempt to rest. It had been a long day since he'd been at the hospital waiting on Carol Rider to be aware enough to answer questions. Sleeping in the uncomfortable chairs in the waiting room didn't provide restful sleep.

Then they'd raided the warehouse with the blood in his body thumping as though his veins were going to burst. After documenting what they could of the old building, including the note the killer left him, they had returned to the office to hold another quick briefing.

With a yawn, Aidan stepped inside the quiet house around noon. He followed the muted sounds of the television into the living room.

Cheyenne was snoring on the couch, her workout clothes clinging to her sweaty skin. Aidan figured she must have been working through her aggression, most likely still upset with him for disappearing the night before and not returning her frantic calls immediately.

He grabbed the quilt from the back of the sofa and covered her before returning to the kitchen for a Coke. What he really wanted was a beer, but since he was still on duty, Aidan decided to bypass it.

Maybe later tonight.

Aidan went upstairs to lie down, but he tossed and turned until he finally turned to his back and stared at the ceiling.

Since sleep didn't seem to be an option, he rose, deciding to call his sister. With all that had been going on, he hadn't checked in to see how married life was faring.

Aidan took his Coke and returned downstairs to sit outside on the deck.

It was nearing a hundred degrees and seemed hotter due to the humidity. The sky was a crisp blue with a few thick clouds. Aidan felt a few brief wisps of cool air against his skin, but it didn't hang around long enough to cool him down.

It wasn't perfect. Not for him, anyway. Memories haunted him, and he couldn't seem to shake them free. Even if they did catch The Carnations Killer, the memories were now a part of him. He'd become so used to waking in a sweat, he thought he would become nothing without it.

As Aidan listened to the dial tone on the line, he considered what life would be like if he were someone else. What life would be like if he wasn't an agent and he didn't deal with the dangers slinking around every corner?

"Aidan!"

He heard his sister's chirpy voice, and as usual, it brought a smile to his face. The lilt of Irish brought a sense of home to him. And Mairead had dealt with so much in her life—it was good to hear happy.

"Hey, beautiful," Aidan said. "How are you?"

"Never better. We got back in town from our honeymoon last month," Mairead said. "I really wished we didn't have to leave."

She began to talk about the things she saw while on the African Safari. Aidan hung onto every detail, letting her story take him away to the jungle seeing zoo animals in the wild.

"I'm glad you had a great time, Mairead," he said.

"How are you guys?"

A pause filled the air. Aidan wondered if she heard about the latest murders he'd been investigating and decided she likely hadn't since she and her new husband spent the past month in another country.

"We're good," Aidan said.

"I miss you," she said. "I wish you'd move back home."

"Two weeks was long enough for me, Mairead," Aidan said with a pause. "You know, you could move here."

He could almost see his sister's frown on the other end of the line.

"This is home," Mairead said quietly.

Aidan let the silence take over the lines again.

"He's back," he said, finally. "I wasn't sure if you've heard."

She didn't respond, but he heard the sniffling over the line.

"I'm going to get him. I promise."

"Come back home, Aidan," Mairead said. "Bring Cheyenne. I'd love to get to know her better. We could be a family again."

"I can't," Aidan said. "I came back only for you and your wedding. But I can't go back."

"Can't you see I need you here? I don't want you to keep searching for him!" Mairead's voice echoed through the phone, and Aidan could tell she'd begun crying. "Please. Candace was my closest friend. But it's not going to change anything. It's not going to bring her back."

Tears burned in Aidan's eyes and he blinked them away.

"He's got to be stopped. Don't you get it?" Aidan said with a hiss. "I have to find him! I promised I wouldn't rest until I did."

His body burned with rage, and he gripped his phone tight.

"I love you, Aidan, I do," Mairead said. "But I can't watch as you destroy yourself."

Why did everyone have to keep saying that?

Aidan knew frustration was on the verge of exploding, but he forced it down.

"Mairead—"

She didn't hear because she was already gone. Aidan set the phone on the table and paced the deck, trying to calm his nerves, but it wouldn't happen.

The next thing he knew, he tossed the table on its side and kicked the chairs around the deck. Laura's potted plants shattered, fragments of clay slinging across the ground.

Aidan fell to his knees and grasped the back of his head with an agitated groan. He cursed, then released another one.

"What in the world is happening out here?"

Aidan rested against the overturned table, unable to focus on Cheyenne's voice. He shook his head and rubbed the corners of his eyes. All he could remember was the pain he saw in his sister's eyes at losing her best friend to a sadistic killer. No matter how hard he tried—and he did try—he couldn't erase his sister's hurt. He longed to find relief from the memory, but Aidan knew only the capture of The Carnations Killer would make it happen.

Aidan glanced around the deck and his eyes rested on Laura's shattered pots.

He cursed softly and apologized, promising Cheyenne he'd buy her sister new plants.

"Aidan, I'm not worried about the flowers." He looked at her. Cheyenne had her hands on her hips, eyes narrowed out of concern, rather than anger. "What happened?"

"I'm fine," he said. Aidan pulled himself to his feet and started cleaning the mess he made, beginning with the glass table. Thankfully it hadn't broken. "I talked to Mairead and we argued. That's all."

"Are you sure that's all?"

Aidan rested his palms on the table and pulled in a few heavy breaths before he turned to envelop her in his arms.

She smelled of sunflower and sweat.

"I'm fine," he whispered in her hair. "I can handle it. I'm sorry I worried you."

"Do you want me to make you lunch?"

Aidan pulled away from her. "No, I'm not hungry. I'm going to finish cleaning up this mess, then head back to the office."

"I'll get it, honey," Cheyenne said, her voice lowering an octave. "Okay? Do what you need to do to end this."

Aidan regarded her, seeing the change in her eyes.

She was no longer worried or concerned.

It wasn't fear he saw in her anymore.

It was faith.

Before returning to the office, Aidan took a cool shower to refresh his mind. It seemed to make everything go away, even if only for a few minutes.

After Aidan looked around to see the mess he'd created only moments before, he'd begun to realize the murders had already begun to destroy his psyche. He'd become obsessed with a ghost and he was losing a sense of who he was.

Aidan owed it to himself to make a change. He knew if he didn't, if he continued to allow himself to slip into a world filled with demons and pain, everything would have been for nothing, and he would lose everything and everyone he loved.

Aidan wouldn't exist any longer.

That's what the killer was preying on.

Now Aidan knew.

He had friends over the years who'd committed suicide or changed careers because of the things they'd seen. Or because of the things they'd had to do to bring justice.

Aidan contemplated a time when a friend of his, an agent with many commendations in his twenty years of service, killed a suspect in cold blood because of the man's involvement in child pornography. Once, when Aidan visited him in prison, he told him that killing the suspect was the one good thing he'd done in his life.

He hadn't thought about his family. He hadn't thought about his son and daughter. Or maybe he had. Maybe killing the man who made a career out of exploiting children was a way of protecting his own.

Aidan had wondered over the years if he could ever go that far. Could he take a life without blinking an eye because he'd murdered more than fifty people including his sister's closest friend?

Or would he start contemplating suicide because he couldn't handle the suffering in the world anymore?

He was raised to believe suicide was a sin. After all, murder was a sin, so it made sense that suicide fell under the same category.

The Carnations Killer knew how to unravel him. He was breaking him.

Aidan imagined him laughing. Laughing at the dedicated agent who had a good life who was trying to figure out how far he'd go to get the murders out of his mind.

Aidan turned off the shower, opened the curtains, and grabbed his towel. Drying off, he stepped out of the tub and caught his reflection in the mirror.

It reminded him of one of the dreams he'd recently had. The one where the killer got in the car and looked into the mirror.

And it had been Aidan instead.

He saw his reflection but didn't recognize himself.

Was this what everyone was seeing lately? A stranger residing in the body of their friend? Their colleague?

Had he really arrived at his melting point? He closed his eyes then reopened them to gaze back into the mirror. He drew in a deep breath, held it, then slowly pushed it out.

"You won't break me," Aidan said through his teeth. "You won't."

"Aidan?" Cheyenne knocked on the door. "I made a quick lunch for you to take with you. I want you to eat."

Aidan opened the door and thanked her, then rummaged in the closet for fresh clothes. After he dressed, he kissed her, allowing his lips to linger. Then he told her he loved her and grabbed the sandwich she'd made.

On his way out, Aidan called Shaun to find out where he was. He told him he'd gone to the office, so Aidan headed his way.

It was then that Shaun informed him their favorite reporter had once again stood in front of the camera and ran his mouth to announce they had a potential victim escape from The Carnations Killer.

Aidan slammed his palm against the steering wheel and let out a round of curses.

He had gone way too far now.

58

SHAUN HAD INSTRUCTED AGENTS to arrest Jordan and take him into the interview room. Aidan stood with him and Tara, watching Jordan through the two-way glass.

The reporter sat back in his chair, drumming his fingers against the edge of the table. He appeared relaxed despite being brought in for questioning again.

"What do you want to do with him?" Shaun asked.

"Lock him up and throw away the key," Aidan said. He'd hoped he'd seen the last of him, but obviously not.

"Hmm," Shaun said, "I think I better go in by myself."

Though Shaun didn't look at him, Aidan nodded, and Shaun opened the door to enter the interview room.

"Mr. Blake," he said as he shut the door.

The reporter smirked and snapped a finger at Shaun. "Henderson, right?"

"Well, there doesn't seem to be a need to reintroduce ourselves," Shaun said dryly as he sat in the gray folding chair. "So, why don't we skip the pleasantries and get right to business."

Jordan scoffed. "So professional. Where's your partner? The one that looks like an extra from *The Walking Dead* half the time."

Aidan scowled. "I don't look like that." Although he said it mostly to himself, he heard a soft chuckle from Tara.

"We're not here to discuss Agent O'Reilly," Shaun said with an edge to his words. "Now, for the purpose of this interview, you're going to be recorded. Got any problem with that?"

Jordan let his shoulders rise and fall carelessly.

Shaun reached over and pressed the button on the recorder.

"This is Special Agent Shaun Henderson on July fourth two thousand and seventeen. The subject of interest is Jordan Blake." He looked Jordan. "What is your age and occupation?"

"I am thirty-five and a reporter for WJFX News."

"Mr. Blake, you recently received a text from the man who the media refers to as The Carnations Killer. When did it come through?"

"About two hours ago," Jordan said. "I'd finished filming a fluff segment and was talking to my cameraman about wanting real news. It was like he read my mind."

"I see," Shaun said. "And it was erased shortly after you received the text?"

Jordan nodded.

"Please say all answers out loud."

"Yes," Jordan said tautly.

"Can anyone confirm you received the text message?"

"My cameraman. Kent Ory."

"And what did the message say?"

Jordan sighed. "Something about me needing to report the real news again," he scoffed. "At least someone recognizes my talent."

"What else did he say?"

Jordan rolled his eyes. "He told me his most recent victim had escaped, but it won't stop him from finding someone else."

"And you have no proof of this text?"

"Nope."

"Okay. And you've received messages from the suspect before, is that correct?"

"What, am I on trial now?"

"Answer the question, please."

Jordan frowned. "Yes. A few months ago, I received a birthday card and then a text. He said he wanted me to let the public know he'd returned."

"That message also disappeared, correct?"

"Yes."

Jordan seemed to be getting bored now.

"Have you ever met a man named Ron Heady?"

"I haven't," Jordan said. He blew out a breath and began drumming his fingers on the table.

Aidan turned to Tara. "Has Shaun *ever* had the desire to punch someone who was annoying?"

"Not that I know of," she said as Shaun spoke again.

"He rented the house owned by your uncle, Thomas Blake," Shaun said.

"So?" Jordan asked. "My uncle doesn't tell me who he rents his house to. I mean, I heard The Carnations Killer used his house to kill those women, but I don't know anything else. I had nothing to do with it."

"Well," Aidan said to Tara, still thinking of the answer she'd given him, "that's an annoying quality."

Aidan watched as Shaun rose and paced the room. He stood in front of the two-way glass. Aidan could see him but knew Shaun could only see his own reflection. To Aidan, he was looking right above his head.

"See, here's the thing I don't get, Jordan," Shaun said. He turned on his heels to face the reporter. "You were on the scene at Maya Gibson's murder, then you claimed to have received a text from the suspect saying he'd returned."

Shaun paced around the table so he'd be at Jordan's back. "You were also at Jane Ridgeway's crime scene while we were processing it, and it turns out the killer used your uncle's home as his home base. Now you know his last victim escaped. Something no one else knows."

He paused and leaned over to speak in the reporter's ear.

"Get it yet, Blake? We don't need too much to try and convict you." He straightened and stepped over to his chair across from Jordan and lowered himself to the seat. Shaun put one leg over the other knee, folding his hands on the table. "We don't even need to inform the jury that you lied about knowing the victim and that you reported on other murders committed by the suspect. We already have enough to charge you. More than likely enough to convict you."

Shaun opened the manila folder that rested on the table and spread the crime scene photos.

Aidan could tell Jordan was trying to remain cool.

The reporter closed his eyes and looked away.

Shaun passed him several sheets of paper.

"These are autopsy reports. Hillary Barnett was his second victim. When she was found, her kneecaps were busted, her ribs broken. Valerie Davis's injuries were so bad that she'd died before he was through with her. Tris—"

"Stop. Please."

Jordan's face turned green. He turned his head away from the photos.

"Look, Jordan. I don't think you could hurt a fly, much less these women. Okay? Don't you want to help give their families justice? Help me help you," Shaun said, keeping his tone compassionate.

This had always been Aidan's favorite part in breaking a suspect.

"How?" Jordan said after a long pause. His voice was low and hoarse.

"I want you to get on the air."

Aidan watched Jordan carefully. After hesitating, he slowly turned his head to gape at Shaun.

"You want me to what?"

"I want you to get on the air, and I want you to tell the public The Carnations Killer's latest victim, Carol Rider is alive, and although she can't do much talking, we expect her to make a full recovery. And say she will remain at Georgia Regents Medical Center until the end of next week."

Narrowing his eyes curiously, Jordan said, "Why would you want me to do that? He would only go after her and finish killing her."

"Exactly!" Shaun slapped a large hand on the table with enthusiasm.

Jordan's eyes grew round. "You want to try and draw him out."

"See? You aren't as dumb as you act. So? What do you say?"

"And you won't arrest me?"

"If you help us, then we'll forget everything you lied about. You can go your way, we'll go ours."

Jordan took the chance to look at the photos of the women on the table. He frowned and asked, "You'll protect Carol, right?"

"Nothing will happen to her."

Another pause.

"Okay," he said. "I'll do it."

59

THEY TOLD JORDAN TO go on the air at six o'clock that night. Before he left the office, Shaun and Aidan told him what they wanted him to say to the camera.

Aidan sent up a prayer that the reporter wouldn't manage to screw up. It was their one good chance to catch the killer. Shaun had thought of it, and at first, Aidan dismissed the idea. He wasn't sure he wanted to chance Carol's life. However, Aidan decided it could be their best chance at getting him.

There was a reason the killer wanted the public to know Carol was alive. They believed the killer was hoping Jordan Blake would be his nosy, self-righteous self and do the work for him.

In telling Jordan to announce the news on the air, they hoped the killer would go after Carol in an attempt to finish the job.

Well.

If their plan in drawing out the killer worked, it'd be a very good plan.

If it worked.

Undercover men were stationed nearby the room, inside, and by the elevators, as well as the stairway. The sentries knew who was authorized to enter Carol's room and who wasn't.

Aidan stopped off at Laura's house to have supper with Cheyenne and watch Jordan report his story.

Then in the morning, Shaun and Aidan planned to meet at the hospital to see how things were going with Carol's recovery. Aidan had informed Cheyenne he may be sleeping in the hospital for the remainder of the week.

"Aidan, honey," Cheyenne said from the living room. "It's on."

Grabbing two beers from the fridge, he made a beeline for the living room and sat next to Cheyenne on the couch. Aidan wrapped his arm around her shoulders and she leaned into him.

"Earlier today," Jordan said, standing in front of a blue backdrop, "I reported that The Carnations Killer had abducted a woman, but according to a text I recently received from him, she escaped. Being naturally curious, I wanted to gather further information. Well, here you are, folks.

"The latest Carnations Killer victim is Carol Rider. She is being held at Georgia Regents Medical Center until the end of the week. According to the doctors, her eyes have extensive damage, and her voice is injured due to the amount of torture received. However, she's expected to make a full recovery, in which case the FBI hopes she can identify her abductor. You heard it here first. This is Jordan Blake reporting live at WJFX News."

It went to commercial, so Aidan pressed the mute button on the remote.

"I have to hand it to him," Aidan said. "He put on a show that was convincing enough, if I didn't already know it was staged, I'd have him in handcuffs."

"You think he'll fall for it?" Cheyenne asked.

"I don't know," Aidan said between sips of his beer. "I sure hope so. We're out of options."

She sat upright and cupped her hand under his chin.

"I know I don't say this enough, Agent O'Reilly," she said, "but I'm proud of you. Everything you are, everything you do. I'm lucky to be yours."

She kissed him.

"I'm the one who's lucky," Aidan said. "After all, you've put up with me for five years. All you know is my obsession with this investigation."

"He murdered someone you cared about," Cheyenne said. She frowned. "I think you deserve a little leeway as far as obsessions go. You haven't let it beat you. I mean, it's come close, but you're still standing. That's something to be proud of. And you're so much more than this investigation. I know that."

She leaned in to kiss his cheek before rising.

"I'm going to take a bath."

As she left, Aidan received a text from Shaun telling him Jordan did a compelling job on his report. Aidan replied that he agreed, and then called his sister.

He hadn't spoken to her since they'd argued and he wanted to clear the air.

60

Jordan hoped his segment of the news was satisfactory. Earlier in the day when the agent held him in the interview room, it suddenly hit him that his head really had been stuck in the clouds.

His uncle was right all along.

It was the photos of the women that finally did him in.

There were so many.

Agent Henderson didn't even show all of them. But he showed him more than enough.

He saw the crime scene photos and even saw Maya Gibson. While all of them were in bad shape, some were beyond recognizable.

Jordan couldn't stop picturing their broken faces. A sick feeling rose in his stomach. It made him want to lose his lunch. Why would anyone want to do that to a woman? To anyone for that matter? What kind of monster hated people so much, they'd destroy their lives and not care?

Did something happen in this guy's childhood that broke him?

Or was he born evil?

He took a sip of his Michelob.

Jordan had asked the agents why they thought The Carnations Killer wanted to contact him. Agent O'Reilly guessed it was because the killer knew he'd do whatever it took to get the story.

It kind of made sense, didn't it?

If Jordan wanted to make sure his bad deeds were being noticed, he'd probably want to find some overconfident imbecile to shout it out.

And if he wanted to remain unknown, then a young reporter yearning to make it in the field was the perfect target.

And the perfect fall guy.

Now everything he'd gone through regarding The Carnations Killer made sense.

One question remained—who was The Carnations Killer?

Would he take the bait the FBI set in place?

Would he finally be caught after all these years?

His cell phone interrupted his thoughts. He glanced at the caller ID, reading *unavailable*. Frowning, Jordan answered.

"Nice try, Jordan. But you don't fool me."

His heart beat against his ribcage as the garbled voice spoke to him on the other end of the line.

"Who is this?"

"You don't know?"

The voice sounded relaxed.

Carefree.

He laughed. "You do know. Tell me who I am."

Jordan swallowed, but he wasn't able to wet his throat. "You're the one who murdered all those women. The Carnations Killer."

More laughter. "See? You've got my number. Now. The reason I'm calling you, I have a message for you to give Agent O'Reilly."

"No," Jordan said. "I'm done being your messenger boy."

"Come on, Jordan ol' pal. We're just having fun, right? Please?"

Jordan remained silent. He wanted to protest, but he couldn't find the words. He clutched the armrest and stared at the muted television.

"I thought so," the killer said. "What I want you to tell Agent O'Reilly is very simple. Are you listening? It's very important he knows I'll be taking a vacation soon. But my last kill will be the biggest thrill of all. I want him to prepare to say goodbye. Oh! I almost forgot. I left you a present out back. Something to remind you of our time together."

"Wh-what what are you talking about?"

When there was no answer, the reporter glanced at his phone screen. The call had been lost.

He sat in silence for a few minutes before jumping out of his chair.

Putting his hand on the doorknob, he drew in a deep breath before he turned. With another breath, he pulled the door open.

He gripped the edge of the door when he saw it.

Slumped in his overgrown grass was his dog.

"Duke!"

The phone slipped from his hand and he rushed outside, but he knew nothing could be done.

A bouquet of white carnations rested on the bloodied golden fur.

Falling to his knees, Jordan rested his head against the dog's still body.

61

"OKAY, JORDAN," AIDAN SAID into the phone. "I'm coming right now. You didn't touch anything, did you?"

"No."

Aidan could hear the strain in the reporter's voice. For the first time since they met, he felt bad for him.

"Good. Keep everything the way it is. We're going to be treating this like any other scene." Aidan paused. "I'm very sorry about your dog."

"Yeah," he said dryly. "Me too."

Aidan ended the call and searched for Shaun's number. Cheyenne lay on her side, staring up at him. He stroked her head as a silent gesture that everything would be okay.

"Yeah?" Shaun answered on the third ring, Aidan could tell Shaun had been woken from a deep sleep.

"I just got off the phone with Jordan Blake," Aidan said.

After he relayed what the reporter said, Shaun released a tired curse.

"Man, he killed the dog?"

"Yeah. Somehow, it seems he knows we were trying to bait him. But I'm going to keep our people on Carol, just in case. We'll need to figure out another way to get him."

"Does Jordan know who the killer is?" Shaun asked. Aidan heard sliding drawers in the background.

"No. The caller had disguised his voice. I'm going to call in a trace, but—"

"Yeah," Shaun said. "I know."

The words that haunted Aidan echoed in his mind.

I can kill, and you can't catch me.

Closing his eyes, Aidan tried to steady his breath.

"We're going to get him, Shaun," he said, his eyes still closed. He had to tell him that as much as himself. But it seemed The Carnations Killer was still ten steps ahead.

"I'm going to head over to Blake's. Take a look."

"I'll meet you there." It sounded as though he was trying to keep from yawning.

"All right," Aidan said.

When he ended the call, Aidan set the phone on the bedside table.

"That's so awful," Cheyenne said, her eyes focused on the blank television. "I can't imagine what that poor man must be going through."

"Me either." Aidan swung his legs over the side of the bed and rubbed his eyes. "I have to go. I shouldn't be gone more than a couple of hours."

Cheyenne nodded as he slipped on a Bon Jovi concert tee and a pair of dark jeans. He wasn't worried about dress code since it was so late at night.

It was nearing ten-thirty when he slipped into the garage. Aidan pressed the button on the wall. The garage door rumbled open, the sudden, loud noise startling him.

Climbing into the car, Aidan pulled out of the drive and stopped at the undercover officers still stationed outside Laura's house, keeping watch over Cheyenne. The one in the driver's seat held a large cup of coffee.

"I've got to run out for a bit," he said.

"Don't worry, Agent O'Reilly," the officer behind the wheel said. He motioned to his coffee. "Double espresso with a shot of Red Bull. My eyes are bulging from my sockets, but I'm wide awake. The little lady will be just fine."

His partner leaned over with a smile on her face. "I only need my Diet Coke and I'm ready to run up the walls."

Aidan snickered. "I hear you. Well, thanks, guys. I'll be back in a couple of hours."

As Aidan drove, he called in a request for someone from the crime scene unit to meet him at Jordan's. He pressed the motorized window button to let the crisp cool air rouse him from sleepiness. He smelled the fresh scent of rain lingering. When he stopped at a traffic light, Aidan leaned over the wheel to gaze at the sky. With lights from the street lamps, it was hard to see, however; he didn't notice the moon or the stars.

He hoped the rain would hold off until they finished going through Jordan's yard.

When the light turned green, he pressed his foot on the gas and resumed his course.

62

He watched as the car pulled away before jimmying the window open. It didn't take much for him to break in.

Quietly and efficiently, he set his supplies inside the house and stepped through the living room window. To be sure the noise he made didn't raise an alert, he stood still, listening to the soundless house.

Well, almost soundless.

He could hear the hum of snoring upstairs.

Taking his time, he looked around the living room.

The walls were a muted green, blending with the pastel colors of the couch against the wall. The coffee table held a *National Geographic*. Big leather chairs sat on either side of the table, and a large flat-screen television hung on the wall, facing the couch.

Various cat figurines were lining the shelves.

He stared into the smiling faces of the photos crowded on the table by the kitchen entrance. They were primarily of his target and her family, including a pretty blonde whom he assumed to be the sister of O'Reilly's wife. It was a shame she wasn't around—he'd have use for her as well.

The countertops in the kitchen were red granite, the chairs stationed by the middle island made of wrought iron with a heart carved in their backings. A rack containing various pots and pans hung above the island. The stainless steel refrigerator, stove, and dishwasher all seemed brand new. Next to the fridge, in the corner, sat a wine rack, containing mostly red, but some Chardonnay. The kitchen walls were cream-colored. Above the back door hung a decorative sign reading *Count your Blessings*.

Next, he peered in the downstairs' half-bath and saw it was wallpapered with black cats. The wife's sister must have a cat fetish, he decided.

He found the stairs and began to ascend. He needed to go slowly because if one creaked underneath his weight, it would alert someone.

The first bedroom he came to looked to be a spare with a framed *USS Enterprise* above the headboard and a poster of dogs playing poker on the adjacent wall.

Then he entered what seemed to be an office. It didn't have a computer but held a desk and a bookcase. Apparently, the sister was a fan of James Patterson and Michael Crichton. He saw a few more photos of his new target and her sister.

The second bedroom he came to was where he wanted to be.

The snoring grew louder.

He stood in the darkened room, his eyes on the lump underneath the covers. It rose and fell in slow, soft movements.

He made his way to the edge of the bed to watch the woman sleep.

He couldn't help himself.

He had to do it.

Clutching his hands around the covers, he pulled it back, revealing a thin nightgown that was just a little too tight around her body.

He put his hand on her. She released a soft moan but didn't wake.

Running his hand against the coolness of her skin, he imagined being with her.

He imagined how exhilarating it would be to put himself inside O'Reilly's wife. Maybe this time. Just this one time, he could make an exception. Break his rules.

But, no.

He had come too far to risk leaving evidence.

"Wake up."

His voice was soft but clear. He sang it to her. He leaned in close to her lips and brushed his against hers.

"Wake up, sleeping beauty."

When her slumber proved to be too deep, he frowned and slapped her.

That did it.

She sprung in her bed, eyes wide. When she saw him, for just a second, she froze.

He smiled at her. "Hi."

His target was about to scream out, but he was too quick. Clamping his hands over her mouth, he pushed her head to the pillow. He straddled her as her arms and legs thrashed wildly.

With expertise, he held her as he pulled off a long piece of tape and placed it over her mouth. He saw the tears in her eyes as she looked at him, trying, but failing, to push him away.

He hit her hard against her temple.

She cried softly in pain, but settled down, the fight leaving her.

He climbed off her. She used the opportunity to attempt to roll off the other side of the bed, but he grabbed her hair and jerked her back.

She tried to scream when the prongs of the taser connected to her neck, but it was a fruitless effort. He paused to watch her convulse, then he zapped her again for good measure.

"We're going to have a lot of fun," he said. Then he scoffed. "Well, I am, anyway."

Making sure it was secured, he tied her hands and feet together.

He walked to the window to look across the street at the men keeping watch of the house. Before he made the call to take them away, he had to prepare to leave.

He carried his target half-conscious down the steps, found keys on the kitchen island, and opened the door to the garage.

He popped the trunk, set her inside, closed it, and returned to the bedroom to finish what he'd planned. Once that task was over, he tossed everything he came with into the backseat of the car. He searched the house to double-check that he didn't leave anything behind.

Now that it was time, he gazed across the street at the unmarked police car and dialed the number.

"Nine-one-one, what's your emergency?"

"Help, please help," he said, in a quiet, childlike voice. "My daddy's hurting Mommy. I think he's going to kill her."

"What's your name son?" The voice on the other end sounded bored, rather than concerned.

"Jay. Please. I think he has a gun. I'm scared."

"What's the address?"

He gave her an address far enough down the road for the officers to leave their station, but close enough for them to have no choice but to be the first responders.

And he'd be able to keep an eye on them in case they returned quicker than he left.

"We'll dispatch someone right away. Remain on the line please."

He stayed on the line as he waited for the car to leave their position. Once they did, he ended the call, hurried down the stairs and into the garage.

He opened it, climbed in the car, and cranked it.

He pulled out of the garage and closed it again as he headed in the opposite direction of the neighborhood, tossing the cell phone in the passenger seat.

63

When Aidan knocked on the door, the reporter opened it.

His eyes were bloodshot, his face wet.

Aidan could tell immediately the dog meant a lot to him.

"This is your fault," Jordan said, jabbing an angry finger at him. "If you and Henderson hadn't coerced me into trying to trap the guy, Duke would still be alive."

"I realize you're upset, Jordan," Aidan said as compassionately as he could, "but no one's at fault here. Let's focus on finding who is."

Aidan tried to pat his shoulder in a friendly way, but Jordan shrugged him off and headed through the house, leading the way to the backyard.

"He's out here."

He tried his best to remain strong, but his voice failed him.

Aidan decided to not make matters worse by playing nice. He was here for one reason, and that wasn't to make friends with the guy who had become his arch-nemesis.

Aidan opened the back door as a knock came from the front.

"That'd be either Shaun or the CSU," he said.

Without responding, the reporter turned to open the door.

Aidan stepped outside and made his way to the dog.

Taking the dried blood from Duke's fur out of account, Aidan would have thought he was sleeping.

A bouquet of white carnations rested next to the body.

No matter what he thought about Jordan, Aidan hated that his dog fell victim to the sadistic killer.

He kneeled next to Duke and laid his hand on the still head.

"I'm sorry, buddy," he said.

Shaun approached with a curse.

"This guy has no morals."

"No," Aidan agreed as he pushed to his feet. "He doesn't."

Aidan noticed a member of the crime scene unit team had also arrived. He recalled her name to be Fallon, but couldn't remember her last name. He told her to keep her eyes peeled for evidence.

"And we don't have much time," Shaun said. "Forecast says rain is imminent."

Fallon nodded, her eyes glued to the dog. She set her kit by her feet and prepared her camera.

Using the beam of his flashlight as a guide, Aidan surveyed the surrounding area while Shaun went in a different direction.

A raindrop struck Aidan's nose. He turned to Shaun but there wasn't a need to tell him what he was thinking. Shaun looked at the sky as if to gauge how much time they had left.

Aidan continued to comb through the tall grass, wishing Jordan took better care of his yard. He felt it would make it easier to find evidence.

Then again, maybe not.

Aidan kneeled where a section of the grass was flat beside the dog house. It had sunken into a soft spot on the ground and left a shoe print. There were also droplets of blood around the area. Shining his flashlight on the print, he studied it.

Glancing up, he saw Shaun and Fallon covering Duke with a sheet. Aidan called out for them, and when they appeared at his side, he gestured with his head.

"Look. I think he stood here, waiting. He likely made the phone call right here to watch Jordan's reaction."

Shaun looked toward the house as another drop of rain fell. "Yeah. I think he had the perfect vantage point. He could see Jordan, but Jordan couldn't see him."

Fallon kneeled to snap a photo of the blood and shoe print. "I'll need to case this. Can you bring me my kit?"

Without answering, Aidan pushed to his feet and hurried to grab the kit. Shaun ran past him to speak to Jordan.

By the time Aidan returned and set the kit on the ground next to Fallon, the rain had begun, and Shaun arrived with a blanket. They worked together to keep Fallon and the evidence dry as the rain broke from the sky.

Despite the warm humid air, the rain felt cold as it pelted Aidan's skin.

After Fallon finished casting the print and collecting the blood sample, they hurried inside from the rain.

"I think that's all we'll be able to get," Fallon said. "I'll take it to the lab and let you know what we find."

Aidan thanked her as she left. Turning back to Jordan, he ran his hands through his soaked hair. "Jordan, did you hear anything? See anything out of the ordinary?"

Jordan shook his head.

"I don't get it. Duke's always barking. But he was so quiet." He sat in his chair. "Do you think he killed my dog when I wasn't home?"

"When did you get home?" Shaun asked.

"Around eight-thirty."

Aidan shook his head and pointed to Jordan's blood-stained shirt. "The blood was fresh."

"I've had Duke for almost eleven years," he said. "He was my dad's dog. Dad lost his battle with cancer three years ago. Duke was all I had left of him."

"I'm really sorry to hear that," Aidan said, rubbing the back of his neck. "Do you mind if we check the rest of your house? Make sure nothing is disturbed?"

Jordan shrugged, so Shaun and Aidan took different rooms to look around.

A few minutes went by and they regrouped back to the living room, neither of them finding anything.

"Try to get some sleep, okay?" Aidan said. "We'll do everything we can. The casting may narrow down a lot of suspects."

Jordan looked at Aidan. "So, you have suspects?"

Aidan swallowed, trying to think of a way to evade the question. It was Shaun who answered.

"Look, man..." He placed a hand on Jordan's shoulder. "Don't worry yourself."

"Right," Jordan said.

Aidan only nodded while he and Shaun made their way to the door. They didn't bother speaking until the agents reached their respective cars.

"I'll see you tomorrow," Aidan said. He climbed into the car to return to Laura's house for the night.

64

When Aidan arrived home, he opened the garage, pulling the loaned company vehicle into his usual spot. Immediately noticing Laura's car wasn't there, he looked at the time on the dashboard. It was after midnight.

Where could she be?

It wasn't like Cheyenne to leave in the middle of the night. Whether she had an emergency or decided on a late-night ice cream run, she would have called or texted. The officers were still across the street, so where was Cheyenne?

And why would she have taken Laura's car and not her own?

Aidan opened the door and called out to her, but his racing heart knew something wasn't right.

Instinct had him drawing his weapon.

He called out for her again, but no response came.

Slowly, Aidan checked each room, but nothing appeared disturbed.

"Hey, honey?" he said again. "Love, are you home?"

His pulse throbbed underneath his skin and his hands sweat. Something was wrong. Aidan could feel it with each breath he took. With one hand holding his weapon, he used his free one to push the door to the master bedroom open.

He almost dropped his gun when he saw the room.

On the wall, were the words *your move.*

It had been scratched out with something sharp. Aidan assumed it was from the kitchen knife left on the bed of white carnation petals.

"Cheyenne!" The silent house unnerved him.

Aidan rushed into the adjoining bathroom, and then rechecked all the other rooms, including the closets.

His heart was now lodged in his throat, beating faster by the second. He tried to catch his breath, but couldn't. Aidan gripped the wall to steady himself but still fell to his knees.

Cheyenne wasn't there.

She was his next victim.

His fingers feeling like putty, he struggled to hold the cell as he called Shaun.

It took a few rings for his partner to answer. "Yeah?"

"He has her."

"What?"

Aidan didn't say anything. He couldn't find the words.

"Aidan, what's going on? I didn't hear you." He clearly seemed annoyed. "Listen, it's been a really long day, and I—"

"He has Cheyenne," Aidan said again. His voice shook, but he knew Shaun heard him because he cursed.

"I'm on my way."

As Shaun ended the call, Aidan heard the screeching sound of tires, presumably Shaun making a quick U-turn. Aidan struggled to his feet.

He went back into the bedroom and looked at the white petals covering the bed, and then the embedded note on the wall.

Your move.

Nothing about Cheyenne's abduction made sense.

She didn't fit the profile of The Carnations Killer: she had brown hair and wore glasses—none of the others did.

So why did he go after her?

Because you love her.

The words echoed in his head.

Aidan scanned the room for anything out of place but found nothing. He wanted to grab the petals from the bed and toss them in the trash, but he needed to wait. The room had to be documented.

"Aidan!" Shaun's voice bellowed from downstairs as the door banged open.

He shouted to Shaun that he was upstairs. Aidan stared at the words on the wall, hearing several footsteps before Shaun rushed into the bedroom, backup trailing after him.

Shaun sucked in a heavy breath, then released another curse.

He instructed one of the agents to begin processing the room. Aidan allowed Shaun to guide him by the elbow downstairs. He told him to let the guys take charge for the time being.

Shaun sat on the couch and urged Aidan to do the same. Instead, Aidan paced the living room, almost burning a hole in the carpet. The things the women before Cheyenne endured flashed through his mind and he couldn't turn them off.

"We've got to find her, Shaun. I can't lose Cheyenne this way."

"We'll find him. I promise."

His words did little to assure.

The living room spun faster, and Aidan sat on the couch, his head between his knees.

Shaun said nothing more. Aidan figured it was because there was nothing he could say to make the situation okay. Instead, Shaun placed a hand on his shoulder and squeezed gently.

Aidan sucked in several deep breaths, trying to contain his fears. He couldn't fall apart. Not when it was more important than ever to find a killer.

"I've got to find her," Aidan repeated, raising his head so he could look into Shaun's eyes. "She can't become just another face on the news. She can't—"

Still rambling, Aidan rose and made his way back to the bedroom. There had to be something that would tell him where to find Cheyenne.

Aidan stood in the doorway and watched as the agents murmured to one another about the writing on the wall. One of them looked his way and he saw pity in the agent's eyes.

"Did you find anything?"

They shook their heads.

"Wait," said an agent who was putting the carnation petals in a plastic bag. He used the camera he held to snap a photo of a brown book. Skimming it through, he said, "It's a photo album. And there's a note for you."

Aidan stepped to his side. Because he wasn't wearing gloves, he grabbed a couple of tissues from the bedside table and took the album.

FBI Special Agent O'Reilly—

Surprise! I left a very special gift for you: all the women I've killed in my lifetime. You think the fifty I have attached to my name is enough to make your skin crawl? Well, enjoy a little light reading. Now, your wife is such a lovely young woman. Lovelier than the others. I suppose it's because she's yours. Well, I have her now, so I guess technically speaking, she's mine. I'm going to enjoy your little wife. And I'll be thinking of you all the time. I wonder if she'll cry out your name. I'll let you know. Anyway, this is our end game. Thank you for playing, and I do hope we'll meet again.

Your friend,
The Carnations Killer

Aidan's hands shook as he read the letter.

The Carnations Killer wanted Cheyenne to be his last victim. Then he was going to vanish in the night.

Again.

Aidan skimmed the pages of the album. He could feel Shaun's breath against his neck.

All the pages contained full-spread bodies of women, most wearing black dresses, holding the token bouquet of white carnations against their chests.

He recognized some of the women, others he didn't.

Aidan heard Shaun curse under his breath.

"There's got to be more than a hundred pages in that book," the agent who found the album stated. "If they are all of women he killed, then—"

"He's telling us who he killed," Aidan finished. He went to the front of the book, and read the first page: *Washington: May 2000 to July 2000 (3)*. He turned three pages, which contained three different women, and found another title page on the fourth page: "California: *January: 2001 to June 2001 (5)*. Six pages later, he found dates for the next year in Colorado, indicating he'd murdered ten women. The other title pages followed the same suit. Finally, the last entry was more recently in Georgia and had the photos of Maya Gibson and Jane Ridgeway.

"He's sick," the agent with the camera said. "He needs to be stopped."

Aidan ignored the comment of the obvious and flipped through the book until he stared at the photo of the one victim he was the most familiar with.

The album slipped through his fingers and he hurried out of the room. Aidan fell to his knees and emptied his stomach. After he heaved a second time, he placed his palm against the wall, trying to compose himself. Aidan heard the agents muttering amongst themselves, but he couldn't make out what they were saying.

Sounds seemed to be distorted.

His mind raced.

He felt a massive hand on his shoulder, but he couldn't move.

Aidan heard the door open from downstairs, following the sounds of Tara's voice.

Finally, he found the strength to climb to his feet. Aidan ran a hand through his hair and straightened his shirt.

Without a word, he made his way down the steps to brief Tara about the situation.

65

Aidan's cell vibrated on the table, but he continued to stare at the ceiling. He was spending the night on the couch. Shaun had offered his house to him, but Aidan didn't want to leave. He'd hoped Cheyenne would come waltzing through the door and what he'd seen in the bedroom was only a figment of his imagination. He'd hoped it, but knew it wasn't true.

Instead, Shaun stayed the night, despite Aidan's protests. He wasn't sure where Shaun slept, whether downstairs or in the spare bedroom.

Although Aidan tried, he couldn't find the means to sleep. Each hour on the clock ticked by one millisecond at a time as he lay listening to the rain against the roof. He wondered if he'd ever sleep again. Every time his eyes closed, every time he blinked...he saw Cheyenne. He saw her being tortured then murdered.

He wondered if he should call Laura and let her know what was going on. Then he decided to wait for a little bit. She'd only worry and there wouldn't be anything she could do. Besides, he knew she'd be home soon and he'd rather tell her in person, instead of over the phone.

Aidan sat upright to look through the window leading to the backyard. The full moon was the only light, hazily illuminating the area.

The silence mocked him. Aidan was so used to being annoyed by her snoring, he wished he'd hear the sound again.

But no.

It was quiet.

It was then he realized the phone stopped vibrating.

He wasn't sure what time it was. His eyelids grew heavy, but he couldn't sleep. He didn't want to even try. He didn't want to close his eyes and see the empty shell of Cheyenne's body.

The phone vibrated once more.

This time, he looked at the caller ID, and it read *unavailable*.

Frowning, he chose to answer it, wondering who would be trying to contact him at two in the morning.

"Yeah? O'Reilly."

"I don't want to do this anymore."

Aidan's heart seemed to skip several beats.

"Then turn yourself in," Aidan said, baiting the caller. "We can end it now. Tonight."

"Do you know the worst thing, Agent O'Reilly?" He continued to speak as though Aidan hadn't said anything. The tone he gave seemed as if he thought he was playing a children's game. The thought of that alone sent chills crawling up Aidan's spine.

"What?"

Aidan hoped if he could get him talking, then he might get enough out of him. Maybe he'd make a mistake. Say something he didn't intend to say. On another hand, Aidan felt beaten. Whoever The Carnations Killer was, was winning, and he knew it.

This person had been taunting the FBI and law enforcement for years. He'd killed countless women without batting an eye. Then he'd slink into the shadows unnoticed to watch as he fooled the world. And then he'd re-emerge once the fear he'd caused finally simmered down.

"It's not really that I don't want to do this anymore," he said. He'd begun lowering his voice, almost as though he was attempting to mask remorse. "No. It's not that."

"Then what is it?" Aidan's throat was dry and he yearned for something to drink. But the glass on the coffee table was empty. He retrieved it and took it to the kitchen, quietly filling it in the sink.

"I can't stop," the killer whispered after a long pause. "It's a disease. You know. Like cancer."

"No," Aidan said through his teeth. The glass of water shook violently in his hand. He clutched it tight. "It's not a disease. You're a sociopath."

"What's the difference?"

Aidan wet his throat with the glass of water.

"Why'd you hurt Jordan Blake's dog?" He worked at keeping himself composed. He wanted to show the killer he wasn't going to get to him, no matter what he did. Aidan's hands shook as he held his cell to his ear.

"It wasn't fair that I never did anything for the reporter," the killer said simply. "But I admit the dog was not nearly as satisfying as my women." His laugh was haunting. "And nothing was as satisfying as my new woman. She's lovely."

Keep calm, Aidan.

"Why did you go after Cheyenne?" Aidan asked. "Why her? She doesn't fit your profile."

"Ah."

The way he said that one simple word sounded as if he was smiling into the phone. Aidan's blood boiled, and he gripped the phone tighter in his hand.

"Cheyenne. Is that her name?"

"She doesn't deserve what you're doing to her."

It was becoming harder and harder to control his emotions. Aidan's legs wobbled, so he returned to the couch and lowered himself to the seat.

"I wish you could see her. See Cheyenne." He smacked his lips. "She asks for you, you know. I have something special prepared for her. When I saw you and her together, I knew—I just *knew*—that she was the perfect choice. Because she's special. Cheyenne is *very* special."

"Let her go," Aidan said through his teeth. "I'll give you whatever you want."

"Didn't they teach you to never negotiate with terrorists?" he asked.

"You're not a terrorist." Aidan wanted to try and appeal to his human side. Maybe he could get him to feel enough to let Cheyenne go. He knew it wouldn't work, but the non-federal agent in him had to try. "I think you've been hurt by someone. Maybe your mom, when you were little."

There was a slight pause.

"What did she do to you?" Aidan continued. "Maybe she beat you. Is that it? When you see a blonde woman walking by, you get flashbacks, right? So you take the women and hit them over and over again. Then after they barely have a leg left to stand on, you strangle them. Because that's what you always wanted to do, right? Strangle your abusive mother."

Another pause filled the phone line.

The rain continued to drum against the roof.

"You think you've got me all figured out, don't you?" He laughed softly and continued, "After ten years of the hunt for the infamous Carnations

Killer, you think you know the depth of the destroyed soul. Let's get back to the purpose of my call, shall we?"

The killer fell silent for a few seconds. Aidan could hear breathing on the line.

Finally, after what seemed hours ticked by, the caller continued. "Do you think you can save her? Cheyenne? I don't think so. I mean, of course, you're welcome to try, but just remember that as good as you think you are, Agent O'Reilly, I'm better. Actually, I can see the headlines now: wife of FBI agent brutally left for dead." He released a sigh of contentment. "The gist of the story will of course read that said federal agent failed to save the love of his life. So, tell me...if even she couldn't be saved, then what hope is there for the rest of the world?"

Aidan had had enough. He clutched the phone tighter to his ear. Closing his eyes, he reminded himself to not allow the killer to get under his skin.

"I will find you. And I will kill you. You'll never hurt anyone else again. Sooner or later, you *will* make a mistake. And I'll be there to catch you when you do."

"Really?" His laugh was dark and demeaning. "No, Agent O'Reilly, you won't. I've escaped the clutches of the world for sixteen years and going strong. You don't know me. Know who I am." Then he said, his voice almost like he was singing: "But I know you." He sighed again. "I know your strengths and I know your weaknesses. I know your fears. You think you're hunting me. But you're wrong—I'm hunting you. I'm your shadow, Agent O'Reilly. I'm your worst nightmare." Another sigh. "Well, it's been such a pleasure chatting with you. We'll have to do it again sometime soon."

He ended the call.

Aidan sat in the darkness, staring across the room. His phone vibrated, and he looked down. It said he had one text message.

He opened the text.

Just wanted to send something as a show of good faith. Take a good long look, because it'll be the last time you'll ever see your lovely Cheyenne.

Your friend,

The Carnations Killer

Another text followed a few seconds later. It was an emoticon of a smiley face. The third was a video of Cheyenne chained to a wall. She was crying, dirty, and had minimal cuts and bruises.

"I'm going to find you," he promised the video of Cheyenne. "I. Will. Find. You."

His heart hammering, he fumbled with his phone, cursing as he attempted to forward the messages to his email, but the texts had disappeared two seconds too late.

He stared at the blank message screen on his phone, replaying in his mind what he'd just seen.

66

Aidan woke the next morning in a daze and wasn't sure where he was. He wasn't in his bed. He was laying on something hard and something heavy seemed to be weighing him down.

He blinked his eyes to clear his vision.

It was dawn.

Aidan sat upright and realized the hard surface he slept on was the floor, next to the couch. The quilt was tangled between his legs.

The light was on in the kitchen.

His first thought was that he'd fallen asleep on the couch and Cheyenne had gotten up early to make breakfast.

Well, one of two theories was correct.

He started remembering the night before.

Jordan Blake had called him to tell him The Carnations Killer murdered his dog, and then when he returned home, Aidan found Cheyenne missing.

Your move.

Aidan shivered as a wave of cold air climbed up his back.

He struggled to his feet to peer into the kitchen.

Shaun's back was to him and he was pouring himself a cup of coffee, staring at a bunch of papers.

Aidan assumed he was searching for answers, determined to find something—anything—to find the killer or Cheyenne or both. But the answers just weren't there.

They never were.

Aidan remembered Shaun had insisted on staying the night, despite being told his partner and friend was fine to be alone.

Rather than letting him know he'd woken, Aidan turned to ascend the stairs. The crime scene unit had cleaned the bed of the carnation petals and taken the book with them. The only reminder that the killer had been in the room were the words on the wall.

"There you are," Shaun said as he came up the steps.

Aidan kept his focus on the wall, tracing the letters with his eyes.

Shaun remained silent before placing a hand on Aidan's shoulder.

"Do we know anything yet?" Aidan asked, his eyes still glued to the words.

"No," Shaun said. "I'm going to head over to the office and see what they found."

"All right," Aidan said. "Let me take a quick shower first."

"Tara wants you to have the day off," Shaun said. "She's insisting."

Aidan shook his head with determination. "No way. This is *my* case, Cheyenne's *my* wife. She's *not* going to remove me! I won't let her."

"Aidan, you need to—"

"I need to what?" Aidan turned to face Shaun, his arms crossed over his chest. Narrowing his eyes, Aidan added, "Need to sit around in this empty house? Need to do nothing while a psychopath is doing whatever he wants to Cheyenne? Shaun, I'm not going to sit back while he's holding her. He took her only because she means something to me. He only did it to try and hurt me. I'm not going to sit around and let him think he's succeeding."

"I'll be downstairs, then," Shaun said after a brief hesitation.

Aidan went into the bedroom, a coldness enveloping him. Gathering clean clothes, he left the room to shower in the guest bathroom.

It only took a few minutes to clean up, so he went into the kitchen and poured a thermos full of coffee.

Despite the dreams the night before—most of which he'd begun to remember were about Cheyenne—he slept a good while. But he continued to feel sleep deprivation over the last few years, so he relied on caffeinated coffee to keep him alert.

Aidan resolved to work today, no matter what anyone said. Even if he were forced to leave and work from home.

He wasn't going to let Cheyenne become another victim of this lunatic.

He couldn't.

Fired with determination and strong coffee, Shaun and Aidan left the house.

67

Early that morning, Tara held a press conference informing the reporters they had reasons to believe The Carnations Killer had murdered not fifty, but a total of eighty-nine women, not including Keisha Moffett or Jamal Foster. The killer hadn't included them in his collection of photos, and Aidan guessed it was because he didn't care to claim them. After all, they were only collateral damage.

She'd also mentioned Cheyenne had been abducted and asked the public to notify the FBI if they see or hear anything that may lead to her safe return and the capture of the serial killer.

Last night, Shaun had questioned the two officers who were supposed to have kept an eye on the house. They had told him there was a report of domestic abuse down the street, and since they were the nearest unit, they went to check it out. The report was false, and by the time they'd returned, Cheyenne had already been taken.

Shaun was looking into the nine-one-one call.

Aidan began studying the photo album the killer had left him. He went through the FBI database and scrolled through the cold cases to see if anything matched the victims in the album.

So far, he came across a few of the faces he recognized throughout his career. They were all murdered in 2003 or 2005. The interesting thing was that the cold cases Aidan matched said the victims hadn't been tased. Strangled, yes, but not tased. And although they were strangled, they weren't strangled by a thin wire. The reports suggested the killer had used something to the effect of a stocking.

And the very first victim was stabbed. The crime scene photos showed blood staining the walls and sheets. The next five victims had been beaten and then strangled with bare hands. Aidan could see the prominent finger marks wrapped around their necks. The fourth one started with the stockings and that lasted until 2003. The wire came after, and when the year 2006 rolled around, he'd continued with the use of wire and added using a taser.

It was unusual for serial killers to change the way they committed murder, but not unheard of. Although there were typical ways a killer killed, the sky's the limit on how it's done.

But Aidan kept wondering why the sudden changes in MO? Was he bored with his methods of torture and killings? Did they become close to catching him at some point, so he decided to rise as someone completely new?

Aidan considered why he stepped out of his comfort zone to take Cheyenne.

From the get-go, The Carnations Killer had wanted *his* attention, even if Aidan didn't realize it until a few years ago.

Well.

If he didn't have it before, he sure had it now.

"You okay?"

Aidan looked up to see Shaun looming over his desk.

"I'm fine."

He grabbed a chair from the empty cubicle nearby and sat at the desk, all the while gazing at Aidan. Shaun shook his head.

"I don't believe you."

Aidan gave him a weak smile, hoping it would assure him he was fine.

Shaun's lips turned down in a frown. "Are you sure you're up for this, Aidan?"

Sighing, Aidan leaned back in his chair.

Instead of answering him, he told him about the call the night before. Shaun's eyes grew with curiosity as he listened with intent.

After Aidan told him about the texts, Shaun cursed and drew in a heavy breath.

"Did you ask for a trace of the call?"

"First thing I did this morning before I took the shower. I'm waiting on the techs now. Chances are it was a burner. But with any luck, we'll be able to pinpoint where the call was made. I tried forwarding the messages to my email, but they disappeared seconds after it played."

Aidan tapped his pen against the edge of his desk with a despondent sigh as Shaun continued to scrutinize him.

"Everything will be fine. I'm going to find Cheyenne, and I'm going to find the killer."

Shaun hesitated, and opened his mouth, then closed it as though he wanted to speak, but thought better of it.

"What? Go ahead and say whatever you're thinking. Tell me you think I'm not capable of focusing on work."

"Look, it's not that," Shaun said. "But you can't treat Cheyenne as your wife. She's going to have to be another—"

"Stop." Aidan held his palm in the air. "Just stop."

Aidan flipped the photo album shut and sat straight in his chair. He ran a hand through his hair.

"Don't talk to me about Cheyenne, okay? Let's move on. Now, I've matched a good amount of the victims in the album he left us," he said. He mentioned the differences in the murders. "I've marked them, but we'll have to scan the others into the database and see if we can find any matches. I've already started contacting the local police departments. They're sending over some of their cold case files."

Shaun leaned over and grabbed the album. "I'll take a look at this. Tara wants to speak with you."

Aidan watched as he walked away, and then headed to the special agent-in-charge's office. When he arrived, he knocked and opened the door when he heard her tell him to enter.

Tara flipped a folder shut and opened her file cabinet. After thumbing through her confidential files, she slipped the folder in its slot and turned back to Aidan, muttering something underneath her breath, then rolled her chair to the side.

"Have a seat, Agent O'Reilly. Would you like coffee?"

"Please," he said, as she grabbed two Styrofoam cups and began pouring the coffee.

As she did so, Aidan told her about the phone call and texts from the night before, and that they were in the process of tracing it.

She nodded as she set a cup in front of him and sipped from hers.

"Is there anything else I need to know?"

Aidan wondered if she was going to insist he go home and take a few days. He knew she wanted him to, but he hoped that wasn't the case. He wanted nothing more than to keep his promise to Candace's killer: be there when he was caught.

The promise to kill him was still up for debate.

Aidan cleared his throat. "No, ma'am."

Tara turned her red lips to a frown and stared at him.

She looked at him disapprovingly while she asked why he was at work today. Aidan explained to her the same thing he did to Shaun earlier that morning.

Unlike him, she was hesitant about letting him stay.

"I understand that you want to find Cheyenne," she said. Her words were soft but full of authority. "I think you should take a little time. It's personal now."

"It's always been—" Aidan stopped himself short. Admitting it had always been personal was a sure way to be sent home. Instead, Aidan drew in a breath, rubbed his hair. "Let me stay. I can't sit around and do nothing. The best I can do is keep busy. If you don't want me to investigate Cheyenne, fine. I trust Shaun enough to do that. But he killed Jordan Blake's dog. I *can* look into that."

She reached for her phone, dialed an extension.

"Can you come here for a second, Agent Henderson?"

They waited in silence until there was a knock on the door and Shaun stepped into the office.

Tara sighed and looked around her desk and began to straighten files and papers. The expression she gave showed she was considering what it was she planned to say next.

"Okay, Aidan, I'm not benching you. "As much as I hate to admit it, you do know this guy better than anyone." She paused before continuing. "However, I'm making a change in this investigation." She nodded toward Shaun. "I want Shaun completely in charge from here on out. Understood?"

Aidan opened his mouth to speak, and then closed it again. He turned to Shaun and saw he was staring at Tara and then glanced at him. It was hard to tell what he was thinking.

"This is *my* investigation," Aidan said, returning his gaze to Tara.

"It's still your investigation," Tara said. "Except Shaun is in charge. You're too invested in it now. He's not. I'm not so sure you can remain objective, Aidan. He can. I'm not going to risk you endangering yourself or anyone else."

Aidan gaped at Tara, then narrowed his eyes at Shaun. "You knew about this?"

"No, he didn't," Tara said before Shaun could reply. Another sigh. "If you want to remain on this investigation, this is the best you'll get. I already spoke to Zane and Hansford this morning on how to proceed. They both suggested you sit back, but I convinced them you should stay on. After all, you've come this far. However, if you don't like the terms, you can go home—Henderson will still be in charge."

Tara's eyes were firm, but at the same time sympathetic.

Aidan wanted to protest but thought better of it.

"Yes, ma'am," he said.

"Is that okay with you, Shaun?"

When Shaun replied it was, she dismissed them.

Without another word, Aidan left the office, knowing Shaun was following close behind.

"Aidan," he began. "I didn't know she—"

"I really don't want to talk about it right now," Aidan snapped. He turned to face him, hands on his hips. "So, boss, what do you want to do next?"

Shaun told him the call and texts did come from a burner, but the nine-one-one was traced to a guy named Gary Short. They also learned Gary worked at WJFX News. He was in charge of the sound check.

As they left the office to interview him, Aidan tried pushing his anger out of his mind. He reminded himself it didn't matter that he was no longer running the investigation as long as he found Cheyenne.

But he didn't appreciate the feeling that he had been stabbed in the back by a man he'd come to think of as a friend.

68

AT WJFX, THEY QUESTIONED Gary Short about the phone call and he informed them he'd lost his phone sometime yesterday afternoon. He didn't remember where he left it and had figured someone walked off with it.

"Where were you last night at nine o'clock?" Shaun asked.

"I went to the movies with friends," Gary said. He jammed his hands into his pocket and pulled out a crumpled movie ticket.

"You always keep your stubs?" Shaun asked.

Gary shrugged. "A lot of people do. I don't really think about it."

"You're a field technician, right?" Aidan asked.

He nodded.

"So, you know technology pretty well, huh? Do you know how to send and delete a text remotely?"

Gary released an awkward chuckle. "Yeah, Jordan mentioned those texts he received from the killer. I didn't send 'em if that's where you're heading."

"But you do know how to do it?" Shaun said.

"Yeah, guess you could say I do," Gary said matter-of-factly. "But I didn't. And I wouldn't hurt an animal."

"Okay," Shaun said, passing the stub back. "Thanks for your time."

After they finished questioning him, they proceeded to leave the station but were stopped by Thomas Blake calling out to them.

They waited as he jogged in their direction.

"Sorry to bother you," Thomas said. "How are you coming along with finding the SOB who murdered my nephew's dog?"

"We're working on it," Aidan said. "We've got some leads that might prove useful."

Thomas looked around and then lowered his voice.

"Is it true The Carnations Killer has your wife?"

Aidan considered bypassing the question, but instead, he nodded.

"I just hope for her sake you aren't as incompetent now as you've been the last...how long are they saying he's been killing now...fifteen years."

Aidan tried to think of something professional to say other than "screw you." He came up empty.

"We know a lot more about the cases than we used to," Shaun said hotly. "He's making mistakes. We're confident we'll find something that'll lead us to him."

Thomas raised his eyebrow. "What kinds of mistakes?"

"Well, he took *his* wife for one," Shaun said pointedly, crossing his arms. "Now, if you'll excuse us, Mr. Blake, we have work to do."

They left Thomas standing in the hallway glaring after them.

"Thanks," Aidan said.

"The Blake family gets on my nerves."

"I hear that," Aidan said as Shaun's phone rang.

He answered, said a few words, and then ended the conversation with a thank you.

"The casting of the print was a size ten-and-a-half. We believe it's from a pair of running shoes. Nike's or something like that. The blood by the dog house was canine."

"Do we have any suspects left?" Aidan asked. "It's not Jordan. Unless he killed his own dog and is an extremely good actor, he's not our killer. Thomas still doesn't have an alibi, and the killer used his house. And no paper trail from the rent money is curious."

Shaun shook his head. "I don't know. To kill his own nephew's dog? That's just plain heartless."

"Because he's been showing true heart all these years," Aidan said dryly.

Shaun didn't reply to the comment. "Maybe it's someone we haven't interviewed yet. Maybe—"

"Killers—especially when it's planned—become invested in the investigations. They are either the most helpful witnesses, watching from nearby, or both. The Carnations Killer is proud of what he's done. He's proud that he eluded us for so long. Why else would he hand over the album of all eighty-six of his victims?"

Aidan shook his head slowly, trying to unravel the mystery.

The killer used a taser to subdue his victims. He moved them to a location where he abused them with a tire iron. After a week, he would strangle them until they were dead, then dump them at a chosen location.

As far as Aidan could tell, the victims had no relationship to each other. The crime scenes were chosen at random. He still believed that whoever he was, he had a job that allowed him to travel.

Aidan continued to stare through the windshield at the WJFX News studio.

"We know who he is. But—"

"We just don't know who," Shaun finished his thought.

Shaun pulled out of the parking lot so they could grab an early lunch at McDonald's, then take it to the office and review the files once more.

69

"TWO MONTHS AGO, MAYA Gibson was murdered the same way most of the other victims were: tased, beaten, strangled. Same MO with Jane Ridgeway. We had believed Sherry Finch was his first victim, but when he took Cheyenne, he told us every woman he'd murdered."

Aidan glanced at Shaun, who stared at his computer screen.

"Who was the first?"

"Um..." Shaun flipped through the database. "...Georgia Rivers."

"What do we know about her?" Aidan jammed a stale French fry into his mouth.

Shaun said she was born in Manhattan in 1972 to John and Marcia Davis. Her parents divorced in 1978. Georgia's mom remarried a man named Ben Rivers and they moved to Aiken, South Carolina in 1983. They adopted a five-year-old boy who had been in and out of foster care since he was three.

"This is interesting...apparently, Georgia was telling her mother her new brother had issues. She'd seen him throw the family cat across the yard, threw rocks at the birds in the trees. They even had a dog, but he went missing. Georgia claimed her brother had killed him. But there was never any proof."

"What do we know about the brother?"

Aidan waited until he searched for the information.

"He'd been sent to the Troubled Teens of North Carolina, a small boot camp in Morganton. There's no more mention of the brother anywhere beyond that."

"Are the parents still living?"

"The mother is in a retirement center in Charleston. Her husband was killed in an accident five years ago, and Carol's biological father died twenty years ago from lung cancer."

"Let's go visit the mother and see if she can tell us anything about her son."

◈

The Charlotte Retirement Center was an appealing place, its trees and flowers gave visitors and occupants a sense of security and peace. Even the warm breeze of the South seemed inviting.

In the courtyard, Aidan noticed a young couple sitting by the fountain with an elderly man in a wheelchair. They had a little boy with them and it looked as though he was reading a book out loud.

Shaun and Aidan stepped inside the doors of the retirement center. To the left was the reception window. To the right were four chairs and a table. Directly ahead were various halls leading to what Aidan guessed to be rooms for those who lived there.

They walked to the window and showed the clerk behind the glass their ID badges as they introduced themselves.

"We're looking for a woman named Marcia Rivers," Shaun said.

"Oh, sure," the middle-aged woman behind the glass chirped. She kept her voice low. "Let me contact my supervisor first and let her know you're here."

"No problem," Aidan said. "Thanks."

They waited, and a few minutes later, the receptionist informed them that her supervisor would be right with them.

Aidan used the time to reread the information about Georgia Davis. She was murdered in her bed during the summer of 2000. Georgia was found by her mother, beaten then stabbed numerous times. If this indeed was the killer, it appeared he was spending his early years trying to perfect his method of torture and death.

Aidan presumed he decided using a knife on his victims proved to be too messy. Or maybe it was nothing more than a fit of rage. The crime scene photos revealed blood on the walls, sheets, and nightstand. The second victim in the album was strangled.

At the time of her death, Georgia wasn't married, but she was dating a man named Dave Brinkley. He'd been in trouble with the police a few times before with petty theft. Brinkley was arrested, tried, and found guilty of her murder. After a month in prison, he was shanked by another inmate and died in the hospital a few hours later.

"Agents O'Reilly and Henderson?"

Aidan glanced up to see a young woman heading their way. She looked to be in her early twenties, but by her confidence and authority, he guessed her to be in her early thirties. She kept her dark brown hair in a tight bun and the only makeup she wore was light pink lipstick. She had diamond studs in her ears that sparkled with every step. Her name, Edith, as stated on the pin she wore.

"Yes, ma'am," Shaun said as he rose.

They shook her hand and she asked what she could do for them. Aidan told her about their interest in speaking with Marcia Rivers.

"I don't know if you'll be able to get anything out of her," Edith said, "but I'll take you to her."

"How long has she lived here?" Aidan asked.

"Since her husband died," she said as they began walking. "She has had a lot happen to her in her lifetime and couldn't be left alone. She found her daughter in bed, murdered. When her husband was killed, she closed herself off to the world. She wouldn't eat, she wouldn't sleep. She even cut her wrists two days after she buried her husband."

Edith kept talking as they turned a corner. "A neighbor found her when she went to check on her and called for an ambulance. After she was released from the hospital, she was taken to a mental institution. She'd been saying, 'if I don't kill myself, he will.'"

"Do you know who 'he' is?" Aidan asked.

She stopped at their destination with a frown. "She kept muttering, 'The Carnations Killer will come after me."

"Does she know who The Carnations Killer is?" Shaun asked, still staring into Aidan's eyes.

"If she does, she never mentioned his name. But I've kept a close watch on her for years." Edith sighed. "The mental health facilities wouldn't keep her because when she stayed there, she seemed fine. So they released her to us. She wants to go back there."

"It's the only place she ever felt safe," Aidan said. "Mental health facilities keep a close watch on their patients to be sure they don't hurt themselves. And they do hourly rounds to make sure everyone's accounted for. Even if The Carnations Killer wanted to go after her, it wouldn't be very easy to kill her with eyes everywhere."

Edith nodded. "While we do periodically check on our patients here, it's less secure. We have cameras at the exits and in our PT room, and we make sure they don't need anything before lights out. But we like to give our patients a sense of freedom. When I first met Marcia and heard her story, I decided to watch her myself. It helps her feel a little safer."

"That was nice of you," Shaun said.

"I saw something in her eyes when she mentioned The Carnations Killer. He scares her. It's almost like something takes over her and she becomes fanatical. I care for all of the elderly we have. If one wants 'round the clock care, well, I'm going to make sure they have it."

Edith opened the door and they piled into the small room.

A stick of a woman sat in a wheelchair, gazing out the window. Her white hair glistened in the light. Aidan couldn't tell if she was alive or not.

"Marcia?" Edith said softly. "You have company. They're FBI agents. Will you talk to them?"

Marcia slowly turned her head. Aidan could see the sleepiness in her black eyes. Her face was wrinkled and pale, and he saw the terror that took permanent residence. Her lips quivered.

"Mrs. Rivers?" Aidan said. He continued to stand a few feet away. He didn't want to risk frightening her. "My name is Agent O'Reilly. How are you doing?"

She didn't respond, only stared at them unblinkingly.

"We have a question for you," Aidan said. "It's about your daughter."

"My daughter." Her voice was low and harsh. "He killed her."

Inching closer, Aidan asked, "Who killed her, Mrs. Rivers?"

She shook her head as though memories she'd long since forgotten forced themselves to the surface. Tears slipped from the corners of her eyes and her bottom lip quivered.

"It's okay, Mrs. Rivers," Edith said. She reached for the elderly woman's hand. "You're safe here. They want to help you. Can you tell them who killed your daughter?"

"My daughter," Mrs. Rivers repeated. "He killed her."

"Who?" Aidan asked again.

She shook her head, whimpering. "I can't, I can't!" Mrs. Rivers grabbed a fistful of her silver hair and pulled. She rocked her body, a moan escaping her lips.

"Who killed your daughter?" Aidan said.

She kept her head covered in her hands when she answered: "He did. My son."

"Your son?" Shaun echoed. "Do you know why he did?"

"She tried to warn me. I didn't listen," Mrs. Rivers wailed. Her words quivered as she spoke, a mixture of fear and age. "I should have listened. And now, now he's going to kill me."

"Why would he want to kill you?" Aidan asked.

She didn't answer.

"What's your son's name?" Aidan said.

She lifted her head and Aidan saw the tears fall from her eyes as she continued to moan.

Edith kneeled next to her, putting a hand on the elderly woman's knee.

"It's okay, Mrs. Rivers," Edith said. She turned to Aidan. "I think that's enough for now. She needs to rest."

After a hesitation, Shaun put his hand on Aidan's shoulder, and when he looked at him, he motioned with a tilt of his head that it was time for them to go.

Aidan frowned but followed until Mrs. Rivers spoke again. He needed to strain to hear what she was saying.

"I think he was born evil. I didn't see it. Not until he hit me with the knife." She paused, another tear sliding down her cheeks. She rocked back and forth, hugging herself. "Georgia told me he needed help. So we took him to a psychiatrist. But it didn't help."

"What did you do with him after that?" Shaun asked.

"We put him in a boarding school, but they kicked him out." Each word seemed to cause her more pain. "Then we put him in the hospital. He said he was going to kill us. He hated us so much. I just wanted to love him. He called me. Said it was done. I went over. I saw her laying there. He'd killed her!"

"What's your son's name?" Aidan asked her again. He kneeled by her side. "Tell me."

She moaned softly before speaking. "Grant."

She reached into the pocket of her pants and pulled out a photo. She stared at it before passing it to Aidan.

Shaun and Aidan looked at the face of a young boy. He looked to be four years old. Aidan could see the smile on his face, but there appeared to be darkness in his eyes.

There was something familiar about him. He couldn't put his finger on it.

"Do you have a picture of your son that's more recent?"

"Burned," she said. "I burned them all. Except that one. He was happy then. He was happy. I wanted him happy."

"Do you know if there was any significance about your son and carnations?"

Mrs. Rivers shook her head, her eyes toward the window.

"Thank you, Mrs. Rivers," Aidan said. He squeezed her arm gently before pushing to his feet.

Shaun and Aidan walked outside where they thanked Edith for her assistance, and they left the retirement center.

70

JORDAN TRIED TO FOCUS on the latest *Playboy* issue, but he couldn't. His mind was on Duke, his beloved dog, the one he'd cared for since his dad died. He'd always loved him and couldn't imagine what his life would be like without Duke.

After the agents left, Jordan buried him next to the doghouse and set a few bricks over the grave to make sure an animal wouldn't break into the yard and start digging him out. He also created a headstone and set it at the head of the grave.

Next to burying his dad, this was the worst thing he'd ever had to do.

He called his mother to tell her what had happened. That was the second-worst thing. Jordan and his mother hadn't spoken since his dad's funeral. But for some reason, he needed her at that time.

She seemed apologetic, but he couldn't tell. He never could tell with her. His mother was always wishy-washy when it came to him. And it seldom failed that he wished he'd never picked up the phone.

Almost immediately, she changed the subject, telling him she'd seen him on the news and how proud she was of him.

Proud.

Was she really?

He spent his entire life trying to make people proud of him: his mother, his uncle, his grandparents.

The only person who breezed into Jordan's life that seemed to be truly proud was his dad. His dad had always told him to shoot for the stars, that he could be and do anything he wanted.

Jordan closed the magazine he held and tossed it on the floor next to him with a frustrated groan.

Rubbing his eyelids, Jordan tried to recall the events leading to the murder of his dog.

He'd gotten home shortly after filming the segment the agents wanted him to do, then The Carnations Killer called him. He told him he knew the report was only meant to trap him. Then he told Jordan there was a present waiting outside for him.

How did the killer know it was a trap?

Why didn't Duke bark? Did he not get the chance to fight for his life?

Duke wasn't accustomed to strangers, so anytime anyone came close he'd bark, letting Jordan know things were awry.

Jordan took a swig of his Michelob, rose from his chair, and made a beeline for the back door.

It was dark, so maybe Duke didn't see the killer in the shadows.

No.

That wasn't it.

Duke didn't bark.

He knew that was the key.

Whoever the killer was knew where Jordan lived, and he knew he had a dog. He knew Duke would have torn him to pieces if he'd approached.

So it made sense Duke knew the killer.

There was a very small handful of people who would have been able to get close enough to Duke to kill him.

His uncle was one, but he wouldn't hurt the dog, would he? He was very fond of Duke. At least that was what he'd always said.

Jordan clutched the neck of his beer bottle as his mind once again ran through the night his dog was murdered.

Duke was innocent. He didn't deserve it. And neither did those women, for that matter. Now, The Carnations Killer had Agent O'Reilly's wife.

Jordan started thinking that he might know where to find her. Or at least how. He considered calling Agent O'Reilly but decided against it. If he was right, he wanted the revenge of The Carnations Killer all to himself.

If he was right, he could be the hero by saving the woman and get justice for Duke at the same time.

Jordan threw the beer bottle across the room, screaming as loud as he could muster. Upon impact, the leftover liquid splattered against the wall and along the furniture.

There was only one person whom he'd confided in about what really happened during the FBI interview.

And that person murdered his dog.

71

As Shaun worked on aging the photo they kept from Mrs. Rivers, Aidan contacted the Troubled Teens of North Carolina.

Kyle Laurel was the director of the Bootcamp. He'd worked with teens for fifty years, and seemed to remember Grant well. According to Mr. Laurel, Grant came into the program when he'd turned fourteen years old. His mother and father didn't know how to handle him. He'd been getting in trouble in school and at home.

"I always felt sorry for the poor kid," Mr. Laurel told Aidan. "He went from foster home to foster home at a very young age, and when the Rivers finally adopted him, they immediately wanted to be rid of him because he was too much of a problem child."

"Did he ever cause you trouble?"

Mr. Laurel paused.

"Grant came to us broken. He kept to himself most of the time and was often picked on for being too skinny. He also had trouble seeing. That was part of the problem. Grant tended to be clumsy, couldn't see at a distance. When we realized it, we took him to an eye doctor who issued him glasses. Unfortunately, it only added to being picked on even more."

"His file states he was kicked out of the program. But it doesn't say why. Only that he was a risk."

"He'd begun to get into fights with the other kids. We tried to prevent it, but when he tried to cut a little girl with a kitchen knife, I knew we couldn't keep him. He was growing increasingly dangerous to others. I couldn't risk their lives."

"He went after a girl?"

"Yes," Mr. Laurel said. "She tattled on him once—we have pets to give a sense of normalcy and he'd kick them around purposefully. Sometimes they'd have to be taken to the vet for a broken leg. I remember asking him why he wanted to hurt the girl. He told me he needed to kill her for getting him in trouble."

"Do you remember what this girl looked like?"

"Pretty, she had blonde, curly hair."

"Blonde hair," Aidan said. His sister also was blonde. As were his victims. "Is there anything else that you remember, Mr. Laurel?"

"After he left the program, I think he was sent to the hospital for behavioral tests." Mr. Laurel sucked in a deep breath and pushed it out. "I wish I could have done more for him. He just needed the same as all kids do—to know that he was loved. But Grant was broken."

"Okay, I appreciate your time," Aidan said.

Ending the call, Aidan walked over to Shaun's desk. He told him about the conversation, but it didn't seem as though he was paying attention.

"Are you even listening to me?" Aidan asked him.

"You're not going to believe this," Shaun said.

"What is it?"

When Shaun leaned back and pointed to the screen, Aidan walked around the desk to take a look.

His heart skipped a few beats.

Shaun had finished aging the photo of the four-year-old boy.

And they knew him.

But they didn't know him as Grant Rivers.

They knew him as Kent Ory.

72

Aidan found an empty chair and rolled it to Shaun's desk as he pulled up Kent's background information.

The cameraman first appeared in 1997, three years after Grant Rivers left the mental hospital. During the first three years, he'd been arrested for assault with a deadly weapon twice. After he assumed the name of Kent Ory, he'd attended college and graduated with honors as a photography major.

He traveled across the United States taking photos for magazines and travel blogs until he met Jordan Blake in 2005. Soon after, he accepted the job as the reporter's cameraman, which provided him another cover to be able to travel the states and continue his killing spree.

"It makes sense," Shaun told Aidan. "He fits your profile. Man, he's been right under our noses the entire time."

"And he's virtually invisible," Aidan added. "Your everyday nice guy. Cheyenne and I saw him at the grocery store not too long ago."

Shaun looked over at him. "What happened?'

"Nothing," Aidan said. "He was talking to Cheyenne when I walked up. He apologized to me for the way Jordan Blake had been acting. He seemed sickened by how those women were treated. I never even suspected a thing."

Aidan cursed.

"Calm down, buddy," Shaun said as he rose. "He's been at this for almost twenty years. He snowed us all."

Aidan knew he was right, but he couldn't help but be angry at himself for not seeing the answer when it stared him right in the face.

They left the office for WJFX in hopes of finding Kent.

They didn't, but found themselves inside the conference room speaking with Thomas Blake.

Aidan asked Thomas what he knew about Kent.

"He's a good guy," he said. "Very kind, charming. Dedicated to his job. And he's a great husband and father."

"Have you ever seen Kent lash out? Has he ever threatened anyone?"

Thomas narrowed his eyes with a scoff. "Kent? Oh, he wouldn't hurt a fly. He's quiet. Very mellow. If I had a son, I'd want him to be just like him. I was glad when he and Jordan became friends. Kent's a good role model. And to think of everything he has been through in his life—well, I admire the kid."

"What has he been through?" Shaun asked.

They were curious about what Kent had been telling his peers. Aidan figured he told juicy stories that were enough of the truth to be believable, but also to draw out sympathy.

"Well," Thomas said with a sigh, "he'd been to several foster homes by the time he was three. No one seemed to want him until he was finally adopted. Eventually, his sister was brutally murdered by her boyfriend, I think it was. And his adoptive parents were killed in a car accident shortly after that. He was only seventeen back then."

Thomas sat back in his chair.

"Why are you suddenly interested in Kent? You don't think he's involved in these murders, do you?"

Ignoring the question, Aidan asked, "Has he or your nephew ever mentioned the name, Grant Rivers?"

"No," Thomas said, his eyes narrowed. "Who's he?"

"Kent's birth name," Shaun said. He explained Grant had been in foster care, his sister murdered, and his adoptive father killed five years prior.

Aidan added that Grant was arrested for assault twice in the following three years after being released from the hospital, and told him Kent Ory first arose shortly after that time.

After they finished speaking, Thomas let the information sink in before he slowly shook his head. "I don't believe you. He's a good man. He's Jordan's best friend and he has a lovely family."

"I'm afraid it's true," Shaun said. "We came from visiting his adoptive mother in a retirement center. She's living the remainder of her life in fear that her son will come to murder her."

Aidan told him how Kent had been everywhere since the murders began, how Jordan was so adamant Duke didn't bark before he was killed.

Thomas frowned. "Jordan always kept Duke outside because he hated strangers. There were only a few people he was accustomed to."

"Was Kent one of them?" Shaun asked.

With hesitation, Thomas nodded, his lip turning to a frown.

Aidan set the photo of the eight-year-old and the aged printout of Kent on the table.

"Does he look familiar?"

Thomas gazed at the two photos before cursing underneath his breath. He ran his hand over his face and sighed.

"Do you know where we can find Kent?" Aidan asked.

Thomas shook his head. "No, I don't. But his wife might."

Aidan handed him a sheet of paper and told him to write Kent's address down. Then they thanked him for his time and left the news station.

73

Before going to Kent Ory's home, they waited for a search warrant. Then, with a team of federal agents, they arrived at the two-story house that stood at the end of a cul-de-sac and knocked on the door. A second later, a little girl holding onto the neck of a purple bear appeared in the frame.

"Hi," Aidan said, attempting to flash her a friendly smile. "Are your parents home?"

"Mommy!" she shouted over her shoulder.

When her mother appeared, Aidan explained to her who they were and asked if they could come inside. With a frown, she allowed them in and told her daughter to go to her room and play.

Once they settled in the living area, Kent's wife asked what it was they needed. Aidan handed her the warrant and she took it, staring at the document with a frown. Looking up, she watched as the agents began searching the house.

"Do you know where your husband is?" Aidan asked.

Her eyebrows were knitted together, and her mouth hung open slightly. She swallowed hard. "Why? What's going on?"

"We have a few questions for him."

"I'd say he's working. He's a cameraman for Jordan Blake at WJFX News."

"We have suspicions that he may somehow be involved in the murders of two women and the kidnappings of two more," Shaun said.

"What?" Mrs. Ory's eyes grew round. Then she did something unexpected: burst into tears. "Oh, Kent. What have you done?"

"Ma'am?" Shaun asked. "Do you know something we should know?"

"No. I mean, yes. I don't know." She lowered herself onto the couch and put her head in her hands. Her body shivered slightly. Aidan sat next to her.

"If there's anything you know, Mrs. Ory, now's the time to say." Aidan kept his voice as compassionate as he could. He didn't want to spook her if she was involved or if she was only looking the other way because she loved her husband. Maybe he held something over her and she was afraid of him.

There wasn't a way to know unless she talked.

"I don't know anything," Mrs. Ory said. "It's impossible, right? I've known Kent for years. He couldn't have done any of these things. My husband's a good man."

"But you think something's off with him," Aidan said.

"What can you tell us about Kent?" Shaun sat on the opposite side of her.

Mrs. Ory set her head in her hands again and sobbed a few seconds more.

"A few years ago, we were on vacation in New York, then the following year he was in Texas. Women died in both states. The news reports said it was The Carnations Killer. I began to wonder about it. It wasn't the first time The Carnations Killer appeared when we were there. A feeling grew inside of me. I mentioned it to him. He laughed it off and said it was only a terrible coincidence. So, I just let it go."

"Had he given you any other reasons that he may have committed these murders?"

She shook her head. "I love him. He's not the killing type. He doesn't look like it, he doesn't act like it. He volunteers for others. He doesn't even get angry. Why would I believe the man I married is a killer? We have a child together, for goodness sake."

Her eyes shined with tears as she gazed at Aidan.

"Sir."

Aidan looked up to see one of the agents appear in the living room.

"There's a locked door."

"That's his office," she said. "He's very particular about his privacy. He gets confidential information from work and tells me to stay out. He says it's for my safety."

"Do you have the key?" Shaun asked.

She shook her head.

Shaun nodded at the agent. "Break it down."

Aidan followed the agent to the back room while Shaun stayed with Mrs. Ory.

The agent connected the heel of his foot to the office door and it splintered open. They had their weapons ready in case Kent was inside waiting but now slipped it back in the holsters.

Aidan stepped into the office and looked around the small room. It held camera equipment, files, and a bookshelf of tapes. They were labeled by dates. Aidan retrieved one of the tapes and stuck it into the TV/VCR combo.

It played automatically, and he recognized one of the victims. Her name was Nora Drake. She was the one found in the Hudson River a few weeks after he'd killed Candace.

"Sir." Aidan looked at the officer who spoke. He held a shoebox full of women's undergarments each separately contained inside ziplock backs with dates.

Aidan turned his attention to the video.

Nora was chained to the wall of what looked like a cabin. She'd already been abused for some time. Her legs held deep gashes and her abdomen had a large cut over her belly button. Nora's eyes were swollen shut.

Kent stepped in front of the camera and stared at his helpless victim hanging against the wall.

"Are you ready for some more?" he asked.

"Please. Somebody help."

The words sounded rash.

Weak.

Kent laughed.

"Help?" he repeated. "Oh honey, no one's going to help you. We're alone, you and me."

He walked to the woman and rubbed his hands on her cheek. He leaned in close. Aidan couldn't tell if he said something before pulling away.

"Tell me you love me."

The woman cried harder.

Kent connected the tire iron he held against her stomach. Blood shot out onto the floor.

Aidan heard the agent next to him gasp and from the corner of his eyes, he saw him cover his mouth with both hands.

"Tell me!"

"I love you!"

He swung the tire iron across her knees, requesting she tell him she loved him over and over again. She did until she shouted it out from the top of her lungs and he leaned over, panting from exertion.

"Oh, my goodness!"

Aidan turned to see Mrs. Ory standing in the doorway, eyes wide, hands covering her mouth.

"Oh, my—"

"Get her out of here!" Aidan said.

One of the agents obliged, leaving Shaun standing next to Aidan. The other agent had turned away, his head lowered to the carpet.

Aidan's stomach took a dive as he turned back to the video.

Kent had released Nora from her chains and used the fishing wire to choke her.

According to the time stamp, it took two minutes for his victim to breathe her last breath.

After there was no movement left from Nora, Kent ran his hand across her body. He whispered something, but it was too low for the camera audio to catch. Slowly, Kent rose and strolled to a wooden trunk. He opened it and brought out the black dress.

"You're going to look so—"

Aidan turned off the television, his eyes closed. He knew he wouldn't be able to stand to see more.

He now saw firsthand how his sister's best friend, Candace, died at the hands of The Carnations Killer.

And that was how he was treating Cheyenne right this second.

Aidan needed to find her.

Shaun told the remaining agents to collect the tapes and they left the room to find Mrs. Ory in the living room, tears streaming from her face. "What's going on? I don't understand! Who was that man in the video?"

Aidan sat on the couch next to her.

"Your husband's real name is Grant Rivers," he explained. "He changed his name a few years back, so he could get a fresh start." Aidan told her about his time during foster care, the troubled teens' program, and being sent to the hospital when nothing else worked. He told her about the assault with a deadly weapon charge.

Mrs. Ory put her head in her hands as her body shook more violently with each word Aidan spoke.

"Mommy?"

Aidan looked to see her daughter standing in the doorway, holding her bear. Her eyes drooped, and her lips turned to a quivering frown.

Shaun led the girl out of the room, telling her they needed to talk to her mom for a little bit longer.

Aidan put his hand on Mrs. Ory's shoulder.

"We need your help now. He has another woman. And if we don't find her—" Aidan swallowed, then cleared his throat. "—If we don't find her, he'll kill her. The same way he murdered that woman on the tape. Please. Do you know where your husband is?"

She looked into his eyes, blinking back tears. Finally, she shook her head. "He said he'd have to run out for a little bit. But he didn't tell me where. I assumed he and Jordan were working on a segment."

"Can you call him?"

"Is there any chance you're wrong?"

Aidan could tell in her eyes she knew the truth but needed to hold onto the hope that the father of her child wasn't a serial killer.

"I'm afraid not. I'm very sorry you're going through this right now. And I'm sorry to be insistent, but time is running out. If you call him, we can run a trace on his cell phone to find out where he is."

Mrs. Ory put her head in her hands again and let out a tearful groan. Aidan heard her mutter something underneath her breath, then she lifted her head.

"Okay." Mrs. Ory wiped her face dry of the tears and pushed to her feet. She went into the kitchen and then reappeared with her phone. "What do you want me to say?"

74

Jordan had watched Kent leave his house earlier and then followed him to the West Lake subdivision. Despite the woman in the booth, he gained entry easily. After Kent went on his way, Jordan stopped to speak to the woman.

Flashing his best Jordan Blake smile, he said, "Good evening, ma'am. I'm with the guy in front of me. He's my cameraman." Jordan showed off his credentials.

"Ah, I've seen you on TV," she gushed in a thick southern accent. "You've been reporting on The Carnations Killer."

"Right," Jordan said with a chuckle. "Yeah, I'm actually on the way to interview one of his victims. So, can I get through?"

"Sure!"

The arms blocking his way lifted. Jordan thanked her, then took off to catch up with his cameraman.

He spotted Kent before he turned left, then a right, and into the driveway of a large house.

Jordan pulled to a stop at the edge of the street to watch as Kent parked next to a golden Camry. He climbed out of his car and went inside.

Jordan got out of his car and jogged toward the house.

All the shades were drawn, so he wasn't able to see inside. Slowly, he turned the knob and opened the door. He kept his ears out for sound but heard nothing.

The house was dark.

Where did Kent go?

It was cold inside, but he wasn't sure if that was why his back crawled with shivers.

He paused to listen carefully for any noise.

He still didn't want to believe his friend was The Carnations Killer, but the evidence he'd put together told him differently.

After all these years of working with someone, you never know what they're capable of.

Murder.

Torture.

Evil.

All wrapped up in a man who showed his charismatic and good-natured side.

He considered the killers of the past that seemed normal: Ted Bundy, H.H. Holmes, John Wayne Gacy...none of them *seemed* like killers to the outside world.

Now added to the list was his friend and colleague, Kent Ory.

After a few minutes of surveying the house, Jordan wondered if Kent left. But why would he? And how?

He stood in the master bedroom upstairs when he heard a faint scream.

"Help me! Somebody, please!"

The words were laced with tears.

He tried to figure out where the screams were coming from, but he couldn't tell. He followed the sounds downstairs until he spotted a door by the staircase.

Jordan reached toward the knob but froze when there was a tap on his left shoulder. He turned slowly until he was face-to-face with Kent.

"Boo." Kent smiled. "Did I scare you?"

Before Jordan had a chance to react, Kent reached toward Jordan's neck.

A shock of electricity exploded in him, and he released a strained groan, unable to stop the involuntary convulsions of his muscles.

Jordan fell hard to the ground.

"I really wish you hadn't followed me," Kent was saying. "You really need to learn to mind your own business."

Kent grabbed Jordan's arms and dragged him down a few steps, then after a few minutes, he found himself being chained to the wall.

"Wake up, buddy." Kent patted his cheek. "Can you hear me?"

Jordan began muttering and Kent grabbed his chin, shaking his head.

"Wake up, brother. We've got to have a little chat."

Slowly, Jordan's vision cleared. "Kent. What are you doing?" He tried to jerk his hands from the wall.

"I hate having to kill people that interrupt my work," Kent frowned. "Why couldn't you have just left it alone?"

Jordan looked around and saw a woman hanging next to him. Her head hung loosely, but she was alive and alert. Her body shivered either from pain or the cold. Maybe both.

"That's the agent's wife," Kent said proudly.

He walked over and grabbed the woman's neck, turning her face toward him. She was full of tear-stained dirt.

"Beautiful, isn't she?"

"Why are you doing this?" Jordan asked.

Kent shrugged. "It's all part of the game. I was just going to kill her. Leave her for our FBI friend to find. You know, after he got home from looking at your dead dog. I mean, she isn't really my type, you know?"

He walked back to Jordan, his eyes shining with excitement.

"But then I saw her in bed, so beautiful, so peaceful. I figured why not?"

"What about Elaine?"

"What about her?"

"She loves you. And Jamie. How could you do this to them?"

Kent tilted his head back, erupting in a manic laugh.

"They won't know. I'm too good at my job, Jordan, my pal. I am *way* overrated for my uses, and everybody knows it. All we have to do is leave. Trust me. I can always get a job taking pictures. Or maybe something technical. Or something low key such as a waiter. Kent Ory always has a plan."

Jordan jerked at the chains binding him. "Kent, this isn't who you are, okay? I know you. We go to bars after work. You're my wingman, right? I'm your daughter's godfather for crying out loud."

He put on a mock frown. "Unfortunately, I'm going to have to fire you from that job. I'm so sorry. It's because I'm going to have to kill you. Can't leave witnesses, you know."

"Just tell me why. Why are you doing this? If you're going to kill me, I think I deserve that much."

"Yeah," Kent said. "Guess I could give you that much. It's all because of my sister. She's the one who said I was crazy." Kent paced the basement. "Can you fathom that? So what? I threw the cat across the yard. I was only playing. Having a little fun. Isn't that something children are supposed to do? And then when I heard her tell Mom what I did, I was sent to bed without any supper." Kent let out a laugh. "But don't worry—I got even. I always do."

"What did you do?"

"Killed her dog. I buried him somewhere." He laughed again. "I forget where. My sister was so frantic trying to find him. I think she cried for weeks."

"They'll catch you," Jordan warned. "You know that, right?"

"No, they won't. Aren't you listening? I told you I'm going to leave. Get your head out of the clouds for once and pay attention, buddy. I already got offered a job in South Dakota. So, I'll be moving. I told you, I always have a plan."

Jordan decided to play a bluff. "They're onto you now, Kent. They know where I am. They're coming for you."

Kent walked toward him. "Really? Is that so? Well, in that case, I have no choice but to kill you and the girl right now." He looked over at her. "Do you want me to do her first?"

He stepped away to grab a tire iron from the table. Holding it tightly in his hand, he stood in a batting position.

"Batter up!"

"No, don't!" Jordan's heart hammered in his chest. "I lied. They aren't coming. Please don't hurt her."

Kent frowned. "Why do you have to spoil my fun? Aren't we friends?"

"Listen, you can put a stop to this, okay?" Jordan said. "Please."

"My sister was beautiful, you know?" Kent said. "But she was always so jealous of me. That's why she convinced my parents I was crazy. I had finally found a home. You know what it's like being bounced around from house to house with everyone calling you *evil*? I just wanted a place to belong! Somebody to just accept me for who I was! But she wanted me out of the picture. And her little scheme worked. But I got my revenge. I stabbed her to death. Her white-trash boyfriend got the blame for it, too."

"Okay, so you killed your sister because she hated you. What did the other women do to you?"

Kent smiled. "They reminded me of her. I just couldn't escape dear sweet Georgia. Then I soon found something out."

He walked back over to Jordan and leaned into his ear to whisper the words.

"I rather liked it."

75

"Kent," Jordan said. "Stop what you're doing."

"Why?" Kent asked, pretending to whine. He stamped his foot. "Why is it every time a prisoner knows they are going to die, they have a tiny bit of hope that if they beg like worthless dogs, they'll be freed?"

Jordan didn't respond. Despite the cold, beads of sweat trickled down his forehead.

"I really want an answer," Kent said. He went to work at unchaining the FBI agent's wife's wrists.

Jordan's wrists were sore from trying to break his chains.

Kent tossed the girl onto the tarp like she was nothing but a rag doll. He grabbed the tire iron from the table and turned to stare at her. She tried to roll to her knees, but each time, she fell back down.

"Don't do it, man," Jordan said when Kent neared the girl.

Kent ignored the plea and connected the edge of the tire iron to her knees. The only sound the woman made was a sharp, agonizing gasp.

"Stop it!"

Kent landed another blow against her temple. She fell backward, hitting her head on the cemented ground.

"Kent!"

"Will you *shut up*?"

Kent ran to him and slammed the tire iron against Jordan's temple.

Stars exploded in front of his eyes.

Kent hit him again and now Jordan could taste blood in his mouth.

Jordan fought against the pain and looked into Kent's angry face. He forced a weak laugh, which was even more painful, but he didn't care.

"Is that all you've got, friend?" He lifted his head to see the chains. "You've got me chained to the wall and you're beating me. Why is that? Are you afraid I'll manage to defend myself? Come on, man. You want to act all macho and everything, fight me like a man."

"I'm going to tape your mouth shut." Kent grabbed a roll from the nearby table and drew out a long slip of tape.

"That's right, I forgot," Jordan said. "You're not a man. You kidnap women, beat them until they can't take anymore, then you murder them."

Kent jerked the piece of tape from the roll.

"You want to know the real reason you never could find a happy family?" Jordan taunted. "It's because even at a young age, they knew you wouldn't grow up to be a man. They knew you wouldn't be worth it. That you weren't worth loving."

Kent placed the tape over Jordan's mouth.

"I said shut up," he said.

He turned to face the girl.

"Reporters ruin all the fun, don't they, Cheyenne? I'm sorry about that. Where were we? Ah. Yes. Now I remember."

He swung the tire iron against the woman's shoulder.

Kent's laugh faded as Jordan fought against the pain. He couldn't pass out. He refused.

He looked around the dark basement, trying to figure out a way to save the girl and himself.

But unless Kent unchained him, he was helpless.

Something vibrated against the far table. Kent stepped over to retrieve the phone.

"Y'all sit still, all right? I'll be back in a second."

Kent disappeared up the stairs and then the door closed behind him.

Jordan watched as Agent O'Reilly's wife lay on the ground.

She turned to face him, her face shining with blood and tears. She crawled to the table where the keys were, but she couldn't stand to grab them.

Come on, you can do it, he thought.

As though she read his mind, she tried to lift herself but again failed.

This time, she stayed on the floor and continued to cry.

He spoke through the tape but knew she wouldn't be able to understand him.

"I can't do it," she cried. "I think he broke my knees."

He wanted to tell her that if she could get him down, he'd protect her.

The woman's eyes skirted to the door before she tried to heave herself to her feet again. Finally, she was able to grip the keys in her hands.

Jordan watched, silently urging her not to give up.

O'Reilly's wife crawled to where Jordan hung, but she still couldn't stand long enough to unchain him.

She paused to cry some more, then she used his legs to pull herself to her feet. She slipped the key into the slot and turned. Jordan's right arm was now free.

They looked over at the click of the door opening.

Footsteps descended the stairs.

76

"SORRY GUYS, THAT WAS my wife—" Kent stopped speaking when he saw Jordan fumble with the key to get his other arm loose.

Jordan managed to unchain himself and fall to the ground with a soft thud.

"Really?" Kent said with a smirk.

Jordan ripped the tape from his mouth, glaring at the killer.

"I'm going to kill you," Jordan hissed. "You killed Duke."

Kent saw the anger flash in the reporter's eyes.

It was amusing.

"Go ahead, then," Kent said, spreading his arms. "You want to fight? I'm right here."

With a growl, Jordan lurched toward him, but Kent dodged out of the way. Jordan ran headfirst into the wall.

Kent grabbed a fistful of hair and pulled him to the ground and kicked him in the face, then kicked him again.

He continued kicking him until Jordan blocked one of the kicks and pull Kent on top of him. They rolled along the floor until Kent found Jordan's neck and began squeezing.

"I don't have time for this," he hissed.

Jordan grasped at Kent's hand, but couldn't get him to let go. Finally, the reporter passed out. After making sure his old friend was still breathing, Kent dragged him back to the wall and heaved him to the chains to secure him.

He turned to face Cheyenne, who had curled herself in a ball against the far wall.

"That was a mistake."

"Please," Cheyenne whispered as he neared.

Ignoring her, he kicked her in the face.

"You must be punished."

He walked over to Jordan.

"For attempting to help Mr. Hero escape, he will take the punishment. And you have to watch. Then I think I'll take off early today. The wife wants me to run a few errands for her."

He looked at Jordan, who was slowly coming to.

"You ready for your punishment, buddy?"

"You're insane," Jordan said, his voice above a whisper.

"Well, that's not a very nice thing to say." Kent turned his lips to a frown. He grabbed the tire iron and swung it across Jordan's knees.

The reporter cried out in pain.

"That's so if you do manage to get out of your chains again, you won't be able to walk. You'll crawl. Like the disappointing slug that you are."

Kent hit him again.

"You know," he said after Jordan finished screaming, "at first, I didn't want to let you in on my little secret because I really liked you. But truthfully, I think this brings us closer together, right?"

Jordan glared at him. "You know what, *buddy*?" he said through his teeth, "I feel sorry for you. I feel sorry for whatever happened along the line that made you pathetic."

Kent only laughed. He looked back at Cheyenne. "Can you believe this guy?"

He began walking toward the agent's wife. As she whimpered, he pulled her back to where he had laid the tarp and tossed her on top.

"No one made me this way," Kent said, his eyes on Cheyenne. "A man has needs. You know, like you need to feel important at the top. Agent O'Reilly needs a chill pill. This is mine."

"You need to grow a pair," Jordan said.

Letting his shoulders rise and fall, he said, "Well, anyway, I need to finish up so I can take off."

77

THE TRACE ON KENT'S cell phone led the agents to the West Lake subdivision. They pulled their vehicles to the next neighborhood. They didn't want to risk tipping off Kent by moving in too close. It was still daylight, so they didn't have a lot to their advantage.

Shaun and Aidan, along with a few other federal agents and members of the SWAT team, put on their vests and trailed along the sidewalk, weapons ready to fire if needed.

Aidan hoped it wouldn't come to that, but they were given the authority to use whatever force necessary.

Aidan spotted a little girl peering out her window in the house at the left. A few seconds later, an older boy looked out, then jerked her by the arm to pull her away. Aidan instructed some of the agents to start clearing nearby houses. Aidan didn't want to chance they would find themselves in the line of fire.

They were now at the front of the house. Ten agents and SWAT members circled the back of the house, five taking the sides and the rest, including Aidan and Shaun, were stationed in the front.

Aidan reached over and tried the knob slowly, but found it was locked.

He nodded to the men holding the battering ram. Once they rushed the door, flash bangs were tossed inside, then the agents filed into the residence.

They continued to maintain radio silence as they spread throughout the house.

Inside was dark and cold—Aidan could see his breath climbing the air.

A few men headed up the stairs while the rest took the bottom level. Shaun noticed the door by the staircase.

Standing to one side of the door, Aidan held his weapon at the ready and he let Shaun reach for the knob.

Then the lights went out.

EXCEPT FOR JORDAN'S ARRIVAL and stupid attempt to escape, Kent decided things went pretty well today.

He was happy.

And the escape attempt allowed his adrenaline to rush. It was exhilarating.

Turning to face the reporter, he said, "You've been quiet, my friend. I'd almost forgotten you were here."

Jordan didn't seem to be in the mood for chatting since he'd taken the harsh punishment for trying to escape. The gray duct tape was now red due to the blood.

"What do you think of this idea?" Kent said. He stepped over to where Jordan hung and leaned against the wall next to him. "How about I do both Agent O'Reilly and his little woman a favor and go ahead and kill her? I can do that when I come in tomorrow. I'll bring you some pain killers and we can make a party out of it."

Jordan's eyes were closed, so Kent slapped him until he woke.

"Don't fall asleep yet. I really want your opinion." He smiled and leaned into Jordan's ear. "We can catch it on camera. We can film her taking her very last breath. Then I'll leave it for our FBI friend to enjoy." Kent laughed. "It'd serve him right, wouldn't you agree?"

Kent stepped away from the reporter and moved to where the girl lay semi-conscious. He kneeled and placed his hand on her chest to be sure she was still breathing.

She was.

"After all," Kent said, "he did accuse you of killing those women."

He heard a loud bang coming from upstairs, followed by a pop and soft creaking.

Placing a finger to his lips he said, "Shh. I think we have company."

Kent ran to the fuse box, switched the lights off in the house, and hurried to grab a fistful of brown hair in his hands. He dragged Cheyenne to her feet and backed away toward the desk where he had created an ideal exit.

He'd learned the last time not to have a point of operation unless there was an easy escape.

He gripped Cheyenne's hair and prepared for whoever it was that decided to visit.

He secretly hoped it was the agent.

SHAUN OPENED THE BASEMENT door and Aidan pointed his gun down the stairs. It was dark below.

With Shaun close behind him, Aidan took one slow step, then another until he reached the bottom. He heard a sound to his left, and when he looked, he saw Jordan Blake hanging in the dim light of the flashlight.

Through the blood trickling down his eyes, he saw Aidan too.

He motioned toward the back of the basement. Aidan nodded that he understood.

"Grant Rivers," Aidan said into the darkness, edging closer to the back. "Show yourself."

KENT WAS PLEASED THAT Agent O'Reilly knew his real name.

Go figure.

He continued to prove he was a worthy opponent.

"Okay," he said. "We're coming out. But let me warn you, I wouldn't start shooting if I were you."

WHEN KENT SPOKE, HE sounded as though he were singing.

Well aware of the blood pumping in his veins, Aidan gripped the gun's handle, trying to steady his shaky hands.

"We're coming out," Kent said again.

When he appeared, he held a woman in his arms.

But not just a woman.

Cheyenne.

78

Cheyenne's face was almost unrecognizable. One eye was swollen shut, the other swollen but open. Her lips were torn and bleeding. Her knees were a mess and Aidan could only imagine what the inside of her must look like.

The nightgown she still wore clung to her body and had begun to tear. He saw the bruises on her skin and he wanted to shoot Kent square in the head. But he couldn't risk that he'd hit Cheyenne.

She cried as Kent held her in his arms.

"Let her go," Aidan said.

"I do that, and you'll shoot me." Kent smiled. "So, guess we're at a standstill."

"You let her go and I won't," Aidan said. His vision clouded. He couldn't see anything except the serial killer who held onto his wife as if she were a shield.

"But we're having too much fun," Kent said in mock excitement. "You know, you have excellent taste in women."

Cheyenne shrieked as he jerked her head back.

"This one really is something special."

Aidan's mind raced, trying to figure out how to get Cheyenne away from him.

Shaun moved to the side, while another agent flanked Kent from the other direction. Aidan remained in the center.

"Uh-uh. Get back," Kent said. He revealed a switchblade and positioned it against Cheyenne's throat.

Shaun and the agent stopped moving.

"Okay, Kent," Aidan said. "Why don't we talk about this? Okay? I'm setting my weapon down now."

Kent watched as Aidan did as promised.

"Send everybody else up."

"Forget it," Shaun said, his weapon still pointing at the target.

Aidan kept his hand in front of him to show he wasn't going to do anything rash. His eyes on Kent, he told Shaun to go back upstairs. "I'll be fine."

"I'm not leaving you with this maniac," Shaun said.

"Go," he said. "Please."

Shaun hesitated, then backed away, ushering the others to follow.

He kept his eyes on Kent the entire time.

Using his thumb, Aidan pointed to Jordan. "How's he doing?"

"He's fine, aren't you, buddy?" Kent said. "We had a few issues here and there, but I think he finally figured out for once to just shut up."

Aidan glanced at Jordan hanging on the wall, trying to keep his head up.

"I'm sure the tape helps." Aidan turned back to the cameraman.

"How'd you finally get smart enough to catch up with me?" Kent asked.

"Your first victim. She was your sister."

"Adopted sister," Kent corrected. "I could not stand her, you know? Always gotta be in my business."

"So you took care of it."

"Yeah. I did."

"When you killed her, was it planned? Or did something she say set you off?"

"Well," Kent said with a sigh. "I'd fantasized about it. But I was only seventeen, you know. I didn't know what I was doing. I grabbed the knife and just started poking her with it until I realized she was dead."

"Then you killed Karen Jones by strangling her with your hands a few days later."

Kent shrugged. "I had an itch. After my sister died, I felt...excited. Hey! A little trivia for you! Did you know Karen was my first real girlfriend?"

"No."

"Well, now you do. She nagged me the same way my sister did. I think she wanted to break up with me that night. I can't really be sure."

"Why did you keep changing your MO? First, you used a knife on your sister, then you used your hands, then stockings, until you decided on switching to fishing wires and tasers."

"The knife was too messy," Kent said as though they were having a normal conversation. He gestured with the knife he held as some did with their hands. "I got blood on the walls, sheets, myself. Let me tell you something, it is not as easy as it looks getting blood stains out. Even with Clorox 2, which my dear mother worshiped. Or plain ole bleach. The whole thing was too messy to bother with."

Kent laughed as though he told a joke. Aidan kept an eye on his weapon in case he found an opening to dive for it, but Kent was careful. He seemed to know he was only trying to distract him. Despite being figured out, he appeared confident things would still turn out the way he wanted.

Aidan started wondering if he planned on them finding him here.

If he wanted to take things to the next level.

"And it took too long for them to finally die if I strangled them with my hands," Kent continued. "Even my third victim, I had to beat a brick over her head because she was just too stubborn to die. The stocking did the trick, but it was too clean. I liked seeing a little blood. So, enter the fishing wire."

Cheyenne squirmed in his arms, forcing him to pull her hair back.

"It was enough blood to satisfy me while not leaving a mess."

Kent put his lips to her neck and bit her.

She whimpered.

"And the tasers, I thought it'd be interesting to try. I saw a man get tased once by the police. He was a big man too. Like a sumo wrestler or something. Anyway, when he got tased..." Kent chuckled at the memory, "...he squealed like a pig. So, I thought it'd be interesting to try. Some of my women passed out, which was a bit disappointing. But most of the time, it was fun."

He sighed.

Aidan still didn't have a way to get to Cheyenne without risking her life.

"Well, it's been loads of fun. I hate to cut and run, but, well, I've gotta run."

Before Aidan realized what was happening, Kent sliced Cheyenne's throat and pushed her toward him.

He caught her before she fell to the ground. Aidan held her throat to keep the blood from oozing out.

"Shaun!" With one hand on Cheyenne's neck and the other on the radio, he said, "He's escaping from an opening in the basement. I repeat the perpetrator is escaping."

When the last word came out, Shaun and a few of the agents flew down the stairs, weapons at the ready.

But Kent had already gotten out.

"We need a bus," Shaun called through the radio. "Person of interest Grant Rivers aka Kent Ory is en route. He's wearing a plaid blue dress shirt and a pair of jeans. He has wire-rimmed glasses and auburn hair. Use whatever means necessary to bring him down."

"It's okay," Aidan said to Cheyenne. "You're going to be fine, love. I've got you."

Shaun found a towel to place on the neck wound.

Douglas was in the process of unchaining Jordan from his shackles.

Aidan looked at Shaun, who gave him a quick, solemn nod, letting him know he understood what Aidan was thinking.

Kent Ory was escaping again.

79

Aidan rode with Cheyenne in the ambulance as Shaun remained behind to process the crime scene.

The EMTs had patched Cheyenne's neck and gave her medicine to help ease the pain, but keep her alert. Aidan held her hand.

"You're doing good, love," he said.

She still couldn't speak, but the tears behind her smile told him she felt safe. He told her he loved her, and he wasn't going anywhere.

When they arrived at the hospital, the orderlies worked together to rush Cheyenne to the operating room. Since Aidan couldn't go inside, he lingered outside the door, pacing the floor.

His phone vibrated against his hip, so he answered.

It was Laura.

"I just got home, what's happening? Where's my sister? What happened to my bedroom? Aidan, answer me!"

"It's okay," Aidan said, trying to calm the frantic girl. It didn't work, and he understood what she was feeling. "Cheyenne's fine. She's in the operating room now at Georgia Regents."

"She's what!" Aidan heard something bang on the other end of the line. "I'm on the way."

Before he could respond, Laura ended the call.

Aidan leaned against the wall. Despite saving Cheyenne, he felt defeated.

Kent escaped their grasp again. However, now that they knew who killed ninety-two people and attempted to kill three more, they had the upper hand.

"Agent O'Reilly."

Aidan glanced over to see Tara and Zane walking his way.

"Agent Henderson briefed us. How is Cheyenne?"

"Still in surgery," Aidan said with a frown. "I haven't heard from Shaun yet. He got away, didn't he?"

Zane nodded. "He escaped on foot through the neighbors' yards. But we do have an APB out on him and alerted security at the airports, as well as set up roadblocks. I'm confident we'll get him."

"I don't know," Aidan said, staring across the hall. "He's smart. He doesn't do anything unless it's planned. That includes his escape." Aidan looked at Tara. "I have a feeling he was glad we found him."

Tara narrowed her eyes. "You're saying he wanted us to catch him?"

"He didn't want us to catch him, really," Aidan said. "I think he wanted to up his game. Push himself close to the edge and see how far we'd go." Clearing his throat, Aidan said, "To see how far I would go. When he left that album, he had to know we'd find out that his first victim was his sister."

"Agent O'Reilly?"

They looked at the doctor stepping out of the swinging operating room doors.

Pushing himself off the wall, he asked, "How is she?"

"She'll be fine. We're going to take her to recovery, then move her to a room where she'll stay for about a week or so for observation. But there shouldn't be long-lasting damage. Just a lot of physical therapy. She has a long road ahead of her."

Relief coursed through him. He tapped his head against the wall, then looked back at the doctor. "Can I see her?"

The doctor nodded and took him into the recovery room. Cheyenne was medicated but seemed to be sleeping peacefully. They'd stitched the cut on her neck, as well as some of the deeper cuts on her skin. His heart broke as he scanned her bruised body.

He put his hand in hers and leaned close to her ear to tell her she was safe now and he loved her.

After minutes passed, one of the orderlies arrived and Aidan was told she needed to be moved. He kissed Cheyenne's forehead and left the room.

"Aidan!" Laura came rushing toward him, eyes clouded with hysterics.

He wrapped her in a tight hug and whispered that Cheyenne was out of surgery and would be fine.

"What happened?" she said through her tears.

Tara motioned that she'd touch base with him later and he took Laura's hand and led her to a nearby bench. He told her most of what he was allowed to say to the family of victims, which was that Cheyenne had been kidnapped, but she survived.

Laura's eyes filled with tears.

"Why didn't you call me?"

"Everything happened so fast. I didn't want to worry you," he said. "And I was too focused on finding her. But Cheyenne's fine. She's strong."

"Did you catch him?"

Aidan swallowed, knowing the question was coming but wishing he could avoid it.

"Not yet." Wrapping his arm around Laura's shoulder, he kissed the top of her head. "But we will. We know who we're looking for now. It's only a matter of time."

80

It had been a week since they've discovered the identity of The Carnations Killer. They still hadn't found him, despite stationing a good number of law enforcement on every possible exit route including all airports in the state of Georgia.

Tara made arrangements to place Kent's wife and daughter in protective custody and stationed men outside his house in case he returned.

There were speculations that Kent had escaped before they'd issued the blockades, but Aidan still believed he was somewhere in the state.

Possibly still in this very city.

Kent liked to lay low, so Aidan figured he'd find a place to do just that if he hadn't already planned one in advance.

The question was where.

Cheyenne was still in the hospital recovering from the injuries she had sustained. Laura and Aidan fussed over her to be sure she didn't need anything, and although she told them they didn't need to, Aidan was pretty sure she enjoyed the attention.

He was torn between the need to stay with Cheyenne as she healed or joining the manhunt. In the end, it was Shaun who insisted Aidan deal with family first and let him handle business.

It didn't keep Aidan from digging deeper into Grant Rivers' past, however. Because his records were sealed, Aidan had to cut through a lot of red tape at the hospital Grant was admitted to in order to learn that he spent months in shock therapy. His parents had hoped to "shock" him into getting rid of the desire to inflict pain on others.

Aidan also learned that when Kent was a child, he'd suffered sexual abuse by his sister. He imagined that had elicited the desire to hurt women who resembled her. It was undetermined whether his adopted parents knew it and looked the other way or were blind to what their older daughter was doing.

His biological parents had been murdered when he was a child. He and his biological brother had been placed in foster homes, and eventually were separated. His brother was privately adopted by a family who could only take one child, leaving Grant in foster care. Very often, foster situations weren't the best for a child, which was in the case for Grant.

Except for one.

According to the families of Grant's foster parents, they adored the four-year-old. It was said that Grant was a bright child, and fun-loving. The couple who took him in had been murdered, along with the three other kids who lived with them.

The first responders to the murder found Grant hiding inside a wooden chest. The young boy didn't say much of anything about the incident. Inside the chest was a bouquet of carnations.

Because Grant's foster mother was found a few feet away, it was assumed she'd attempted to hide Grant. It was unclear whether the killer knew Grant was inside the chest or not.

After the murders, Grant was moved to two more foster homes until he was adopted by the Rivers.

Aidan wanted to feel sorry for him. He really did. But he didn't believe people were born evil. Neither did he believe that the situations they are put through make them evil.

Every human being is given a choice whether to be good or bad. Grant Rivers made his, and more than ninety people paid the price.

Aidan rubbed his tired eyes. He started realizing how little sleep he'd had since the hunt began ten years ago.

And it had only been a week since Cheyenne was kidnapped.

A lot had happened.

His cell phone vibrated, and he looked at the caller ID. It read *unavailable*. He glanced at Cheyenne, who slept, and her sister, who sat next to the bed, reading a magazine.

The phone continued to ring as he told Laura he was going to step outside. After he entered the hallway, Aidan pressed *accept call*.

"O'Reilly."

"How is she?"

Kent didn't bother disguising his voice this time. They knew who he was, so why should he even bother?

"She's doing great, no thanks to you."

"Ah, that's wonderful," Kent said, masking joy. "I'm so glad she's back with you, Aidan...you don't mind if I start calling you by your first name, do you? I mean, after all, we've been through a lot over the years, haven't we? Anyway, I have to admit, it didn't turn out exactly as I'd hoped, but it has been dreadfully fun working with you. But you don't have to worry about me any longer."

"Why? You going to do us a favor and kill yourself?"

Kent released a low snicker.

"Not quite, friend. Not quite."

Aidan heard a whistle in the background, but couldn't make out what it was, or where it was coming from.

"Well, Aidan, I believe this is where we part ways," Kent said. "I'll have to catch you one of these days and see how you're doing. Enjoy your lovely Cheyenne."

He ended the call as Aidan spotted Shaun walking toward him.

"How's Cheyenne?" he asked.

Looking at him, his mind reeling, his question barely registered.

81

THE STEAM ENGINE BLEW smoke into the clear blue sky and the whistle echoed into the distance.

Kent leaned against the wall of the empty boxcar, ready to leave Georgia for his next adventure. He knew he couldn't accept the job in South Dakota like he'd planned, so he decided to try something new. Maybe he would spend a year, possibly two, in Hawaii.

He unzipped his backpack and pulled out his passports. He had four different names to choose from. Kent decided it'd be interesting to build a brand new career as Caleb Jenkins. He figured Caleb could be a great writer. He could see it now: a writer of mysteries. He could even draw from his own experiences. After all, write what you know, right?

Kent chuckled at the thought. It was a grand idea.

So, he put his new identity in his shirt pocket and slipped the others back in the bag. Next, Kent took out a photo album. It was his original of all of his women. He was disappointed he lost two of them. And he wished he could have retrieved a few of his tapes so he didn't have to rely on his memories.

But it would have been a major risk going back.

He needed to get to the train before it departed, so he could get over the state line. Kent had disguised himself with a mustache and goatee. If one of the engineers happened to discover him, he wouldn't be immediately recognized.

From the rags he stole, he'd look like a homeless man trying to find a place to sleep.

So far, most everything had gone according to plan.

He'd gotten under O'Reilly's skin. He could tell by the strain in his voice. And that day when they came face to face, the look of fear in his eyes was priceless.

Even Kent had to admit he was lucky to escape. Thankfully there were enough trees around to conceal himself as he ducked behind the other houses.

Kent looked at his watch. It was seven-thirty. The train should have started moving by now.

He frowned.

It seemed quiet outside the walls. The whistle didn't sound anymore.

After waiting another five minutes, Kent decided he should take a peek outside to see if he could tell what the holdup was.

He pushed to his feet and slid the door open.

"Can we see your ticket please?"

Agent O'Reilly stood before him, with what looked like an entire army. They had their weapons drawn, pointed directly at him.

Well.

That's interesting.

Kent smiled at O'Reilly. "You're smarter than I give you credit for. How did you know where to find me?"

"Next time you call, I suggest you end the call before your transportation toots its horn," O'Reilly said.

He heard the sense of satisfaction lacing his words.

"Thanks for the tip," Kent said.

"Grant Rivers, step off the train," O'Reilly said.

Kent did as he was told and stood in front of the agent who had spent ten years of his life tailing after him.

"Well, guess all good rides must eventually come to an end," Kent said with a smirk.

"Turn around."

When he obliged, O'Reilly cuffed him as another agent read him his rights.

"I figured you'd want to kill me, Agent O'Reilly," Kent said, "If you ever got this close to me again."

"I'd thought about it," O'Reilly said. "But then I decided my idea of fun is watching you rot in prison. So, that's exactly what I'm going to do."

Kent snickered. "Want me to bring the popcorn?"

O'Reilly pushed him toward another agent and he was led away from the train yard.

82

"So, WHAT WAS IT like when you caught him?" Laura's tone was evident of excitement. "Did you have to fight him?"

Shaun laughed, and Aidan rolled his eyes.

"No, I think all the guns in his face kept him from resisting," he said.

Laura turned her lips to a frown. "I thought you guys had action in your type of career."

"Trying to find the identity of one man for ten years isn't action enough for you?" Aidan said.

"How does it feel to finally have caught him?" Cheyenne asked.

Aidan considered the question. He knew some of his peers would begin to feel empty after hunting a killer for so long. They searched for them relentlessly until it engrossed them, and they'd forget who they were before.

So how did he feel about it?

Aidan regarded Cheyenne, remembering the pain his sister felt when she learned of Candace's murder, how he felt arriving at the crime scene and seeing Candace. He reflected on the chase and remembered the fear when Cheyenne was missing.

"Relieved," Aidan said. "Like I can finally rest."

She smiled at him and reached for his hand. He kissed her.

"Oh," Aidan said, suddenly remembering the bet he and Cheyenne had made a while back. He turned to Laura. "So, you were dating someone in Florida, right? A heart surgeon. How'd that work out?"

Laura shrugged. "Turns out he wasn't my type."

"How long did it last?" Aidan asked.

"I don't know, a month?"

"Oh, really," Cheyenne said, her face brightening in amusement. "You chucked him to the side before you returned home?"

"Well, *chucking* is kind of harsh," Laura said defensively.

Shaun chuckled as he watched the banter.

"Either way, I have a slave for a month," Cheyenne said. Aidan could hear the edge of satisfaction in her words.

"What's that supposed to mean?" Laura said, narrowing her eyes. She looked from Aidan to Cheyenne, whose smile stretched from ear to ear.

"Well, doesn't make much of a difference," Aidan said, pointing to her leg. "You can't walk anyway, so I'd say you've got a slave no matter."

Cheyenne shook her head with admission. "Nice try, buddy. But this doesn't count."

"Aww, c'mon," he said. "Not fair."

"Well," Laura said. "While you two work that out, I'm going to run to the cafeteria and get myself some lunch." She looked at Shaun. "You seem like you're aching to buy. Care to join me?"

A broad smile spread across his dark face. "I'd be honored."

"Well, what's the holdup?" Laura said, a smirk forming on her lips.

"I like her," Shaun said to Aidan as Laura went ahead of him.

"I like her, too," Aidan said. "But I also like you, so let me warn you. She goes through men like people goes through underwear."

Shaun let his shoulder rise, then fall as he made his way for the door. "Who knows? I just might be the one. Catch you later."

When the door closed after him, Aidan climbed onto the bed to get close to Cheyenne.

"I was really scared I'd never see you again," he said. "I didn't know what I'd do without you."

"I wasn't," Cheyenne said. "I knew you'd find me."

"You did? How?"

"I had faith in you even when you didn't," Cheyenne said. "I always did."

"I'm sorry I worried you all this time. Things will change from now on. I promise."

"First," Cheyenne said, running a hand through his hair, "don't make promises you can't keep. Second, don't change yourself for me. I love you for the man you are and the compassion you show to others. And third, I think you should turn down the Quantico job."

Aidan pivoted so he could see her better. "When did you come to that decision?"

"When he was holding me. You had just lowered your gun."

"So...he was about to kill you in front of me and you made the decision that you didn't want me to be a teacher at Quantico?" Aidan laughed, but it was an uneasy one. The image of seeing her in Kent's grasp was still unsettling.

"I've never seen you work in situations like that," Cheyenne said. "You were amazing. And this is something you've done for ten years. It's something you love doing. If you go to Quantico, you won't be happy."

"You're a hard woman to figure out," he said.

She laughed and linked her fingers with his.

SHAUN AND AIDAN BRIEFED Tara and Zane, with Hansford on a conference call about the events at the train yard. They'd congratulated Aidan for a job done well.

Aidan told them it was a team effort. Shaun told Aidan he was only being modest, but Aidan didn't want to take all the credit. It didn't sit right with him.

Afterward, he took Cheyenne home to Laura's house and helped settle her on the couch. The doctors told him to be sure she kept her knees elevated and on ice. She was going to have to walk with a cane around the house and ride in a wheelchair if she happened to go out.

Shaun had asked Laura out on a real date and she accepted. Aidan was being honest to Shaun about wanting him to be careful where Laura was concerned, but he figured Shaun was a big boy. He'd been warned and as a federal agent hunting serial killers, Aidan was sure he could take care of himself against Cheyenne's wild sister.

Aidan stepped into the kitchen to get Cheyenne a glass of water she'd requested.

When he got the ice, his cell phone rang. Multitasking by filling the glass with water, he answered the phone without first checking his caller ID.

"Hello. This is a collect call from 'Kent Ory' at Georgia State Government Corrections. Press one to accept, two to decline."

Aidan set the glass on the island and gripped the edge.

He was calling again.

Why?

Curiosity had him accepting the call. Once he agreed to the payment, Aidan was connected.

"Hello, Aidan. It's Kent." His voice appeared undisturbed despite being in prison awaiting trial.

"Grant," Aidan said, keeping his voice collected. "Why should we keep beating around the bush? Your name's Grant."

Kent sighed. "Very well. Call me whatever tickles your pickle."

"What do you want?" He stepped out back so Cheyenne couldn't hear the conversation.

"Oh, you know. Just wanted to have some decent conversation," Kent said with a heavy sigh. "It's just so *boring* in here. Once you've lived certain ways for so long, you get accustomed." He clucked his tongue. "You know exactly what I mean, don't you, Aidan? In the end, you're *just like me*."

"I'm nothing like you, Grant." Aidan forced himself to compose his breathing.

"But you are," Kent said. "I saw your eyes that day at the house. When Cheyenne was close to me. If you could have, you would have killed me."

Aidan swallowed hard.

Yes, I would have killed him, he admitted to himself. *But would that have made me the same as him?*

"You're wrong," Aidan said. "The difference between us is you kill for sport. You've brutally abused and murdered ninety-one people. You tried to kill three more. Anything that happened to you would be considered justified."

"Justified?" Kent laughed lightly. "Call it what you want. But you know the truth."

Aidan ground his teeth together and gripped the cell phone in his hand. He heard the door open behind him but didn't turn around.

"Tell me something. Why me?"

"You?"

"You always left me a message. You wanted me to be sure I was chasing you. Why?"

He heard a breathy chuckle.

"Well, I'm sorry to say I must cut this conversation short."

"Wait," Aidan said. "Grant...Kent...tell me. Why did you want me investigating you?"

"I don't want to be a phone hog," Kent said. "But, don't worry. You'll be seeing me again, Agent O'Reilly. I guarantee it. Maybe then we can talk specifics. Until that day comes, keep a lookout for a parting gift I sent especially for you."

Kent ended the call and Aidan sat staring across the yard.

Shaun sat in the chair next to him.

"Was that him?"

"Yeah," Aidan said distantly.

"Hope life on the inside is treating him unkindly," Shaun said.

"Hey, Aidan," Laura said from behind, handing him a box.

"This just came for you."

Aidan accepted the unmarked box and opened it.

"I don't believe it," Shaun whispered.

Aidan stared into the box, his throat raw.

Inside was a bouquet of white carnations.

"The man's got some nerve," he said.

Aidan pushed to his feet and made his way to the trash can. He tossed the box of carnations inside.

"I think we'll rest better knowing he'll answer for what he's done," Aidan said. "He can't do anything to us any longer."

"No, he can't," Shaun said.

"Laura's got a Wii system," Aidan said, making his way to the living room. "Wanna play a little bowling?"

"Sure," Shaun said with a coy smile. "But I should warn you, I'm a master."

"Sounds like a challenge," Aidan said.

Grabbing two beers from the fridge, Aidan led the way to the living room to set up the game.

FBI Special Agent Aidan O'Reilly engages in a game of wits against a serial killer with a vendetta. How many lives will be lost before justice is served?

Keep turning the pages for an exclusive excerpt from book two in the Aidan O'Reilly serial killer thriller series:

A Killer's Vengeance

Sneak Peek of A Killer's Vengeance

"Hey, Rachel." Aidan lowered himself to sit in the kitchen chair directly across from her. "I want to start by thanking you for talking with us. We'll try to make this as quick as possible. How are you doing?"

Rachel Amos remained silent, looking as if she'd been without a shower for several days, and Aidan supposed she had been. She wore a blue tank top with black shorts, both wrinkled as if she'd been sleeping in them. When Aidan first looked into her eyes, they were dark and sad. She now stared down at the surface of the table, tearing a napkin into small pieces.

"I know this is hard for you," Aidan said. "You've been through so much, then having to be questioned time and again. But, my partner and I, well, we'd like to find out what happened that day at Phinizy Swamp. To do that, we need your help. We need to hear your side of things. You're the only one who can tell us."

Rachel continued to maintain her silence, and her father, sitting next to her, wrapped his arms around her shoulders.

"I'm sorry, agents, but my daughter has been through a lot this past week. Can we—"

"Phil," Mrs. Amos said sharply, standing in the corner by the sink. She crossed her arms over her chest and glared at her husband. "One of her friends is dead. Another close to death. These agents want to know what happened. *I* want to know what happened."

"Krystal, she needs time," Mr. Amos said, his voice cracking. He looked from Aidan to Shaun and back again. "My daughter just needs time. Can you try to understand that?"

"What *our* daughter *needs* is to talk about what happened that day!" Mrs. Amos cut her hand through the air as if making a point. "I know you want to protect her, Phil, but what good is it if she's not talking about it? She hasn't spoken a word since it all happened. And... and... one of her best friends is dead! Leon's in a coma... and..."

Mr. Amos pushed his chair back, screeching it angrily across the floor. "You don't have to spell it out for me, Krystal! I know! I *know*!" He spewed out a curse. "I'm trying to protect my daughter."

"Mr. and Mrs. Amos," Shaun said, although the bickering of the parents overtook his voice. "Mr. and Mrs. Amos, please—"

Mr. Amos continued to ignore him. "I know exactly what the stakes are—"

"Obviously, you don't—"

"Krystal—"

"Stop it!" Rachel gripped the sides of her head. "Stop fighting! I'm sick of listening to you! That's all you ever do! I can't take it anymore!"

Rachel let out a bloodcurdling scream before pushing out of her chair, forcing it to fall back against the floor with a clatter. She jerked the kitchen door open, eyes streaming with tears, and stormed out, despite the protests of her parents. The door bounced off the table against the wall, then slowly closed, settling against the doorjamb.

"Let me talk with her if you will," Aidan said, holding up his hand to prevent Mr. Amos from chasing after his daughter. "If you don't mind."

"She's not ready to face it."

"The sooner she talks about it, the sooner she can focus on healing," Shaun said. "And the sooner Agent O'Reilly and I will leave your family to your grief. Think of your daughter, Mr. Amos. Think of her friends. Ray Parsons deserves justice, and Rachel may be a way to get it for him."

There was a long silence. Mr. Amos stared at his wife, whose face twisted in pain and stained with tears. Finally, he nodded at Aidan, pulling his wife into a tight hug.

"It'll be okay, sweetheart," Mr. Amos said, his words muffled in her hair. "We'll get through this. I promise."

"Thank you, Mr. Amos," Aidan said. "Do you know where Rachel went?"

Rachel's dad raised his eyes to Aidan. "She'll be in her treehouse out back. It's her safe place. I built it for her a few summers ago. But if you ask her, we built it together." He smiled wanly. "A little girl with a hammer, and me holding the nail."

Shaun smiled. "And you'd do it a thousand more times."

"A million," Mr. Amos said and gently kissed his wife's forehead.

Aidan found a glass and filled it with iced water before walking out the door. He shut it behind him, staring toward Rachel's treehouse.

He slowly walked toward it.

"Rachel?" Aidan said as he approached. "It's Agent O'Reilly. Do you mind if I come up there?"

When she didn't respond, Aidan climbed to the top, holding the glass of water in one hand.

"Wow," he said as he stuck his head inside. "This is an impressive hide-out."

Rachel sat on the floor in the corner, a blanket covering her body, her eyes red and cheeks soaked with tears. She was shivering with anguish, rocking back and forth.

"I thought you might be thirsty, so I brought you a glass of water," Aidan said. He set it next to her, then went to another corner to give her a little space. A table sat underneath a window with a photo of Rachel, Leon, and Ray. Beneath the table were stacks of board games. "Did your dad build you this treehouse?"

He looked her way and waited until she finally nodded.

"That's great. Really cool. I never had a treehouse like this, but back in Ireland, my sister and I used to hang out in an abandoned cave. That was our clubhouse."

Rachel seemed to pay attention, however, made no effort to talk, so he continued to carry the conversation.

"We'd have passwords for those interested in coming in. I can't remember what it was, though. Something silly like colcannon."

Aidan allowed his speech to lull, giving her a chance to respond.

"You're Irish?" Rachel asked shyly. "You don't sound like you are."

"I am and I'm not," Aidan said with a smile. "I was actually adopted by an Irish family when I was really young. I don't remember much, but my biological parents were murdered. I spent a brief time in foster care. My parents couldn't have children, so they adopted me. A couple of years my sister was born. My adopted folks would say I'm the blessing and she's the miracle."

"I'm sorry about your real parents," Rachel said with a frown. "That's so sad."

"Thanks. It's part of what drove me to wanting to be in law enforcement." Aidan paused. "But I admit my temper seems very much Irish, if you know what I mean." Aidan winked, pleased when Rachel snickered. "My sister, she sounds a little Irish, though as she got older, it started to fade slightly."

"Does she live here, too?"

"Mairead's in Boston. I don't think she ever intends on leaving. Much of our childhood, we'd alternate between Cork and Boston for Dad's job. She likes it there. I lived there for a while as an adult, but eventually I had to transfer to Atlanta."

"Your job made you leave your sister?"

Aidan frowned, his heart growing heavy at the memory which still resurfaced when he wished it didn't. "Actually, not directly. A close friend of ours was killed. She was a victim of a serial killer called The Carnations Killer."

"I'm sorry," Rachel said.

"Thanks," Aidan said.

"Did you find out who killed your friend?"

Aidan nodded. "We caught the killer. It took about ten years, but he's in the federal penitentiary in Atlanta now, where he'll stay for the rest of his life."

Silence passed through them before Rachel finally looked up at him, through her long eyelashes. "Will you catch who killed Ray?"

"I'd like to," Aidan said. "I'd like to very much, Rachel. But I need you to help me. Do you think you can do that?"

Rachel diverted her eyes again and sniffed, before nodding.

"Why don't you start from the beginning?" Aidan said. "You and your friends went to Phinizy Swamp for a class trip, right?"

With hesitation, Rachel nodded.

"We left the group."

"Why?"

"I'm not supposed to tell. It's all stupid, really. But..." She trailed off, trying not to cry again.

"Go on," Aidan said. "I won't talk about anything to anyone unless it is directly relevant to the case."

Rachel looked back at Aidan and studied him, then sighed, wiping her eyes. "A few weeks ago, Ray had gotten involved with a game."

"What kind of game?" Aidan asked.

"A scavenger hunt," Rachel said. "It was kinda like Pokémon Go, except the game started out in the emails. If you're interested, you have to sign up. So Ray did. Only certain people were eligible to play."

"What was included in the emails?" Aidan asked. "Did it come with instructions?"

"It had a map of the search area. There would be miscellaneous hidden items. We'd have to solve a riddle, and the answer would be what we needed to find."

"When you found the object, how did you notify the person in charge of the game? Or were you given another riddle?"

"They gave us twelve hours from the time we opened the email to finding the item. Then we're supposed to email a picture of ourselves with the item. And the next clue would come in a new email. When we got the map of Phinizy Swamp, Ray started thinking it was someone in our class. We knew we needed to go to the bridge because there was a red *X* over it on the map."

"Interesting," Aidan said, rubbing the nape of his neck.

Rachel narrowed her eyes. "Why? Did I say something helpful?"

"Maybe. When was the first time Ray started getting the emails?"

Rachel was silent for a few minutes before she frowned with a shrug. "I don't know. Two weeks? Three ... it's a blur. I'm sorry."

"And neither you nor Leon received the emails?"

"No."

So, Ray was no doubt the target, Aidan decided.

"Did you find any other clue at the bridge?" he asked.

Rachel nodded. "Leon found it. It was a photo of some guy. That's when I heard the gunshot. I turned around and saw Ray falling to the ground. He...he'd been shot."

She paused, her bottom lip quivering again.

"It's okay, honey," Aidan said. "Take your time."

She began to cry. Aidan had to strain to understand her near unintelligible words.

"I remember... screaming. I remember... Leon... he... he froze, then he ran. But he... he tripped and hit his head. I-I tried to get him to move, but he was ... wouldn't. Ray, too. They weren't moving, so I ran. I-I-I left them."

Tears came full force, and Aidan left his corner of the treehouse to go to her. He wrapped his arms around her and allowed Rachel to let loose the tears.

When she was able, Rachel pushed herself away and turned to look at him, blinking back tears the best she could.

"I don't understand why anyone would want to kill us," she said. "We never hurt anyone. It doesn't make sense. Do you think the killer will come after me?"

"No," Aidan said. "I don't think he will."

Of that, he was certain.

Rachel wiped her eyes with the heel of her hands.

"Can you answer a few more questions for me?" Aidan asked her. When she nodded, he said, "Have you ever seen the guy in the photo before?"

Rachel shook her head.

"Can you describe what he looked like?"

"I-I-I don't remember," Rachel said. "Light brown hair... maybe blonde? I don't know. I'm sorry."

"It's okay. I don't want you to force your memory. It may come back to you later. You can let me know then. You're doing good, honey."

Rachel wiped her tear-stained face with her hands.

"Tell me a little about Ray," Aidan said. "Did he get into a lot of trouble?"

Rachel shook her head. "He'd never been in trouble before. Ray never really talked with anyone except me and Leon."

"What about Leon? Does he ever make trouble?"

Rachel shrugged carelessly. "I guess he was more outspoken than either of us. He thought the emails Ray got were exciting. At first, Ray didn't want to bother with the game at the swamp because we were supposed to stay with our class, but..."

"But what?"

"But like Leon, Ray wanted to keep playing."

"How do you know when and if the game would end?"

"I don't know. I kinda thought the whole thing was weird. I had a feeling about it. But we played Pokémon Go many times, so I didn't think too much about it."

"Think back to the day you and your friends were on your class trip," Aidan said. "Do you remember if anyone spoke to you before parting from your class? Or afterward?"

Rachel considered the question. "I don't think so. I'm sorry."

Aidan gently squeezed her shoulder. "Don't be sorry. Be glad you're okay."

"I don't think I'll ever be okay again. Ray's dead. And Leon... they said he might not live."

"Rachel, I promise we'll do all within our power to find out who did this to you and your friends. Okay?" Aidan hesitated a beat. "I have one last thing I need to ask you. We heard you've been having some trouble at school with a kid named Mitchell Garvey."

She nodded, wiping her eyes with the heel of her wrists. "He's a jerk. No one cares that he's been bothering me. At least not until Ray and Leon got involved."

"Have you had issues with him since the altercation at school?"

"No. Not really."

"Do you believe he has a reason for picking on you?"

"I went on a date with him once," Rachel said. "It wasn't really a date, though. We went to the movies with some other couples. He tried to get me to sleep with him, but I said no. I wanted to save myself. He got rough. I never told Ray and Leon about that part." Rachel paused, drawing in a long, shaky breath. "But ever since, he started spreading rumors that we...kind of slept together...and that he taped us. It was all lies, but the kids in school believed it and called me a slut. And other things."

"And a few days before your field trip, Garvey cornered you in the locker room?"

Rachel nodded. "He started touching me while his friends watched and laughed. I kneed him and got away. Ray and Leon saw me and asked what was wrong. I told them then."

"And they defended you?"

She nodded. "I didn't know they'd gang up on him. I didn't want Ray and Leon to get into trouble. But Mitchell was getting worse. He scares me sometimes. I couldn't face school the next day."

"All right," Aidan said with a smile. "That's useful information. What do you say we go down now? Talk to your parents? I'd also like you to look at a photo. See if you recognize someone. Maybe you saw her at school, or someplace else."

"Okay."

Aidan let Rachel climb down the ladder first, then followed her into the house.

Her parents watched them, keeping their concerns quiet as Aidan showed her the photo of Stephanie Carpenter.

Rachel studied her for a long few minutes before finally looking up at Aidan.

"No," Rachel said. She looked down again, as if trying to be sure. "I haven't seen her before. I'm sorry."

"It's all right," Aidan assured her. "Thank you, Rachel. You helped shed a lot of light on a few things."

Aidan thanked Rachel's parents for allowing him to have the time with her, then he and Shaun left.

◈

Buy book two now!

Acknowledgments

Special thanks to Diana Ridenour for your time and input in the specifics of the FBI. Very special thanks to Mom and Joe. Last, but certainly not least, an extra special thanks to God for never ceasing to make Yourself known to me in everyday life. You're my Rock and my Comfort.

Also By Angela Kay

Series

Jim DeLong Mysteries

Aidan O'Reilly Thrillers

Standalones

Whispers of the Dead: A Crime Thriller

Kept in Silence: A Gripping Psychological Thriller

Novellas

The Naked Eye: A Locked Room Short Story

Author's Note

Thank you so much for reading *A Killer's Mark*, the start of it all. I truly hope you enjoyed it and leave a review on Amazon. I think among the books I have out so far, this is my favorite.

Writing Aidan's and Shaun's investigation into serial killers is both fun and nightmarish. I spend so much time invested in learning more about real-life serial killers and watching the *Investigation Discovery* channel daily. Why are serial killers so interesting? I don't have an answer for that. I suppose it's human nature to be engrossed in the darkness of the mind.

Thank you again for turning the pages! If you haven't already, don't forget to get *A Killer's Vengeance*, book two of the Aidan O'Reilly serial killer thriller series.

Sincerely,
Angela Kay

Made in United States
North Haven, CT
25 January 2024